The Glorious Adventures of the SUNSHINE QUEEN

Other Books by
Geraldine McCaughrean

The Glorious Adventures of the SUNSHINE QUEEN

Geraldine McCaughrean

HARPER

An Imprint of HarperCollinsPublishers

NEW HANOVER COUNTY PUBLIC LIBRARY
201 Chestnut Street
Wilmington, NC 28401

Library of Congress Cataloging-in-Publication Data
McCaughrean, Geraldine.
The glorious adventures of the Sunshine Queen / Geraldine McCaughrean. — 1st
American ed.
    p. cm.   Sequel to: Stop the train!
  Summary: When a diphtheria outbreak forces twelve-year-old Cissy to leave her
Oklahoma hometown in the 1890s, she and her two classmates embark on a wild
adventure down the Missouri River with a team of traveling actors who are living on a
dilapidated paddle steamer.
  ISBN 978-0-06-200806-0 (trade bdg.)
  [1. Adventure and adventurers—Fiction. 2. Theater—Fiction. 3. Paddle steamers—
Fiction. 4. Missouri River—History—19th century—Fiction.] I. Title.
PZ7.M4784133Gl 2010   2010021958
[Fic]—dc22   CIP
                                                                                          AC

Typography by Torborg Davern
11 12 13 14 15   LP/RRDB   10 9 8 7 6 5 4 3 2 1
❖
First American Edition
Originally published in 2010 by Oxford University Press in the U.K.,
under the title *Pull Out All the Stops!*

*For Ailsa Joy
and all her fellow actors*

CONTENTS

CAST OF CHARACTERS

In Olive Town

Cissy Sissney

Hulbert Sissney, her father, the grocer

Hildy Sissney, her mother

Habakkuk (Kookie) Warboys

Pickard Warboys, his father, the telegrapher

Blosk Warboys, his mother

Tibbie Boden, a rancher's daughter

Miss May March, a schoolteacher

Chad Powers, a part-time inventor

The Bright Lights Theater Company

Cyril Crew, the proprietor

Everett Crew, his brother

Loucien Shades Crew, Everett's wife

"Curly" Curlitz, front-of-house/accounting/
publicity/prompt/refreshments/property-manager/
walk-on actor

Egil, Finn, and Revere, actors

Aboard the Sunshine Queen

Elijah Bouverie, boiler scraper
The Dixie Quartet: Benet, Boisenberry,
Sweeting, and Oskar
Max the Plank, a Polish clown
Medora and her Photopia
The Dog Woman and her three performing dogs
George, a barber-surgeon and phrenologist
Elder Slater, a hellfire preacher
Chips, a carpenter

Along the way

Sugar Cain, a "rafter," or river pirate
Cole Blacker, son of wealthy parents
Henry, an English butler

and, of course, a host of others . . .

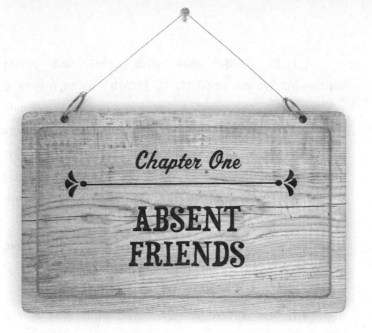

Chapter One

ABSENT FRIENDS

Dear Class Three,

how are you? Aint life grand? Last week we playd Nuorleens. More cokrowches out back than faces out front but foke seemed to lyk us. Leestways they did not thro things like in Toosson. Dearest Everett says not to wurry when they thro things cuz some times they thro the most yoosfull objeckts—suspenders and froot and reel munny even. Says one time a lady throde a cat at him and it was in kitten and the Company kept it and soled the kittens and raysed a good prys.

Tawkin of wich some one of your akwayntens is also in a interestin condishun. what do you no?

Little Annie May (she plays the pritty herroins if you recall?) is leeving us to marry a bank tella next munth. we wish her well naturly. Still it leeves a hole in the Company. A pritty ingenoo is hard to find. Dearest Everett says wors things happan at sea. O Lor if you coud just see him playin Cyrano rite now! be is ~~magin mangif magnee~~ sub lime.

Sorry to heer how Sara waters is sick. Give her a kis from me and say hunny and wisky is best for a bad throte.

will rite from St paul. bope Miss May March is still makin moves to improov on wot God made you.

your everlovin
Loucien Shades Crew

Cissy folded the letter and gave it back to Miss May March, whose thin white face, like a dish towel resting on a puddle of wine, had grown pink around the edges.

"Thank you, Cecelia. You may return to your seat."

Miss May March did not approve of the letters Class Three received from their previous teacher. To give Miss March her due, she never actually binned them, but she did not dwell on their contents either. Talk of cockroaches and "pretty ingénues" and "interesting conditions" was not on her curriculum.

One year earlier, "Miss Loucien" had taught the children the sum total of everything she knew. But she had married a traveling actor and left Olive Academy for a life in theater. Miss May March was well aware of the mark her predecessor had left on Class Three, but to her way of thinking it was the kind of mark that should have been quickly washed away, like the soap ring around a bathtub. There was something shocking about the woman, with her chaotic handwriting and her creative spelling and her gypsy existence. Her misspelled letters always put the children into a restless, contrary mood. This very minute Miss March knew perfectly well they were comparing her with Miss Loucien . . . and marking her a very poor second. Knowing this sometimes made her spiteful.

"Take out your slates and write the following proper nouns: *New Orleans . . . Tucson . . . St. Paul . . . Fuller Monterey*, pray tell me: what does a proper noun have?"

She knew he would not know. (The Monterey boys had less than one brain between the two of them.) Miss Loucien would not have known either. Perhaps this was a chance to impress on Class Three that Miss March alone had the power to make of them literate, civilized citizens. Fuller Monterey drew in his tortoise-shaped head and refused to answer. He looked even more sullen than usual.

"Habbakuk Warboys, then. What does a proper noun have?"

Kookie, however, was quite equal to the challenge. "Panache!" he said.

"Hexclamation marks!" said Tibbie Boden, sticking up her hand.

"Clean linen!" said Barney Mackinley.

"First use of the washroom!" said Fred Stamp.

Cissy Sissney took no part in this. Her soul was still held between the folds of Miss Loucien's letter. She was imagining the footlights, the gilt moldings of the opera boxes, suspenders and kittens flying through the air, the noise of applause. . . .

Cissy lived for the days when a letter arrived from her old schoolteacher. Miss Loucien's letters were an Event, an Occasion almost. Cissy was always given the honor of reading them out loud because her reading was best. And afterward she liked to sit and savor what she had read—to imagine she was there, on the road with the Bright Lights Theater Company, seeing all those charlatans and celebrities, seeing all the big cities and out-of-the way settlements, singing for her supper.

It was so long since the Bright Lights had left town that she could barely remember the pretty

Annie May. How would the Company manage without someone to play the helpless, screaming heroines? Cissy wondered if, at twelve, she was old enough to audition for the job of ingénue. Perhaps she and Kookie could run away to Nuorleens (wherever that was) and join the Bright Lights Theater Company and star in *The Perils of Nancy* and see Miss Loucien and Everett Crew again. Oh!

Beyond the window, a great tidal wave of Boredom rolled in from the eastern horizon, then broke over the school roofs and Main Street and the silo and the umbrella factory before rolling on to the western horizon. Cissy knew the color of boredom; it was the color of prairie. It was the color of northwest Oklahoma. It was the color of schoolday afternoons. Sometimes she thought the sky had been nailed down on Olive Town like a crate lid and that she was suffocating on Boredom.

Then her eye fell on the empty space left by Sarah Waters along the school bench, and suddenly Cissy's eyes felt hot and swollen. No amount of honey and whiskey would ease Sarah's throat now— but then how was Miss Loucien to know that? Since the last exchange of letters, Sarah's sore throat had proved to be diphtheria, and she had moved up to the cemetery, to be planted there like a melon seed that was never going to grow. Surely, if Miss

Loucien had stayed, Sarah would not have died.

Though the school bench was crowded, no one had yet slid sideways to fill the empty space. Fear of infection or just pure superstition had saved a place for Sarah Waters. Everyone was hoping there had been a mistake and that she would walk back into school one day, good as new.

"Kookie," Cissy whispered to the bristle-haired boy beside her. "What's it mean: 'interesting condition'?"

Kookie gave a superior kind of snort. "Interesting condition? That's slang, that is. Means someone's 'specting a baby. Ma's been 'interesting' so often now, she says she just ain't interested in bein' interesting no more."

"Expecting? No, but . . ."

"The ingenoo must be 'specting—now she's marrying the bank teller."

"No, that can't be right," Cissy insisted. "She doesn't even get married till next month. So she can't hardly be expecting a baby now."

Kookie gave this some thought. "Maybe the letter got held up in the mail," he said.

"Cecelia Sissney! Habbakuk Warboys! Go right this minute and sit in Fool's Corner and write twelve times on your slates: I must not talk in class. Next time we receive a letter, Cecelia, perhaps someone else had better read it out," said Miss May March, still pink around the edges.

The town committee was planning to move the grain silo. The speculator who had built it (back when the town itself was being built) had gone broke before the first harvest was in. The town committee wanted to keep the silo, but somewhere else, so that the station buildings could be enlarged. They wanted it moved up Main Street and down West Road to the new railway sidings. There the grain could be funneled directly into open-topped freight cars while they awaited a locomotive. The town committee was also of the opinion that there were enough willing hands in Olive Town to get the job done free.

Suggestions were invited from anyone with a pencil and a bright idea, and various citizens of Olive Town submitted diagrams full of arrows, ropes, and pulleys. Virgil Hobbs was of the opinion it could not be done at all, whereas Charlie Quex, the barber, knew a man who had won fifty dollars one time by moving a barn, intact, from one side of a river to the other.

"How did he do it?" Sheriff Monterey had asked.

"Beats me," said Charlie. "I only shaved the guy. He didn't have time to go into detail."

As Cissy ran home from school that day, she ran through the long black shadow cast by the big metal tower. It chilled her as though she had run through a brook.

"Gonna lower it onto its side and move it on rollers," her father was telling his wife, as Cissy burst into the grocery store and ran through to the rooms in back, where the family lived. "Poppy! Poppy!"

"Hope Chad Powers knows what he's doing," grumbled Mrs. Sissney. "Be a first if he does."

"Poppy! Poppy! A letter came from Miss Loucien today! They're in Nuorleens, wherever that is, but Annie May is marrying a bank teller and leaving a hole, and someone's expecting, but we can't guess who!"

"*Well!*" said her mother, cramming the one word full of outrage and disgust. Hildy Sissney loaded her words like other people loaded cannon.

"That's nice, chicken," said Hulbert.

A sixth sense warned Cissy that all was not well. When her mother began banging the pots around and her father hugged her tighter and longer than usual, she knew something bad was in the air. She wanted some comfort for the humiliation of Fool's Corner and her dreadful loss of letter-reading privileges, but dared not mention either in front of her mother.

"Was a delivery on the morning train," said Hulbert. "Help me stack it onto the shelves?"

"Sure, Pops," said Cissy warily.

"Best get in the practice," said Hildy Sissney under her breath, and Hulbert turned and glared at his wife.

A terrible foreboding flooded Cissy. She went through to the shop to check the new stock of tins and packets and cartons, but though her father coughed several times, and rubbed his bad leg and seemed about to break some news, his courage failed him. Cissy had to wait till suppertime for the axe to fall. Then she found it had more than one blade.

"We thank the Lord for feeding us, body and soul," said her mother in a huffy tone that suggested the Almighty had been shirking lately.

Cissy opened her eyes and picked up her fork, but there was more to come.

"We pray for the soul of poor Sarah Waters and for Gaff Boden's ranch hand and for Sheriff Monterey if it comes to it. Lead him not into drinking, leastways. Amen."

"Sheriff Monterey? Why? How come we're praying for him?" said Cissy.

"His boy Peat. Looks like diphtheria, same as Sarah," said Hulbert. He had forgotten to open his eyes after grace—or perhaps he found things easier to say that way. "So your mother and I have decided to take you outa school, chicken . . ."

"Hotbedda germs," said Hildy.

". . . just till the sickness has passed through," said Hulbert.

Hildy jabbed her fork accusingly at her husband. "Now don't you go doubling back on me, Hulbert Sissney. We agreed. Twelve's plenty soon enough for her to start pulling her weight. She's got reading. She's got her numbers. What more does she want to work in a grocery store?"

The newspapers with which the walls of the living room were papered suddenly seemed to be shouting their headlines into Cissy's face: DENVER'S FIRST WOMAN DOCTOR . . . OKIE CENTENARIAN NEVER LEFT HOMETOWN . . . MEDFORD SCHOLAR ENTERS HARVARD . . . DIPHTHERIA KILLS THIRTY . . .

Through the window, the problematic silo cast its shadow across the street and in at the grocery door, like the index finger of Doom.

So. She was to leave school and work in the Olive Town grocery store, selling beans to cowboys and gingham to their wives. She was to spend her life reading the *Olive Town Morning Star* for news she already knew, about people she saw every day. The Medford State Fair would be the highlight of her year, each passing year. The rolling prairies would crush her days, the prairie moon pull faces at her each night.

Cissy loved Olive Town. She had lived there since the first train dumped its first handful of settlers on an empty wilderness: Claim Nos. 3048—9. She loved all the odd, desperate, varied people who had come there in search of a new life. But keep shop there? Forever? Abandon geography and history and daydreaming and playing "stones" with Kookie in the lunch break and reading the books Miss May March lent her and writing essays entitled "My Life: A Plan"?

"Don't sit there moping. Go fetch in a dozen carrots, Cecelia, thanking you," said her mother sharply, and Cissy gladly bolted out the back door. She disturbed several rabbits that had been feeding on the vegetable patch, and she watched their pale shapes speed away across the prairie, passing far out of sight: lucky rabbits. In between the failed squash and the aphid-covered lettuces, Cissy gave herself up to crying—for Sarah Waters and Peat Monterey and Gaff Boden's ranch hand—and for the end of her childhood.

Her father came out to help her tug up the puny, blunt-nosed carrots.

"I don't want to leave school, Poppy!" she told him.

"I know, chicken. I know. But your ma wore me down. She gets fearful tired serving in the shop all day, you know . . . and if diphtheria's gotten loose in the schoolroom, school'll be shut down soon anyhow. . . . Oh. And Gaff Boden has asked us to take in his girl, Tibbie, till the sickness is past. Your mother said no. Had to reach an accommodation with her, didn't I? 'You take Cissy outa school,' she said, 'and I'll take in Tibbie Boden.'"

"Tibbie Boden is coming *here*? To *live*?" Another blow.

"Sure is." Her father smiled broadly. He thought he had saved the good news till last.

Not Tibbie! Golden-haired, blue-eyed Tibbie off the Boden ranch! The girl Kookie had vowed to marry. The one girl who made Cissy invisible in Kookie's eyes.

"You like Tibbie?" Hulbert said cajolingly. "And she needs somewhere safe from the germs up at her place. You *do* like Tibbie, don't you, chicken?"

"Sure," said Cissy, thinking: I like her right where she is . . . way out of town, on her daddy's ranch. Cissy's sole advantage had been in living a few doors away from the telegraph office where Kookie lived. Now even that advantage was gone, and she would lose Kookie. He and Tibs would marry and move away to Yale and study astronomy or taxidermy or something with a future in it.

A wave of self-pity washed over Cissy. "If I catch diphtheria and die, Poppy, I don't want you to telegraph to Miss Loucien in St. Paul. She would be too upset. She was hoping I would join her in the acting business one day, you see."

"Ah!" said Hulbert. "I see!" And his heart ached for his little girl, whose life had suddenly shrunk in the wash from a costume gown into a shopgirl's apron.

Chapter Two

THE FINGER OF DOOM

*T*he ground under one side of the silo was being excavated, while an A-frame of telegraph poles and a harness of ropes restrained the big metal tower from tilting over. The idea was to lower it gently onto its side. Virgil Hobbs was of the opinion that everyone involved would get killed, but Mr. Powers was in charge, and Mr. Powers was a designer at the umbrella factory: a draftsman and an engineer. People were more inclined to believe him than the bootmaker.

Actually, people spent a lot of time doubting Mr. Powers too, but that was when he was talking up prairie sailboats. Since arriving in Olive Town to work at the umbrella factory, Chad Powers had given over all his spare time to building revolutionary horseless vehicles driven by wind—big, flat rafts on wheels, with masts and spinnakers and booms— sometimes outriggers and other times tillers. So far he had solved the problem of going but not of coming back.

The children of Class Three had lined up, at one time, to test-drive the prototypes. But after one schooner took to the air and another overturned at full speed, the parents had banned any more rides. And so Chad Powers could be seen every weekend when there was a breath of wind, careering over the meadows, colliding with trees and cows and sailplaning into the river. He was forever wrapped up in bandages, splints, and surgical collars, but his enthusiasm was unquenchable. One day, he said, Olive Town would be famous as the birthplace of the Powers Patent Prairie Sailboat.

In the meantime, he had submitted by far the best idea for moving the silo. The tissuey blue design paper covered in neat blue diagrams had convinced the town committee he was the best man for the job.

A series of telegraph poles was laid on the ground for use as rollers. The huge metal body of the silo was to be lowered onto this rolling raft and pushed, like some ancient juggernaut, toward its new site by the railroad sidings. Everyone had offered to help—the children had been particularly keen—which was why Miss May March had organized a long exam for them to take, so that they couldn't. She said they would get in the way.

All day Kookie Warboys sat adding nonexistent lengths of rope together, measuring the perimeters of imaginary fields, labeling the states of the Union, and listing the plagues of Egypt, while out in the spring sunshine, men hauled on real lengths of rope and grappled with a genuine Tower of Babel. The silo was giving problems.

As Kookie huffed and sighed and pushed his way through a barbed-wire entanglement of sums, a minefield of questions, Miss March's pen scratched away covering page after page of lavender writing paper. She had a pianist's hands, flexible and strong, and played the portable organ on Sunday in Olive Town's one and only church. Her handwriting looked like rows of bedsprings. Page after page she covered with her even, bedspring writing. Kookie looked down and found a puddle of ink where his pen nib had bled into the blank test paper. Where was Cissy? That's what he wanted to know. How were you supposed to copy from a person if that person did not turn up at school?

From outside the window, Cissy spied on the roomful of bent heads, the tufts of home-barbered hair, the shoulders hunched as if against bad weather. Her schooldays were over, and suddenly there was nothing she craved so much as taking an un-do-able exam in an unknowable subject. She should never have learned to read, she told herself, and then she could have kept on going to school, year after year, until she was thirty-four and too big to fit behind a desk.

"Pencils down, and rest your hands on your heads," said Miss May March (who had theories about the circulation of the blood and also liked to keep children's hands in plain sight at all times).

Beyond the window, Cissy dodged out of sight. She bit her lip. She wished she had found the courage yesterday to go over to the telegraph office and break the news to Kookie. But telling it would have made it true, and yesterday Cissy had still been hoping to wake from a bad dream. Besides, Kookie's sweet-natured mother would have kissed Cissy and hugged her and started her off crying in front of Kookie. And Cissy knew she looked like a sucked plum when she cried.

"You came back then?" snapped Hildy Sissney when Cissy clattered into the shop. Cissy flinched from the reproach and from the noise of the bell over the door. "A fine lot of use you are to a business, I must say!"

"Sorry, Ma. I just went—"

"That you did! Just up and went, without a word! Left me to bag the orders single-handed! You're not at school now, girl, learning sloth and idolatry."

"Idolatry?"

"Well what else are you, if you ain't idle? I've a good mind to—"

"I sent her over to the print house with a message, Hildy," said Cissy's father, emerging from the back room. "No need to carry on at the child."

Cissy thanked her father with a smile and slipped the loop of her apron over her head once more. It was stiff and scratchy with starch, and it felt like a hangman's noose as she tugged her hair free. "Why is the silo outside our place, Poppy?"

"That's as far as they got it, chicken. Mr. West put his knee out pushing one of the rollers. So they've wedged it where it is: all set for the last few yards tomorrow."

At the end of school, Kookie came tearing up the street to discover by what ruse Cissy had escaped Miss May March's exam. Mrs. Fudd was standing in the doorway with two skeins of knitting yarn in either hand, showing them to the daylight, comparing them with a jar of jam. "Damson, my sister wants. Reckon that's damson?"

"I'd say it was, kinda." Cissy tried to sound helpful but sounded simply unconvinced. When she saw Kookie on the boardwalk, waiting to get through the door, her cheeks flushed the color of strawberries.

"Depends if it's in the jar or on the tree, I guess," said Mrs. Fudd. "Ya think my sister meant damson in the jar or on the tree?"

Cissy had to confess: "I couldn't say, Mrs. Fudd. It's a pretty enough color. I think the Romans liked it. They dyed their best clothes in plum." Her education might have foundered, but Cissy struggled to keep its little flag flying.

"*Romans?* Save us all! Clementine wouldn't want nothing as foreign as that!" And Mrs. Fudd hung her skeins over Cissy's hands and left the shop.

Cissy's mother uttered a gasp of exasperation. "First I knew the Romans wore *cardigans*. Thank you kindly for edifying us, miss." As she said it, her eyes flicked between Cissy and Kookie, hovering in the doorway. "Well? Set the wool back where you found it, and next time remember: keep your Romans to yourself, you hear?" It was said for Kookie's benefit: Mrs. Sissney might just as well have embroidered SHOPGIRL on Cissy's forehead with purple wool.

Kookie frowned. "You shorthanded?" he asked. "You got a rush on?" His eyes drifted around the empty store, took in Cissy's apron. "One of my brothers could help out, maybe."

Cissy said nothing. She tried to edge Kookie out through the door onto the sunlit boardwalk, away from her mother's withering stare, but he stayed put, obdurately looking about him, putting two and two together.

"'Nother letter came today from Miss Loucien," he said. "Shoulda been there."

Cissy gave a little cry of anguish. The news felt like the last and unkindest cut. "So soon? Who read it out?"

"I did, course. Seemingly, Curly got thirty days for profunnity (whatever that is) in a place called Salvation (wherever that is), so the rest of the company is camping out in a shipwreck till he's served his time!"

It was impossible to picture. Almost. In Cissy's imagination, mild-mannered little Curly (ticket seller of the Bright Lights Theater Company) mouthed at her through the bars of a jail window, while Miss Loucien picnicked on the seabed off open clamshells. "Shipwreck?" she whispered.

"Some old boat in a field."

"What's a boat doing in a field?"

But just then Tibbie Boden came toiling up the street, carrying a big, tightly stuffed carpetbag. Kookie, seeing an opportunity for chivalry, ran and snatched the bag from her. "Where d'you want I should take it?" His day took on a further strangeness when she nodded toward the store. "You stopping over with Cissy?" Behind her glasses, Tibbie's blue eyes rolled, like those of a horse smelling smoke. Everyone in Class Three was more afraid of Mrs. Sissney at the store than they were of the diphtheria. Nobody would *want* to stay over at the store.

The silo, lying flat along its rollers, pointed at the three children like heavy artillery.

Not wishing to go inside the shop, Tibbie also began to talk about the new letter from Miss Loucien. She could remember parts Kookie had left out.

Fuller Monterey, on his way home from school, shouted something vile and kicked a can at them. It hit Cissy in the ankle, then spun to a standstill. Their eyes trailed after the scowling, blaspheming Fuller. "Miss May says we got to make allowances since his brother's sick," said Tibbie. "Peatie might be dead, even this minute!" she added, wide-eyed.

"Mad coot," said Kookie uncharitably. "Fuller don't need an excuse to be nasty."

"You coming back to school tomorrow, Ciss?" said Tibbie.

"No, she ain't!" crowed Mrs. Sissney from inside the shop. "So unless you got something to buy, Hosea Warboys, I'll thank you to git off home!"

Oh, couldn't she even have gotten Kookie's name right? Cissy wanted to be at the bottom of the sea with Miss Loucien, cooking pancakes over the vent of a volcano.

"You never coming back to school then, Ciss?" said Kookie with open jealousy.

"Looks that way," said Cissy, trying not to cry.

After supper, she crept away out of the back door of the store. Her father was plying Tibbie Boden with kindly questions: "What's your favorite subject at school? Which books do you like to read? You wanna help me hang up a hammock for you alongside Cissy's?"

The only person she passed on the street was Mr. Powers, who explained he had just been checking the wedges. He had one wrist plastered and the other in a sling; clearly he had been out testing another prairie sailboat.

The schoolhouse was not locked, but Cissy climbed in at the window anyway, so as not to be seen going in. Two flies were following each other around the center of the room, flying in perfect squares as if they were using a ruler. She could see her story about Chinese dragons still pinned to the wall. When she slid open Miss March's drawer, a smell of Parma violets and chalk came up at her. She stabbed her finger on the tines of a comb. But not one of the homemade envelopes bearing Miss Loucien's big, wild handwriting lay among the chalk and confiscated playing cards, the coffee beans Miss March chewed on for her complexion, the pencils and red ink bottles. Had Miss May taken it home, then? Was it, like dear Miss Loucien, gone forever?

No. One page at least was in the bottom of the wastepaper basket, along with some peanut shells and a dead mouse.

. . . be wonderful to reflote it and werk the river, putting on shows all the way from here to Saint Looee? Teribal waist just rotting here but I spose it keeps the rain of our heds. Por Curly. be was only tawkin Shakespeare, the way he does, giving out with some purple passedges. Don't think the pasters wife had herd much Tyoodor powetry bifor.

Lor I do miss you fokes. Lifes indoobitably grand but it would be grander with out the rats and with out feeling so sick all the . . .

A clammy dread swept over Cissy. Her diaphragm quaked. Miss Loucien, if she was feeling sick, must have diphtheria! Rats were nibbling the glittering sequins from the costumes in the property box! The Bright Lights Theater Company was breathing its death rattle among heartless, soulless people who thought quoting Shakespeare was a crime! And Cissy, in the Olive Town Store, was in prison, as surely as Curly was in Salvation town jail.

She slipped the page into her scratchy apron pocket. Her mother wore a Bible against her stomach (to let the holiness soak through). Well, Cissy would wear a letter from the Bright Lights Theater Company. Unpinning the dragon story, she took that too, and gave the globe a last spin. (Everyone in Class Three knew that spinning the globe could sometimes grant a wish.) Then she started back through the window, smearing her apron with dead flies from along the sill.

There was a hooting, as though she were being mobbed by owls; someone tumbled out of the shadows and away down the street. It was Fuller Monterey. And when Cissy looked down, there was a wet red wound in the center of her apron. Fuller had been daubing paint on the outside of the school he hated so much, and her unexpected appearance had frightened him into a clumping, yelping run. She thought he must have been drinking cider or some of his father's homemade hooch, because he seemed hard put to keep his balance. Cissy craned her head to see what he had written. *you are de* said the unfinished graffiti. She started back up Main Street. Ahead of her, the silo lay on its hard mattress of rollers, its great circular base looking like the entrance to a dark gigantic tunnel; or hell, perhaps.

A thin liquorice whip of smoke rose up from behind the shining cylinder—nothing much. Just a rope or two on fire.

With a noise like the twang of a bow, the rope gave way. The silo rocked and stirred. One by one, the telegraph poles on which it rested began to roll—to separate and splay out—letting the silo tip and grate. The metal capping—huge as a mill wheel—sheared off the silo and bowled away, down West Street, over the new sidings and out onto the prairie. But the bulky trunk of metal bent and bowed and bounced its way across the sloping street, until, like some monstrous, flaccid battering ram, it gouged its way end-first into the Olive Town Store. One building eating another. The raw metal edge was so sharp that it sliced the entire building out of the ground. Solid timbers, struts, and batons took on the grotesque softness of a shelled oyster, as glass shattered, cloth rippled, wood crumpled, and counters and racks spewed their contents. Five thousand nails streamed to the ground, spread out into a silvery puddle, and slopped against Cissy's shoes, while dust rose up around her, swallowing the daylight, the detail, everything. The vast metal tube of the silo bent in and out of shape, giving off a deafening, unearthly *wow*ing noise. And then the telegraph poles came piling in too, flattening the boardwalk, turning it to matchwood, piling up on top of the vacant plot that had, a moment before, been her home.

When the dust cleared, Cissy still stood immobile, the sheet of writing paper aflutter in her hand, collecting brown dust out of the air. A burning rope wriggled at her feet, like a snake. In front of her, the silo lay on its side, intact. But of Cissy's home and livelihood nothing remained but a hole in the air. Wanting to fill up the hole—to undo the unbearable— she tried to picture exactly how it had looked before she set off for the schoolhouse. But the only thing Cissy could truly remember was the check of the tablecloth where she had eaten supper with her family.

Chapter Three

THE
EXILES

"It's the mark of the Beast," said Hildy Sissney.

She meant the red paint stain in the center of Cissy's apron. The people who had found her standing in the street—unmoving, unspeaking—thought she had been hit by debris, impaled by some flying pickaxe or set of kitchen knives. Her mother knew better. "Mark of the Beast: that's what that is."

As far as Mrs. Sissney was concerned, the long finger of God had expunged the Olive Town Store. Hildy had been engulfed by the booming, hollow dark of the silo. It had swallowed her, like the whale swallowing Jonah. Not for her the scarlet stain of sin. The only serious injury she had sustained was a purple-ridged bruise to her abdomen, caused by the

Bible she kept, unread, in her apron pocket. To Hildy Sissney (whose mind was swinging like a door in the wind) the sign could not be plainer. Cissy had been daubed by the Devil, but she herself had been poked in the belly by God. The Living Word had delivered a blow to her solar plexus that had emptied her of breath but filled her with the spirit of holiness. She spoke in tongues, most of them angry and shrill, but at least she did not need consoling. Hildy was filled with the zeal of the Lord, and she had no need of knitting yarn, cooking pots, or a bed to sleep in. Even daughters were a thing that somehow belonged to an older, more sinful life.

"Where's Poppy?" asked Cissy. Neighbors were gathering up bits and pieces from the roadway—a spoon, a ball of string, a saucepan, an onion. "Where's my pa?" said Cissy. "Where's Kookie and Tibs?"

Kind Mrs. Warboys from the telegraph office wrapped her in a blanket, and her husband picked Cissy up as if she were a baby. "Kookie was back at our place, thank the Lord, and Tibbie's with him. It's a mercy you were outside as well."

"But where's Poppy?" said Cissy.

Fuller Monterey, for the devil of it, had removed the wedges under the silo and set fire to one of the ropes securing it. But the sheriff made no arrest. Before nightfall, Fuller came down with diphtheria, like his brother; and people never care to speak ill of the ill.

So they turned their wrath instead on Chad Powers, whose plans to move the silo had gone so catastrophically wrong. He was instantly fired from the umbrella factory, and one of his prairie sailboats was found the next morning burned down to its axles.

Hulbert Sissney might have leaped to Chad's defense—he hated to see blame put on a man like a saddle, "because there's no other horse to hand." But, as Cissy found, to her frantic grief, Hulbert was lying in the back room of the barber's shop, both legs broken and his head thickly swathed in bandages.

Fuller's diphtheria sealed the fate of the school, which did not open its doors the next morning. Any child with relations elsewhere was packed off on the train until the epidemic was over.

Hildy Sissney knew that God would be sending five more plagues along any minute for sure, and sat watching for them to arrive, like a child on Christmas Eve waiting for Santa. They asked her where Cissy should be sent—to what relation or trustworthy friend—but Hildy's only trustworthy friend, at that moment, was Jesus, and she did not have a sound postal address for Him.

"I could always go to Salvation," said Cissy, thinking aloud. To Hildy, Salvation sounded next door to Jesus.

"Yea, Lord! She shall! She shall go to Salvation!" she cried and, considering the matter settled, put Cissy quite out of mind.

The neighbors, though, were not happy about it. They were less willing than her mother to put a lone, vulnerable child onto a train bound for a rumor of a place on the Missouri River.

"No, no," said kind Mrs. Warboys. "You and Tibbie can mess in with us, darling. Where you can fit nine, you can fit eleven, if everyone breathes in."

Hulbert, meanwhile, lay in Charlie Quex's back room with an old pair of cavalry field glasses near at hand, so that he could watch the space on Main Street where his home had once stood—watch it for signs of regrowth. His nightmares were filled with noise and pain and panic as he relived the disaster over and over again. But while he was awake, he gave great thought to his daughter and the need to get her away. "If I can just keep her safe . . . ," he kept repeating, as if she were the last and most precious item of stock spared by the collapsing store.

"I can't leave you, Poppy," she told him. "You need me here to look after you!"

"I'd rather have you back safe when there's a roof for you to live under, chicken. Mrs. Warboys comes in every day to feed me, and Charlie is keeping me shaved. Now if we can just fix up somewhere for you to go . . . I'm sending you and your mother to stay with your grandmother—just till the excitement's left her. You and she . . ." The rictus that tugged at Hulbert's face was meant to be a smile.

"Oh please, Poppy! No! Not Grandma Gorgon! Please! She'd be sure an' say everything was my fault!"

For a moment they sat in silence, pretending Cissy had not called her grandmother a gorgon, each racking their brains to find something nicer to call her without actually lying.

"Not Grandma, then?"

"Not Grandma, *please,* Poppy!"

"*I'll* take her, Mr. Sissney. *I'll* take Cissy and Tibs to a place of safety!"

It was Kookie. He was holding himself very erect, so as to look taller than his height, and against the low morning sunshine in the doorway, it gave him a look of martyred heroism. (He knew this, because he had checked it out in the barber's brass-rimmed mirror.) Cissy's heart fluttered a little within her.

"Kind of ya, son," said Hulbert gently. "Reckon you might be up to rescuing a responsible adult while you're at it? No disrespect, but I'd feel easier in my mind if an adult went along with you to this place of safety." Kookie wilted a little. "Miss May March might be willing. Send her to me, and I'll ask her." Kookie wilted even more. In his experience, adventurers rarely took their schoolteachers along on quests into the unknown.

"Take them *where*?"

Miss May March was a Christian soul and took her responsibilities as teacher very seriously indeed. But the thought of evacuating her charges to a riverbank somewhere in Missouri and handing them into the care of "Miss Loucien" and a bunch of strolling actors . . . well, that seemed quite the opposite of a Christian duty. She had met the former schoolteacher once; the memory alarmed Miss March even more than Miss Loucien's awful spelling or the liveliness of her letters. All that red hair, those curving uplands and hand gestures! No! Seeking out the shelter of the Bright Lights Theater Company would be like running in under a burning tree to keep out of the rain. Something inside her twisted up at the very thought.

On the outside, only her lips pursed tight. "If you're sure that is what you wish, Mr. Sissney."

"Cissy thinks the world of those acting folk," said Hulbert, trying to take the schoolmarm's hand but misjudging the distance. "And she's not wrong. I'd trust Loucien and Everett Crew with the eyes outa my head, and that's the truth."

The idea had come to him in the middle of the night, when a man with a head wound has all his best and worst ideas. He should not have quenched his daughter's dreams, he told himself now. He should never have consented to taking her out of school! Sooner than extinguish her spark of Promethean fire, he should have let her run wild, like a bronco, across the lush green paddocks of the world!

"You should never have given him that whiskey for pain-killin'," Mrs. Fudd told Mr. Warboys. "Hildy's kept him strictly teetotal. He ain't used to it."

But whether Hulbert's idea was the result of concussion, whiskey, or a temperature of 104 degrees, the upshot was that Miss May March found she had agreed to deliver Cissy Sissney and Tibbie Boden into the care of the Bright Lights Theater Company in a shipwreck somewhere along a tributary of the Missouri, called the Numchuck River.

Kookie simply invited himself along.

They were not the only passengers to board the Red Rock Runner when it pulled in to Olive Town Station. Chad Powers, hampered with cardboard tubes, an artist's portfolio, a spare crutch, and his arm in a sling, had to make several attempts before fitting himself through the train door.

"You 'scaping the diphtheria too, Mr. Powers?" asked Kookie.

"Me, I'm just escaping," said Chad Powers, his face a picture of fright and confusion. That was when the children noticed that the townsfolk assembled on the platform were actually hissing behind their teeth, hissing Powers out of town. Someone even threw an egg.

Inside the carriage, teacher, children, and inventor stared transfixed as the yellow yolk slid slowly down the glass—a small putrid sun setting on Chad Powers's career. No one commented on the egg. Tibbie, who had a horror of scenes, took off her glasses, the better not to see it.

"I shall be continuing on to Des Moines, myself, to visit my invalid mother," said Miss March, pulling down the window blind with sudden violence. "Where are you headed, Mr. Powers?"

"Somewhere I'm not known," he said, and turned his face to the wall.

"You should come with us to Salvation!" said Kookie. "You could join the theater, maybe!

Cissy stared at Kookie. So did Mr. Powers, unmanned by this sudden kindness. But talk of the Bright Lights had Miss March on her third tirade of the morning.

"Now, this is strictly a *temporary* arrangement, children. I've told you already: I want to hear no talk of theatricals. If your—ahem—*friends*—were not resting from their disgraceful line of work, I could not *possibly* place you in their care. I do hope that is clearly understood. We go in search purely of shelter from the hurricanes of misfortune. If I find this . . . *encampment* of theirs is unsuitable, I shall have no choice but to take you with me to my invalid mother in Des Moines."

The train, in starting to move, jerked Tibbie Boden into the knowledge that she was leaving behind her father, her town, and everything familiar and friendly. She ran back down the train to the rear platform and stood coughing up tears and protests and regrets. Cissy and Kookie ran after her. The little settlement of Olive Town shrank away from them into the distance, as though they had offended it by leaving.

"There are rats in Salvation, Miss Loucien says," Cissy whispered to Kookie.

"Didn't read out the bit about the rats," said Kookie. "When I read the letter in class. Thought it might color Miss March against the Bright Lights."

So *that* had been why a single page had lain in the wastepaper basket. Not for the first time, Cissy was filled with admiration for the sharp thoughts inside

Kookie's spiky-haired head. She had never thought of censoring the letters as she read them out in class. "Do I hate Chad Powers?" she asked him, suddenly needing advice.

Kookie shrugged and pulled his hands up the sleeves of his shirt. "Couldn't say. He draws spackfacious trains and boats and chariots and the like."

"And it wasn't his fault really, was it? It *was* Fuller's doin', really. Wasn't it? The store getting flattened?"

"Mad son of a—" Kookie began to say of Fuller, but he turned instead and went back inside the train.

If it had not been for Curly's prison sentence, Miss March would never have known where to start looking. She and the children might have traipsed upriver and down without ever finding the "shipwreck." As it was, they headed straight for the Salvation town jail, standing on tiptoe in the alley alongside, to peep in at the high, barred window.

So the first happy sight Cissy saw, a week after the demolition of her life, was the top of Curly's bald head shining beyond the prison bars. It looked like the classroom globe, and she wanted so much to give it a spin, for luck.

"How's things, Curly?" shouted Kookie, too excited to keep his voice low.

Curly slopped his coffee and looked up at them through bent spectacles. *"The worst is not, so long as we can say, 'This is the worst,'"* he intoned.

"We've come visiting!" roared Kookie. "Everyone's got diphtheria back home, and school's closed and Cissy and Tibbie's got no place to live, so Miss May's brung us to join the Bright Lights—we had to change trains four times! And this is Chad Powers, who come along for the ride. Where's this shipwreck, then?"

"Kindly allow *me* to communicate, Habakkuk," said Miss March reprovingly, but Curly was already at the window, dispensing quotations like rosettes. He and Miss March shook hands through the bars, while she explained about her mother in Des Moines and how she would not be stopping. Since Miss March was no taller than Cissy, prisoner and teacher were able to see only each other's foreheads, and with their free hands, they brushed away sewage flies from their faces, only to feel them resettle time and again, like kisses.

When Miss March asked him to lead the way to the shipwreck, Curly apologized: "Sadly, lady, I'm in here and you're out there—on account of the profanity."

"And did you speak profanities, Mr. Curlitz?" she replied, tight-lipped.

"Certainly not! I spoke the words of the Bard of Avon! But 'mountainous error be too highly heap'd for truth to o'erpeer.' That's to say, they didn't understand I was speaking Shakespearean—thought I was blaspheming."

"Then let us correct the error, Mr. Curlitz," said Miss March decidedly. "Would you care for a coffee bean?"

It was a tedious walk downriver, their path often blocked by bulrushes as tall as their heads, and by big hunks of driftwood washed up by the last flood. It was made more tedious by a fine, mizzling rain. Their boots sank into the soft black soil, and the footprints, as they pulled their feet free, filled up with shining brown water. The trees changed to a uniform, ghostly gray and hissed like the people at Olive Town Station running Powers out of town. The bulky luggage seemed ridiculous and irrelevant. Who, in this sodden waterworld, would ever need a change of petticoat, a portfolio, a book, a sunhat, a crutch? Curly tried his best to shelter Miss March under her umbrella, but the spokes only snagged on the vegetation and brought extra water cascading off the leaves. At one point a water rat ran across their feet and plopped into the river. At another, a section of bank subsided into the water like a suicide despairing.

Miss May March had harangued the sheriff of Salvation so hard that he had shortened Curly's sentence by four days and released him, just to get her off his doorstep. On and on she had raged about "sacred English literature," "small-minded, small-town busybodies," and "wilful ignorance." Even Curly had been unable to poke a quotation in edgewise. As a result, he was on his way home to the bosom of the Bright Lights Theater Company. As he explained to everyone who would listen, he was now not merely the ticket seller: he was front-of-house/accounting/publicity/prompt/refreshments/property-manager/walk-on actor.

"Well, of course, I shall be on my way to my mother's in Des Moines, just as soon as I've delivered these children . . . ," said Miss May March, unwilling to stray onto the insalubrious subject of acting.

"There it is!" Curly cried delightedly, breaking into a trot and pointing ahead with the umbrella. *"The barge she sat in, like a burnish'd throne."*

And there it was, indeed.

The poop was not of beaten gold, nor were the oars of silver, but the stranded boat was certainly a sight to see: a sight fit to stop Shakespeare dead in his tracks. Like the ziggurat of some long-dead civilization, the paddle steamer lay fringed around with vegetation, its full extent uncertain beyond the shifting curtain of rain: fifty tons of wood, rising in three grimy, mold-stained tiers toward the pilothouse, the twin prongs of its metal chimney stacks and the single curlicued word propped up on the roof: **CALLIOPE**. A single light glimmered on the hurricane deck, but the hiss of the rain obliterated any other sign of life.

"Ahoy there! *Calliope!* Room aboard for a few drowned rats?" shouted Curly, his voice squeaking with happiness.

"Is that its name?" said Miss May, peaking her hands over her eyes to keep out the rain. "Are you sure?"

"That's what's writ on it, miss," said Kookie patiently, gratified that here was a world where schoolteachers knew nothing useful at all.

Up close, *Calliope* was not quite so big. She was not one of the great Mississippi cruise steamers, which had once carried hosts of passengers up and down the country to the sound of large orchestras and a forest of trees burning in the engine furnaces. Just as the Numchuck was a lesser version of the Missouri or Mississippi, so the *Calliope* was built with less ambition. But some time before the flood, it had been a beautiful craft, lovingly turned out. The refugees shinnied over the bull rails, scattering their bags and baggage on the deck, then climbed to the deck above. At the head of the ladder, a figure in a loose dress peered down into the gloom, struggling to make out who they were. To Cissy, she looked like an angel checking the rungs on Jacob's ladder. All that red hair; those red gloves frayed at the fingers' ends; the comforting shape of the pearl-handled pistol tucked high up above her waist.

"Oh, Miss Loucien!" cried Cissy, tripping over her own skirt, stumbling up the last few steps of the ladder and into the arms of her best friend in the world. Saltwater spurted miraculously from eyes that had not shed one tear, and out of her throat came the most unearthly, banshee wail. *"Oh, Miss Loucien, it's all gone! Everything's gone!* Ma's as crazy as rabies and Sarah Waters is dead of the diphtheria and Poppy's all beat up 'cause Fuller dropped the silo on us, and everything's smashed to hell, and I'm not to go to school even when the plague's over—an' Pa's busted past redemption, an' I never learned the end of 'The Lady of Shalott,' an' I missed you SOOO MUCH!"

At the mention of diphtheria, the gloved hands gripped Cissy's shoulders and pushed her sharply away, so that her head snapped back on her shoulders; a leak from the deckhead splashed directly in her face. She found herself looking up into features wearier than she had remembered them, wearier and more anxious.

Then someone turned up the wick in those big lilac eyes, and fold upon fold of the cheesecloth dress enveloped Cissy, and cheesecloth sleeves drew her close. "Well, looky here, Everett—everybody," murmured the voice. "We got visitors from our former lives—when times were easy and the beds were hard. Someone put on a kettle of water, and let's share some news. Is that what we'll do, folks? Is it?"

Crouching with her face pressed hard in against Miss Loucien's front, Cissy was dimly aware that the teacher's familiar curvy uplands had been joined by a bigger hill lower down. After a moment's thought, it was her turn to pull away.

"Sacray blue, Miss Loucien! It wasn't Annie May at all! It's you that's 'specting the baby!"

Chapter Four

CALLIOPE

*T*wice a year, the Missouri rises. As it drinks down spring meltwater or summer rain, it loses its head and runs amok. It swells and throbs like the nightmares in Hulbert Sissney's feverish head. Forgetting the maps drawn up by fastidious river pilots, ignoring the dry, baked levees, it simply gets up and stretches itself. Overspilling its banks, unpicking its neat embroidery of tributaries—tributaries like the Numchuck River—it spreads out over the landscape, engulfing water meadows, swamps, landing stages, and riverside highways. It is an unstoppable surge of chocolate-brown water lumpy with storm litter, staking its claim to everything. And when it has made its point, and withdrawn, it leaves behind flotsam, like a drunkard's tip on the bar: tree stumps, shack roofs, dead cattle, cartwheels. Even boats.

That is how the wreck came to be sitting in a field. After prodigious storms upriver, the ship had broken its tethers, been swept off its moorings, and spun helplessly across a flooded river bend, coming to rest on a spit of land that had two days earlier been dry meadow. As the flood receded, the steamer had settled, like a dinosaur's skeleton in a tar pit, the paddle wheel at its stern snapped from the drive shafts, its frail hull cleaving to every mound and hollow of the ground.

Its fate went unnoticed by the owner of the field, who had died of pneumonia a day or two before. Only his goats and chickens knew of it: they sheltered there from the tail end of the storm. Rats and skunks quickly reconnoitered its three tiers, but apart from them, nobody knew about the ship. The dreary trees, hunching around like a circle of friends, conspired to hide it from sight. For a matter of weeks, neither the town of Salvation nor passing traffic on the river even knew it was there.

It was Salvation's children who sniffed it out. It was they who told Cyril Crew.

Finding no one wanted Shakespeare in Salvation, the manager of the Bright Lights Theater Company had mounted a pantomime for the town's children.

Cyril Crew had a soft spot for children; they were always so ready to steal from their parents' pocketbooks in order to see a show. These ones were no exception. In their wild enthusiasm, swarming over the improvised stage, trying on costumes and playing with property swords, one or two happened to mention the stern-wheeler beached in a field about a mile down the river.

Ah! Free lodgings, thought Cyril, counting the cents, bottle tops, and shirt buttons in the collection dish.

And now the Bright Lights mounted another play— on the spot—to welcome the new arrivals. (Miss May March tried to insist they shouldn't.) It was a piece Cyril Crew had written based on "The Celebrated Jumping Frog of Calaveras County." The five members of the audience had to spread newspaper on their chairs to soak up the damp; the storm outside rattled loose boards against the saloon wall.

But the magic held.

Cissy's dreams had not deceived her. The actors' big booming voices in the big booming space of the saloon deckhouse drowned out the noise of wind and rain. The story pulled her free of her weariness and worry as if she had jumped clean out of herself and landed way over in Calaveras County.

Revere was still so handsome, with his little whippety hips and sailor's blue eyes! Egil could do such interesting things with his face, as well as stand on his head without using his hands! Finn could play seven different people just by changing his accent. And though Cyril's gestures were big and wild, and Curly delivered all his lines as if Shakespeare had written them, Cyril's brother Everett's voice still poured through her like chocolate, and Miss Loucien—the new, extra-added Miss Loucien—still swooped around, graceful as a bluebird. When the champion jumping frog was fed ball bearings before the competition to weigh it down, Cissy laughed for the first time in at least a hundred years.

And when the play ended, she was slow to speak, unwilling to part with the magic of the past minutes. . . .

"Can I be your new actress, Mr. Crew? Can I?" The words fell into Cissy's ear like acid. She looked up and saw Tibbie Boden flash her pretty smile up into the theater manager's face as she asked again and again: "Can *I* be your new ingenoo?"

"Yeah!" cried Kookie. "Tibbie's pretty enough for Broadway!"

Cissy was filled with the desire to smash her damp chair over Kookie's head. She felt herself weighed down, pinned to the ground with disappointment, like an oversized frog stuffed with ball bearings.

Could fame and happiness really be snatched so swiftly away?

"Tibbie, hon," said Miss Loucien cheerfully, "if it don't stop raining soon, you'd be better off growing fins and making a career as a fish." Then her lilac eyes flicked in Cissy's direction, and she gave a wink as swift as a gambler palming a card.

That night, Cissy lay wrapped in a mildewed curtain and listened to the river rush urgently past to its tryst with the sea. She pictured herself riding into Olive Town one day aboard Cleopatra's barge. (The railway sidings had somehow liquefied into a new tributary of the Mississippi.) She was standing on a raised platform, waving an arm gloved to the elbow in purple satin. From the bank, Mrs. Fudd (wearing a starched shop apron) cried excitedly, "Damson! Damson! Those gloves are the very color!" And Cissy the World-Famous Actress drew them off and threw them ashore, tossing her long and (oddly golden) hair and saying, "Have them—I have plenty more like them in Rome!"

Then a noise started up a couple of fathoms below her head—as of giant rats, big as beavers, gnawing through the hull. After that, she lay awake all night, clutching Curly's umbrella to her like the sword of an antique stone knight on a church sepulcher, but twice as cold.

"Picture it, my dears!" said Cyril Crew. "A showboat! A floating treasure-house of the performing arts! A wandering theater, taking drama to the people!"

The rain washed over the wooden roof in pulsing waves, playing a different pitch on the stern deck saloon, the Texas, and on forward to the gangplank at the prow.

"Well, I must be getting on. My mother in Des Moines is expecting me," said Miss May March. In fact, she was effectively pinned in place by the weather and could go nowhere. But as soon as they started to talk of theater, she left the saloon as if in fear of infection.

"We have to be realistic," said Cyril's brother regretfully. "Showboats are all washed up."

"What, *all* of them?" Tibbie peered out through the dirt-caked windows, expecting to see a whole fleet of showboats beached alongside.

"The railroads did them in. Business turned away from the river. The rivers used to be the only way around this side of the world: north to south. Des Moines to New Orleans. Now people who want to get anywhere just board a train and make it inside the day. They can get to the big cities for theater. Even the water rats have turned sophisticate these days. No, the sun has set, I'm afraid, on the showboats and river palaces."

Clearly this argument had been turned over as often as a wet pillow while the Bright Lights sat around, waiting for Curly to be released from jail. But the faded, jaded magnificence of *Calliope* encouraged foolish ambitious daydreams; Cissy and Kookie were quickly caught up by the possibility of joining a floating theater company.

"You could have dances! A band! A circus, even!" cried Cissy.

"Acrobats! Magicians! Chantoosies!"

"Kookie!" Tibbie looked shocked. "Chantoosies indeed! What would Miss May say?"

Kookie was about to describe how little he cared what Miss May thought, when the lady herself came back into the stateroom. Her hair was wetly slicked down against her head, and her bangs dripped. "I would say *chanteuses*," she said reflectively, in a refined French accent. But her mind was not on saloon singers or even French pronunciation. Her mind was on the roof of the Texas. *"Calliope,"* she said in a sleepy, thoughtful murmur. "You truly think that's the name of the boat?"

"Looks that way, ma'am," said Curly through a mouthful of pins.

The rain slid the leaves around on the outside of the windows. Curly was mending costumes. Powers was sketching waterborne sailboats. Cyril was busy writing a new play for St. Louis if ever they raised the fare to get there.

"Are you quite *sure*?" said Miss March, and there was a plaintive note in her voice.

When the rain eased, they carried a chair up to the Texas.

Chad Powers climbed up onto the roof, where the huge placard stood bearing the single word CALLIOPE. What else could it be, after all, but a nameboard for the ship?

Behind the notice rose up an array of little pipes.

"The vents from the boilers, surely," said Finn.

"Look more like organ pipes to me," said Chad.

"Why's it called Texas?" asked Kookie.

"Beats me, Kooks. Maybe from up here y'can see as far as Texas on a clear day," suggested Loucien, holding her aching back.

Miss March made a noise of quiet self-satisfaction, like a duck smacking up duckweed. "A calliope, yes! I cannot wait to tell my mother. It is just as I thought! Yes! What a waste! What a shocking waste! If only we had it back at school!"

Kookie nudged Cissy in the ribs and whispered, "Must be a style of cooker, then. For roasting children."

It was only the discovery of the calliope steam piano that made them venture as far as the boat's engine room. During all their stay on board, the Bright Lights had never braved it, because, despite Cyril's daydreaming, they had never seriously thought of putting out on the swollen, heaving river. (And there is no point in starting up the engines of a boat stranded in the middle of a field.) But finding themselves possessed of a steam piano made everyone hanker after some steam to power it.

"Couldn't we try for just a *little* puff?" Mr. Curly had said, noting the sparkle of excitement in Miss May's eye. *"The man that hath no music in himself is fit for treasons, strategems, and spoils."*

Revere was adamant they should not. Revere had been a sailor before his acting days, and in his opinion, a lit steam boiler was "a bomb looking for somewhere to go off." He lagged behind, laden with gloom, as they descended ladders and struggled aft along companionways blocked with storm debris and crates, to the engine room. Cissy (who had heard all that nighttime gnawing) stayed put in the saloon with Tibbie and Miss Loucien.

As they reached the stern of the boiler deck, dragged open the swollen, buckled boiler-room door, and stepped down three metal rungs into the unlit stokehole, a noise greeted them that made Finn's foot slip off the rung of the ladder, catching Everett a blow in the head; in falling off, Everett dislodged

Chad—"What the—?"—who fell on top of Kookie.

The scuffling coming from the boiler was far too big to be a single rat. Was it perhaps a colony of rats—or a pig belonging to the dead farmer, trapped, unable to get out, and even now crazed by hunger? The pile of men on the floor picked themselves up extremely fast, and Kookie grabbed a log of wood from the fuel pile.

"Maybe it's an alligator!" he suggested. "Maybe it got on out of the swamps, down Deep South way!"

There was another scuffling sound from inside the boiler, and despite himself, Chad Powers started back up the ladder. A shape not unlike that of an alligator slid out of the boiler's round door, then rose onto its tail end.

"Do you feel it?" said the alligator. "She's on the move again."

Chapter Five

CARRIED AWAY

*T*he floor under their feet heaved. Doors throughout the boat banged: a many-chambered heart flickering back into life. At the same moment, water swilled from end to end of the deck below. The *Calliope* was awash.

The swollen river, overbrimming its banks, lifted the hull as the wind lifts a rug, rippling it from end to end. Older, fetid water was swilled through the bilges. But a tree stump had bitten up through her hull; temporarily, the boat was pegged in place by it.

"Everyone off!" shouted Cyril Crew, but the thought of the womenfolk and girls two decks up, plus the company's few scattered possessions, drove the men back up the companionways, hollering and yelping

with alarm as the boat groaned and squealed at every joint and weld.

Impaled on its tree stump, the whole ship writhed like a Roman who has fallen on his sword and failed to die.

Chairs and tables and theater props danced across the stateroom floor. Miss Loucien had gathered both the schoolgirls to her, their heads protruding from under her armpits.

"Everyone off! Everyone off!" shouted Everett. "She's going to wash back into the river!"

"But our movables!" wailed Curly. Already he had gathered to him a cocoon of possessions: a doublet, a crown, Cyril's new script, Mr. Powers's crutch, and a cash box.

"Better off plugging the hull," said the alligator man, who seemed to have stalked them up from the engine room.

Outside, lapping tongues of water were turning the mud to slurry, the undergrowth into streaming tendrils. Skidding and sliding down toward terra firma, the Bright Lights found only terra slimy, terra awash. The young men were the first over the side: Finn and Egil and Revere. Their dark shapes splashed away into the veiling rain, arms and legs flailing wildly. Cyril Crew followed more ponderously, picking his way through the slurping, slippery mud.

Everett picked up his wife and hoicked his long legs over the bull rails, but found himself up to his knees in mud that all but sucked off his boots. After three paces, he could no longer keep his footing. In front of him three trees, their roots washed bare of soil, capsized, falling, sprawling toward him, bouncing on the great gray cages of their boughs. Only by turning his back and enveloping his wife in both arms did he manage to shield her from the whippy lash of their twigs and wet leaves.

The whole world seemed to be on the move, sliming back into the mud God had once used to make it. Everett turned back and returned to the ship: it was the only shelter available. Child-sized hands, cold and slippery with rain, pulled them both back over the rails.

"Be better off afloat," said alligator man, lending a paw.

And whether he was right or not, they had no choice anymore. With a groaning shudder, the *Calliope* began to slip sideways off the spit of land. The men who had gone ashore—Cyril, Finn, Egil, and Revere—also turned back, but the ship dragged herself away faster than they could run to catch up. Frantically they shouted—*"Stop!" "Wait!"*—as though their friends aboard still had any part to play in what was happening. Sharp, hooked little waves, scuffed up by the wind, snicked and grappled the heaving hull, hoicking it back out onto the river, repossessing the wreck after its brief season on dry land.

"But we were snagged!" cried Everett, looking around to see who was left to hear him. "There must be a hole!" And if that was true, then surely that hole, now empty of the tree stump that had made it, was letting the river gush in. Within minutes they would sink as surely as an uncorked bottle tumbling downstream.

And so those aboard scattered in every direction, searching the weather deck and dark cargo space for signs of water pluming up from below—though, as Mr. Powers observed, "God alone knows how we'd plug it!"

"Cyril?" Everett could be heard calling between cupped hands, shouting into the rain. "Cyril, are you all right?"

Kookie lingered, however, and Cissy, too afraid to brave the rolling deck without him, stood clinging to the back of his jacket. He picked up Mr. Powers's damp sketches off the floor. Rolling them thoughtfully into a tube, he put the tube to his eye, like a telescope, which he trained on the alligator. Held at a distance, like that, the creature from the boiler room was less terrifying. He was simply a very old man, encrusted from head to foot in green mold and rust the color of dried blood. His face was streaked with oil, and his eyes had a way of drifting sideways. His mind did not seem to be entirely on the job at hand.

"Bet you know 'zactly where we were snagged," Kookie said.

The alligator, after some difficulty, swiveled his eyes toward Kookie. "Been workin' on it," he said.

Not only did he know, but he had spent several nights sawing and hacking at the tree stump in an attempt to part it from its roots. ("That's what I heard in the night," said Cissy, the noise of giant rats explained at last.) Then he had battened the stump in place, like a giant plug, and packed the jagged hole around it with old rugs and rags, daubing everything with tar.

In the end, the whole stump had pulled out, like a rotten tooth, from the sloppy ground. The mend had held, and the stump was now riding along, embedded in the *Calliope*'s skin, a tumor welling up through the deck.

Kookie, Cissy, and the alligator stood around the mend and watched black water well through the tarry rugs. They could picture, beneath their feet, the bare splayed roots clawing for grip but grabbing only handfuls of rushing river. The top of the stump wagged its head. The alligator wagged his head in reply. "That'll hold it far as Engedi," he said.

The *Calliope* banged and juddered over big, unseen obstacles in the river, which shoved at her and set her spinning. Faster and faster she spun, heeling over to an angle that threw her passengers to the floor and swept them all together in one corner of the stateroom, like pastry trimmings. A tree limb burst through one of the windows—a groping arm—but immediately withdrew as the vessel turned around once more. Chairs and boxes slid from end to end of the stateroom—drunken waltzers stampeding over the fallers on the floor. Beyond the banging doors, great gray waves weltered past, rising proud from the river to punch the hull.

Now and then, across the swell of Miss Loucien's stomach, Cissy glimpsed Tibbie's face, white as milk, and promised God that Tibbie could be the new ingénue if only he would let her see Poppy and home again. She shut her eyes tight and listened to Everett and Loucien Crew saying how much they loved each other and how glad they were to have met.

And Cissy tried to be glad, too.

"There is a tide in the affairs of men," gasped Curly, *"which, taken at the flood . . . ,"* but the shuddering of the ship shook the rest of the quotation out of his head.

The riverside houses of Salvation rushed past,

knee deep in water. There was no living soul to be seen. Cattle mutely bellowed from patches of high ground, their noise obliterated by the racketing river and the clacketing clatter of the paddle wheel spinning unchecked on its axle. In fact the clamor was completely deafening. It harangued the boat from shore to shore, yelling that it was *nothing! matchwood! sawdust! raffia work! history!* Then even the shores receded, and the veils of rain thickened until all Time and Civilization had surely been washed away.

The boat was a crocodile, snaking its flexible spine as it bore them away to its underwater den.

How long they lay there, clinging to one another and under attack from the furniture, no one knew. They tried to judge time passing by how far Curly had quoted his way through *King Lear*. But he had been through the whole of *Pericles* and was halfway out of the Sonnets before they hit Patience.

Like Salvation, Patience stood on a bend in the river. It had only eight houses and, thanks to the *Calliope*, almost finished the day with seven. They hit it nose on, crunching up a timber dock as though it were made of stale bread. The jolt dislodged a little cannon that stood near the prow. It ran backward down the deck, smashed through the wall of the cargo space, and got wedged between two steam pipes.

Up in the stateroom, the last dancing chair fell over onto its back, while the jolt of impact shook a single choking cry of fright from the people strewn around the floor. But though they waited for the *Calliope* to fall into pieces around them, like bad scenery in a play, she did not. Planks slid down the shingles, lamps spewed colza oil down the walls. The clapper fell out of the dinner bell in the saloon. The prow drove itself ten feet into the bank. But the *Calliope* did not disintegrate. She simply stopped dead, while the river boiled by behind her. And the passengers who tottered out of the stateroom onto the hurricane deck found themselves looking into the faces of a large family seated in a row opposite them, at treetop height.

The family was ranged along the roof ridge of their house, wedged between their two dogs, like books between bookends. With the battering-ram arrival of the stern-wheeler, they did not jump to their feet or hurl themselves into the floodwater but solemnly watched it demolish their landing stage, eyes curiously blank, hands folded on their ragged kneecaps.

"Hold on! We'll rescue you!" called Kookie, darting to and fro along the ship's rails, trying to think of a way to fetch the stranded family aboard. The gangplank was long enough, but it was in the wrong place, hugely heavy, and fixed in place by a winch.

"Yes! Never fear!" cried Everett. "We'll get you down from there!"

The Kobokin family gaped back, unmoving. "Same ever' year," said the oldest man resignedly. "It'll pass."

Every year his house was besieged by the river. Sometimes it fell down. Sometimes one of the other eight houses in Patience fell down. What cannot be changed must be endured. The Kobokins were not looking to be rescued. They were simply waiting, up on their roof, for Fate to take a kinder turn.

"Fresh water be welcome," said the mother, who was cradling a baby in her lap. Only the baby's kicking legs were visible, but even from a distance of thirty feet, there was a family likeness in those little pink knees. With an inventor's ingenuity, Powers climbed to the pilot deck, threw over a weighted line, and got the Kobokins to hold it taut. Then he slid a camping kettle of fresh water down the cable. After drinking from it, the castaways balanced it on the chimney to collect rainwater.

"Have you got enough to eat?" called Everett (which, fortunately, they had, because there was no food at all aboard the *Calliope*).

"Is there anything you need?" called Loucien.

A row of Kobokin shoulders lifted in nine identical

shrugs. "Could tell us the news, maybe," said the grandpa.

Everett's eye ran along the row of rheumy, passive faces, the hollow cheeks, the shineless eyes. He glanced once more upriver, for some sign of his missing brother, then drew in a long draft of air through a nose still dribbling blood. And he began to recount the news, undaunted by the fact that he did not actually know any.

He told them about the giant and monstrous Wallergoom shot in St. Paul when it was on the very point of eating the sheriff. He told them about the church that had been washed clear down to the Gulf of Mexico in the floods and been commandeered by the cavalry to fight buccaneers in the South Seas. "I hear it rolls fearfully in a big sea, but the enemy are sure impressed by the ship's bell!" He told them about the hosts of butterflies plaguing Natchez, settling on cattle and carrying them off into the sky, stuck to their millions of butterfly feet. "They don't mean to, but their feet get sticky with nectar, you see, and before they know it . . ."

He told them about nearsighted bandits who had held up the bullion train in Wichita and stolen three hundred eggs, a turkey, and a folding chair, because they got the wrong caboose. He began a report on the Kentucky Derby where the winner had been disqualified for using six legs—"Well, the horse was so short in the legs that the jockey could join in and run as well, and that's just plain contrary to the rules of the sport!"—but by then one of the little Kobokins was laughing so hard that she fell off the roof ridge and slid down as far as the gutter.

The whole row of faces was grinning and scowling in equal parts—struggling to hear Everett above the noise of the river. Ma Kobokin passed the baby into a neighboring lap and shouted, *"Know any songs?"*

So Miss Loucien sang. And though she protested that she could sing properly only when she was wearing a corset, her loose underwear did not seem a serious handicap. Her big, chocolaty voice streamed across the water in a heartfelt rendering of "Flow Gently, Sweet Afton," and even the river seemed to slow a little, like sauce thickening on the boil. When everyone joined in with "We'll Get Home to Heaven By 'n' By," Everett and Powers improvised harmonies, and Kookie produced a harmonica, as if by magic.

All this while, the *Calliope* swung to and fro, as if in time with the music, but (in fact) because her stern was still sticking out into the river. The surge of the current over her rudder was swinging her to right and left, making her bow splinter the last of the landing stage and chew a larger and larger bite out of the riverbank.

Eventually the river drew the boat back out into the mainstream, like a jealous dancer reclaiming a fickle partner. Powerless to resist, the *Calliope* spun around once in midriver, then continued her reckless plunge downstream. From the rails of the hurricane deck, the Bright Lights went on waving until Patience and the Kobokins were completely out of sight.

"You should do something with that voice," said the old man out of the boiler, again reduced to an alligatorish crawl across the tilting stateroom floor. "Dan Rice used to make a mint of money with his floatin' operas, I remember."

"Showboats are all washed up!" called Tibbie, sliding across the planks on her stomach, pursued by a spittoon and a café table.

"Well, this here's a theater company. And for now we're still afloat!" called Kookie, catching hold of Cissy around the waist just as she was about to crash into a wall. "So I don't see what's to stop us being a floatin' theater. Did I happen to say, everybody? I do plumdoodly cartwheels!"

Chapter Six

CASTING ON, CASTING OFF

"*T*hat Dan Rice fella," said Elijah, the boiler scraper and alligator man, "he useta build him a flatboat in St. Louis, put a deck on it and a kinda wood opera house, painted all over. Nothing like this, o' course—no engine, no wheel. Useta to push it along with a steam tug. Then he'd hire himself a troupe and float them downstream, giving shows. Everyone lived aboard, so no hotel bills—no barns or halls to hire neither. Most everything they took was clear profit. Once he got to New Orleans, he'd sell the boat for lumber, pay off the troupe, buy himself a ticket on a steamboat going north again. Buy a new flatboat. Start all over again. Did four or five trips a year, I remember. Made a pile of money. Always said singing went down best.

Especially singing by a woman with a big—"

"Vocal range?" Everett interrupted hastily. His arm circled his wife's shoulders protectively. They looked at each other, like two children tempted beyond endurance.

Somehow when Elijah described that long-gone floating playground, it sounded . . . believable. The great gilded passenger steamers might have sailed away into the past. Dan Rice's push-along showboats might have sailed into history. But one scruffy wreck bouncing its way from bank to bank, just making ends meet by supplying a little joy and excitement as it went? Well, that was a scene they could picture easily enough. How was that any different from a touring theater company living out of the back of a wagon?

"As soon as my brother and the rest of the company catch up with us . . . ," Everett began, glancing yet again toward the bank. All day they had scoured the landscape for waving figures—for the friends who had been accidentally left behind outside Salvation. Perhaps they had jumped some train, stolen horses, stowed away on a coach, and were even now racing to catch up with the *Calliope*.

But the river was moving the boat along at prodigious speed—faster sometimes than a galloping horse—and the floods had washed out most of the riverside roads. There was no telling when or if Finn or Egil or Revere or Cyril would rejoin the boat. All but three of the professional Bright Lights Theater Company had been replaced by an inventor, a boiler scraper, a teacher, and three schoolchildren.

"Ech, you'll need all kinds," said Elijah, rubbing rust flakes out of his iron-gray hair. "Magicians and fortune-tellers and hellfire preachers and quacks and freaks and all such. Put out the word. They'll come swarming like roaches: all evens and oddities." Thunder rolled around the edge of the sky, and lightning flickered. "Course it's gambling where the real money's made."

Everett felt such a jolt shake his wife that he thought she had been struck by lightning.

"No gamblers. I won't have gamblers aboard!" She said it in the way people speak of snakes or head lice. Her lip curled and her teeth clenched, and even her eyes shut out the very word: gambling.

Instinctively the children moved closer together under the table where they were sheltering. It was as if someone had named *Macbeth* inside a theater, or spoken a curse.

Elijah seemed a little old to be a boiler scraper, thought Cissy. At his age he ought to be taking life easier. But she could remember her mother telling her, with bitter relish: "Restin's for the rich. Poor folks like us, we just hafta go on slavin' till we drop." Elijah certainly applied all his frail energy to scraping the boiler, grunting and coughing in the narrow flues of furnace and steam pipe. It was murderous work, and the old man seemed constantly surprised by the unwieldy size of his body. "Musta put on a pound or two," he muttered. If this was true, Cissy could not see where he had put it. Elijah was as thin as a rusty rail.

But thanks to his efforts, when the boat next came to rest, they actually managed to light the boiler and trickle steam through the veins and arteries of the derelict steamboat. They did not even attempt to engage the paddle wheel, drunkenly swinging on its axle, for fear it would smash itself to pieces against the hull.

A dyspeptic bleat rang out over their heads, making everybody duck; next came an eerie, sorrowing howl. Strains of "Guide Me, O Thou Great Redeemer!" wavered across the Numchuck River, and Curly stopped throwing bits of broken windowpane over the side and held his hat reverently over his heart. Miss May March had fathomed the workings of the calliope steam piano and was playing it for the benefit of the herons, water rats, and catfish.

The *Calliope* obliged by putting herself ashore at Engedi. She caused alarm and raised voices by cannoning into the floating wharf and shunting a raft so hard that some of its cargo of prairie grass slumped into the river. The collision was made all the more sorrowful by a rendering of "There Is a Green Hill Far Away," played at funeral speed on the steam piano.

"Doesn't that woman know anything cheery?" protested Everett.

"Nope," said three young voices, as one.

They placed an advertisement in the *Winona Gazette* and telegraphed another to Branko, farther downriver. Chad Powers began painting a sign along the outside of the main-deck cabin:

BRIGHT LIGHTS
FLOATING THEATER

and they put up handbills around the town. Never mind that on the undersides of the handbills were advertisements for *The Tempest*: Shakespeare was no longer on the menu. The advertisements read:

WANTED
ARTISTES, PERFORMERS
& INTERESTED PARTIES
FOR VOYAGE OF FORTUNE
ABOARD THE PADDLEBOAT
CALLIOPE
TALENT THE ONLY REQUISITE.
APPLY ENGEDI WHARF, WEDNESDAY

Then for three days they sat tight and waited.

Elijah could recall auditions fifty years before for jobs aboard the river steamers. "River was a way outa starvin' in them days. Notice went up askin' for a roustabout. all kinds piled up on the bank a-hoping to get lucky. Germans and the Irish, for the most part. Last man standing got the job. Fought each other like jackals. Free-for-all fistfights. Germans and the Irish."

Even Kookie (who was one of nine children and accustomed to competing for anything on offer) was shocked by the thought of it. "You German, Elijah?" he asked.

"Habbakuk Warboys!" exclaimed his schoolteacher. "A gentleman does not ask such things!"

But whether Elijah had ever been either German or Irish, whether or not he had fought bare knuckled for his first job aboard a paddle steamer, was as lost as the date of his birthday or the names of his kin.

A big stack of life rafts had been stowed in the stateroom. On top of these, Miss Loucien spread a plaid blanket for the children to sit on. "Now what I want you to do, fellas, is to sit up here and audition the talent. If *you* like it, it's past doubt the paying public will."

"My wife trusts your critical eye," said Everett from the top of a stepladder, where he was trying to make the mildewed curtains travel along their runners. "Curly's too highbrow, Lou says. I'm too devoted to the spoken word. And your Mr. Powers has broken his glasses."

Once upon a time, a ten-piece band had played on the stage of the *Calliope*'s stateroom. Today it was the turn of would-bes and hopefuls. So Cissy and Kookie and Tibs Boden put on their most severe faces and faced the stage, like cats on a wall waiting for the moon to rise.

The first person to audition was a Chinese contortionist who could hold her head between her knees while playing the xylophone with her feet. She twirled banners, too, but the act was over in a minute and a half.

"Any more?" said Kookie, resting his fingertips together as he imagined a New York impresario might. The girl looked at him from between her knees: a look that said, *That ought to be enough for anyone*.

"I do again?" she suggested.

"Next!" said Tibbie.

"Thank you so much. That looked very . . . painful," said Cissy.

The Dutch clog dancer did not know any dance steps but sounded striking on the hollow wooden stage of the hollow empty room.

"Could you do something with your hands, too?" said Kookie.

"Semaphore or something?" said Tibbie.

"Thank you so much," said Cissy. "That was very . . . loud."

There was a dog act with three rat-sized terriers. The woman had an accent so strange that picking out her separate words was like separating dried peas from lentils. She was wearing around her throat a black velvet choker decorated with crystal buttons, almost as if she were a high-class dog herself. "I had four," she said, choking back tears, "but Twinkle got drowned on the way here." She had to say it four times to be understood.

"We'd love to have you!" said Tibbie, guilt stricken about the lost runt.

"Do they bite?" asked Kookie.

"Yes," said Cissy, who had just gotten down to stroke them.

The talent spotters were happy to see a lantern-slide projector carried aboard. "We have lantern-slide shows sometimes in the storeroom back home!" said Cissy. "Leastwise we *did*."

The projectionist, who had scaly skin and a paunch, hugged the shiny black metal to his chest, and his eyes flickered to and fro between half-closed lids. "My show's not for your sort."

The children looked at one another. Could there

really be a projectionist in the world who did not like other people to see his slide collection? "Do you have any wild-animal ones?" asked Cissy. "I saw a zebra once in—"

"No," snapped the scaly man. "You kids got no fathers?" And he cast about with his snaky eyes for some adult who might appreciate his wares. The comment about fathers did not endear him to Cissy. Nor did his habit of scratching himself with the slide box. But despite disliking his audience, he snapped open the legs of the projector and pointed it at the cleanest, least mossy wall. After a few curses and some complex chemistry with a pellet of lime, which produced a brilliant blue light, he slid home the first slide.

Tibbie closed her eyes and covered her face with both hands. Kookie stared, his mouth ajar, his eyelids fringed with exclamation marks.

"Next!" said Cissy with great presence of mind.

But the projectionist deliberately mistook her, and put in the next slide.

"*Next!*" said both girls simultaneously. The projectionist leered and reached for a third.

"Go away!" they shouted at him, all three.

"You wanna get us all arrested?" squeaked Kookie. Even so, his eyes stayed on the mold-spattered wall for a long time after the naked ladies had faded from view and the projectionist had clattered his way angrily ashore, spilling burning pellets and a smell of graveyard lime.

The *moving* pictures, on the other hand, had all three children enthralled. Medora, who was Spanish and dressed in Gypsy costume, was pretty attention-catching. But they had never seen anything so new-fangled or marvelous as Medora's Amazing Photopia. The images flickering across the wall exceeded lantern slides as far as a horse exceeds the painting of a horse. Tibbie got down and laid her hand to the wall to see if she could feel the fluttering butterflies of light and dark. Instead, the pictures engulfed her, patterning her dress, while human figures strutted jerkily across her smock and the blond curtain of her hair.

"Tibs, you're in the moving pictures!" breathed Kookie . . . and then they were all standing against the wall, watching gray phantoms play across their hands and chests.

The coin-operated, vibrating therapy chair was also immense fun. Since it was designed for adults, it bounced the children around like peas in a drum and dumped them unceremoniously on the floor. "Spackfacious!" said Kookie.

"Can I have another try?" said Cissy.

The chair belonged to a barber-surgeon called George. He was eager to set up a booth on board, offering shaves and haircuts. He rarely used the vibrating facility: customers begrudged another dime on top of the price of a haircut, and while the chair was shuddering its way around the room, it was nigh impossible to give a man a close shave without cutting his throat. Another service George no longer offered was phrenology.

"What's that?"

"It's a science," said George defensively. "Study of the skull. You can tell a lot from feeling a man's skull . . ."

"What, while he's still wearing it?"

". . . health . . . intelligence. But no! Only thing customers wanted to know: was money coming their way. Or love. Like it's fortune-telling or something. Don't do much phrenology lately." He sank into regretful recollection, then suddenly snicker-snacked at the air with a big cutthroat razor. "Could offer bloodletting for the sweating sickness!" Kookie (who was still a long way off needing a shave) asked for advice from Curly, as to whether a showboat needed a barber.

Curly was more interested in hearing about the sweating sickness. "Is it common on the river?" he asked.

"Common as fleas on a dog," the barber assured him. "Farther south you go, the worse it gets!"

"And what brings it on?" said Curly, reflexively turning up the collar of his shirt.

"Bad air. Bad food. Too much sun. Overwork. Who knows? But folk will pay to be bled and physicked!"

"Stick to haircuts," said Curly, running his hand gratefully over his shining, hairless head. He had once read a book about an Englishman named Sweeney Todd and did not care for the idea of a bloodletting barber. Casting an affectionate look at the little impresarios, he murmured, *"Did you ever see the picture of We Three?"* and went back to mending the window.

"I thought there might be ballerinas," whispered Tibbie wistfully as the next applicant came in. He wore a tall black hat, a long black duster coat, and a shoestring tie.

"I am Elder Slater, and I mean to give sermons to the wicked!" he informed them, "and turn them back from the paths of destruction!" His eyes glared with such terrifying zeal that the children dared not argue.

Everett, hearing the preacher's thunderous voice from outside, came to see if the children needed help. "Perhaps we could dispense with the gun . . . ," he suggested.

But the preacher brought his face so close up to Everett's that their noses touched. "I will dispense with my gun, sir, on the day that the Devil dispenses with his traps and snares!" And he went to pitch himself a tent at one end of the hurricane deck. Cissy could not see how money was to be made out of telling people they were going to hell. Kookie suggested it might set his audience shaking so much at the knees that all the coins would fall out of their pockets, but Loucien said it was more a matter of passing around a hat.

"Well, *I* wouldn't pay him," said Kookie obdurately. "Call that an act?"

There were no ballerinas, but there was a deputation of four black men with banjo cases. They were not exactly in the full flush of youth, their hair varying from pepper-and-salt to silver, but they were wearing the nattiest getups Cissy had ever seen—including two-tone shoes. Kookie, though, had begun to savor his power. "State your business and where you done it previous!" he said ferociously, and stood up on the stack of life rafts. (The men were all as tall as scaffolding poles.)

Benet, spokesman for the quartet, gripped the hem of his houndstooth vest with one hand and embraced his straw boater with the other. "Ladies! Suh! We was employed previous by no less than the Hamlin Wizard's Oil, Blood and Liver Pills, and Cough Balsam Show! We been hired out by them to revival meetings 'tween St. Louis and Houston. We's close-harmony an' Dixie—play two instruments apiece . . . 'ceptin' our banjos are presently . . . *sublet.*"

"Sub . . . ?"

"In exchange for a herd o' George Washingtons," said the second singer.

"George . . . ?"

"Left 'em on the peak of the *mont-de-piété*," said the third.

"The . . . ?"

"They gone swimming 'mong the sharks. . . . That's to say, suh, we was obliged to pawn them," admitted the fourth member of the band.

"Can you sing like you talk?" asked Kookie.

"Better, suh!"

And they could. They plaited their four voices around a medley of songs so catchy and cheering that the rest of the Bright Lights were all tempted into the stateroom to listen and clap.

"That's what you want on your bow," observed Elijah, nodding his head in time to the music even after the music had stopped. "Sing you into port. Gather a crowd. That's what we had. I remember."

"When, Elijah?" asked Loucien.

"Was a while back."

Told that they were hired, the Dixie Quartet (late of the Hamlin Wizard's Oil, Blood and Liver Pills, and Cough Balsam Show) bowed smartly, like butlers taking orders for tea, and filed out of the room. It was not until they had climbed to the Texas to sign their contracts that they could be heard soft-shoe shuffling their joy across the roof.

"They never said they could dance!" said Tibbie delightedly, her dreams of ballerinas very nearly come true.

When the next candidate came in, they were quick to tell him (before he could start roaring), "We already have one preacher on board, sir!" This man was dressed identically to the first—shoestring tie, black duster coat—except for his hat, which was low, as if it had ducked to avoid gunfire.

"Always room for both the cloth and me," said the man, looking around the room with expert eyes. "Me, I'd set up down thar." He pointed to the far end of the stateroom. "Put up screens. Discreet. Be sweet. No disturbance to either party. Ten percent to the house. Monte and faro. You know?"

The children looked back at him blankly. "Is that like bloodletting?" asked Kookie, envisaging some terrible surgical procedure hidden from sight behind screens.

The newcomer studied their faces with his head to one side. "Not unrelated," he said. "I'll happily skin a sucker anytime. Why don't we call it five percent to the house, after all? Reckon that's plenty for innocents like you."

"Why don't we call it *time to leave*?" said Miss Loucien's voice, and there was the unmistakable click of a pistol being cocked. "I'll have no gamblers on this boat, mister."

The gambler held his hands well away from his sides, as if to show he had nothing up his sleeves. "Clean! Clean! Nothing sharp about me! Nothing shady, lady."

But Loucien only advanced on him, the gun aimed at the waistband where he carried his playing cards in two leather pouches.

"Enough, ma'am!" he protested. "I'm wise! I'm advised. But you won't begrudge me a ticket as a fare-paying passenger? Carry me down to Mayhew? So long as I *promise* not to play on board, yes? Maybe I'll find me a more obliging boat down there."

"Y' can walk downstream on the water, for all I care," Loucien told him, "or take a lift with a bald eagle. Y' ain't sailing with us. I'm not carrying your breed as far as I can spit!"

The gambler backed toward the door, grinning more broadly than any preacher. "What? A river paddler with no sport? That's like a church with no steeple. People! What can I say? You're fools to yourselves." Skipping nimbly down the gangplank, he escaped with his dignity almost intact.

Meanwhile, embarrassment hung in the stateroom wetter than the condensation on the walls. The crew of the *Calliope*, not liking to meet Miss Loucien's blazing eye, looked at their feet, then slunk back to what they had been doing. Everett, though, studied his wife anxiously for signs that she might be ill. "Why particularly—" he began, taking the pistol out of her shaking hands.

"*I won't have them, I said!*" Loucien stamped her foot and sank her fists in under her cheekbones, which were burning red.

The three children, embarrassed still to be there listening, were glad enough to look up and find that another hopeful had entered the room.

"State your name and what you do and where you done it previous!" said Kookie. "Magic, is it? Magic wouldn't go amiss."

Cissy could not think quite what this one might be about to offer in the way of entertainment, what with his sallow sunken face, limp suit, and straggling mustache overhanging his mouth like a soup strainer. Mind reading? Puppets? Peanuts?

"Do you dance at all?" asked Tibbie of the man in the limp suit.

"Could you give us a taste, maybe?" asked Cissy politely when the man still failed to mount the stage.

"I'm not about to give you a damned thing," said the man, loosening his frayed tie and glaring around him. "But *you* can give *me* back what's mine. You can give me back this boat. I won her fair and square. And she's *mine!*"

Chapter Seven

PATIENCE REWARDED

Something inside Cissy withered and shrank. The back of her neck grew hot and sore, as if a starched apron had chafed it.

Now the *Calliope* would be taken away, just like the store; just like school. . . . Of course the *Calliope* had an owner. Paddle steamers are not thrown away like apple cores, into the long grass of a riverbank. Apparently the *Calliope* had *two* owners to squabble over her, and neither of them was the Bright Lights Theater Company.

The man showed them his gambling marker.

THE SUNSHINE QUEEN
AND ALL THAT'S IN HER.

"We wuz sitting right there," he recounted in his high mosquito whine. "I'm two thousand dollars up, and I want to call it a night. Then in comes this stranger. The house won't give him credit, he says, and he's thirsting for a game of poker. Who'll lend him two hundred dollars so he can join in the game? 'What you got to cover the loan?' I ask him, 'cause I'm feeling flush, right? And he writes this pledge for his riverboat: 'The *Sunshine Queen* and all that's in her—an' that's includin' the safe,' says he. And dammee, but he cleans us out. I watch that two thousand dollars dwindle and dwindle— biggest pile I ever stacked up. You're not telling me he was playing straight: no one gets that lucky without he's carrying five aces up his sleeve! Come the end, I've got a fistful of colors—winning hand!— but nothing to bet on it but his damned marker. An' I lay it down. I gotta! He's skinned me. He's just won every cent I got. Just gimme this one, I'm praying. Just lemme win this hand, God! Then this Black Hand gyp stands up. Puts down his cards and stands up. 'Keep it,' he says. 'I'm gettin' outa the shipping business.' I'm holding this winning hand—three kings and a queen—and game's over and I think . . . But it's okay! I got the boat, yeah? I still got the boat? I seen this boat: it's gotta be worth a sum! I'm off the hook! I'm not busted! If worst comes to worst, I kin mortgage it to the bank! Come the morning, I go down to the wharf to check her over: my ship. An' guess what I find." The man's lip curled with such contempt that his mustache bristled like a hedgehog doing gymnastics. "Gone! He's up and sailed away in the night. He's beggared me, the crimper!"

There was a long pause after the gambler's sad story finished. It was all too plain to see that nothing good had happened to him since.

"I think you are mistaken," said Everett, almost convincingly. "This note refers to a ship called the *Sunshine Queen*. This vessel is the *Calliope*—a derelict we picked up near Salvation." And he pointed at the sign on the roof.

The gamer in the limp suit pulled another face. "That? That's not her *name*! That there's a billboard! Might as well say she's called 'Don't Lean Out' or 'No Spitting.'"

They followed him up the various steps and ladders to the roof of the Texas and the peeling plywood noticeboard proclaiming **CALLIOPE.** On the way, they picked up a train of interested parties: Elder Slater, the preacher; the Dog Woman; Medora (without her Photopia); the Dixie Quartet. The man with the frayed necktie made a few feeble attacks on the placard, trying to pry it off. In the end, Everett felt obliged to help him. By that time everyone knew full well what they would find underneath.

THE SUNSHINE QUEEN
Venice Steamboat Company

The cardplayer's small head wagged in triumph on its long neck. "So you just shift yerselves off my property, and take yer freaks and yer animals and yer undertaker music with you! And count yerselves lucky I don't have you thrown in jail!"

There was another long pause.

"Very well," said Everett coolly. "I'll just go and make up your bill."

"Bill?"

"For salvage, yes," said Everett, raising his eyebrows and widening his large, expressive eyes. "I refloated your ship off a water meadow near Salvation. Plenty witnesses to it. Naturally I have no objection to you taking back what's yours, sir. But the laws of navigation say you have to pay me fifty percent of her value. For salvage."

"Salvage!?"

"And delivery, yes."

"Just cast off the ropes and let's get out of here," said Everett, watching the hunched narrow shoulders of the owner slump away in despair, cheated of his prize once again. The children were as hopping happy as fleas; the quartet were dancing. But Everett froze them with one glance. "The man had hopes, and I just dashed them. I don't find that cause for pride or celebration, do you, people?"

Miss Loucien stroked her husband's sleeve. "He meant to win his luck by turning over a playin' card," she said. "Us, we're meaning to earn ours by hard work, ain't we?"

He looked her over, soothed but not cheered. The look said that he would sooner his pregnant wife did not have to earn her living at all but could be provided for by a better husband in a better place. "I wonder what became of The Hand," he said, picking up the crumpled gambling pledge. Its owner had thrown it down in disgust, too broke to pay salvage on the boat he believed was his by right—and probably was.

"Fancy you knowing that stuff 'bout savages!" exclaimed Kookie.

Miss May March winced. "Salvage, Habakkuk, not savages. It is the act of recovering a wrecked ship. It gives certain rights to the person who saved the ship from being completely lost. Clever Mr. Crew *knew* that. Haven't I told you a thousand times, children? Knowledge is power."

Everett grunted. "It generally beats ignorance. But

to tell you the truth, ma'am, I don't know the first thing about salvage. It works like that at sea. I recall Revere saying something about it, and he was a sailor once."

"Not here," said Elijah, leaning over the ship's rail, measuring the river's depth with a weighted length of cord. "Not on the Numchuck it don't. No matter. It seed off that gambler. Kinder 'n' easier than shooting him in the head and losing the body overboard."

"I was unwilling to part with the boat," said Crew, looking more and more guilt ridden. Then he drew himself up to his full height, gave a shudder, and attempted to justify bamboozling the gambler. His voice was that of Coriolanus explaining why he had turned traitor. "In the absence of my brother, Cyril, I have developed *responsibilities*. Right now that feels a lot like the sweating sickness. I have seventeen souls, three dogs, and an unborn child to shield from the elements, and this derelict washtub of a boat is the only thing that comes to hand. I also think there is more chance of our lost companions finding us again in a large and watery world if we stay aboard her. That was my motive. If I swindled the man to do it, let it be added to my account on Judgment Day, but so help me, if I have to, I shall do it again!"

Having delivered this splendid apologia, he left the saloon deck at speed, a handkerchief pressed to his face.

Loucien hurried after him. "He's real worried 'bout his brother," she explained to those who had not guessed it already.

The *Sunshine Queen* was on her way downriver again, Chad Powers at the helm. But to say he was steering would have been flattery. The ship was zigzagging from bank to bank, sometimes tattering the curtain of willows only to cross back and frighten the birds out of the trees on the other bank. The *Queen* was not navigating the flooded river so much as riding it, bronco style. Every moment they expected to collide with dry land or with some floating tree trunk, and the boat to fall apart around them.

"He's overwinding her," said Elijah, shaking his head disapprovingly.

"Perseverance, dear my lord, keeps honor bright." said Curly.

"But you could maybe do better, Elijah?" suggested Loucien. It did not seem very likely that this raggedy boiler scraper had ever even visited the bridge of a stern-wheeler, but he seemed to think he knew something; and just then the water rats on the bank knew more about rivers than anyone in the Bright Lights Theater Company did. Everyone else looked doubtful, including Elijah. His eyes wandered up and down the ornate metal pillars, the wrought-iron tracery, in that vacant, tell-me-where-I-was-again way that made him look permanently half asleep.

"Could do it better with my feet," he said.

It sounded like bragging, but Elijah was not boasting. He was dredging up a memory of childhood. He contemplated the roof of the pilothouse, head to one side, eyelids drooping. As a boy (he told them) he had been too small to stand at the helm and see the way ahead. So he had sat on the roof and dangled his legs through the hatch, turning the ship's wheel with his bare feet.

"Humdiddly! They *let* you do that?" asked Kookie, instantly desperate to give it a try.

Elijah shrugged. "Don't recall anyone stopping me."

So they helped the old man up onto the roof of the pilothouse, and he dangled his legs through the hatch. His big scuffed boots were too big to fit between the spokes of the oaken wheel, and because the laces were missing, they were soon pulled off by the tug of the rudder. *Clump, clump,* they fell onto the floor. With bare feet, though, Elijah's skill at steering came back to him like a gladsome memory, and a smile settled on his biblical features as he brought the *Sunshine Queen* under control. Chad Powers could have learned a thing or two about steering from those deft kicks of Elijah's large grubby feet, but oddly enough, Chad did not choose to stay in the wheelhouse for long after Elijah's boots came off. He opted for a breath of fresh air instead.

The furniture grew calm and still, like horses after a storm. The crockery in the cupboards stopped jittering. The Dixie Quartet stopped throwing up over the rail; the colza oil stopped slopping out of the wall lamps, and the *Queen* became almost sedate, as Elijah steered a clean line down the center of the river. Now and then a crosswind would shove at her like a playground bully and send her skidding across the surface, but Elijah would simply side-pedal her back onto the straight and narrow, letting only the mildest swear words trickle like tobacco dust out of the corner of his mouth.

A lost brother and a guilty conscience were not the only things troubling Everett Crew. The floods were easing, the banks emerging, littered with flotsam. Trees that had been underwater shook their branches dry. People too would be shaking themselves and looking around. The *Sunshine Queen* showboat now held talent enough to mount a show. What it lacked was an audience. How was anyone to know about the joys in store for them without posters, advertisements in the press, or a lively reputation? All their past was upstream. All their audiences were downstream, ignorant of the existence of the *Sunshine Queen* and all who sailed in her.

As they came into Doldrum, it was sunny again. Elijah sounded the ship's whistle. The Dixie Quartet stood on the bow amid a cloud of midges and sang "O Promise Me" in close harmony. Miss March played harmonious chords on the calliope, and the resident ducks stretched their necks and quacked like little town criers.

But nobody came.

Elijah's steering placed the *Queen* just so—though the berth was shallow, and they could feel the hull scraping over mud. Two dogs sleeping on the pier stirred. Each opened a jaundiced eye. The Dog Woman's terriers barked furiously at them. The hellfire preacher fired his pistol and bellowed a few lines about the loving-kindness of God. The dogs woke up fully and ran off, scared by the gunfire.

Still no one came.

The houses were tidemarked by the flood, but Doldrum had not had it half as bad as Salvation or Patience. Even so, nobody so much as looked out a window.

They tied up and peered for signs of life beyond the dense nettles that grew shoulder deep behind the pier. A locked warehouse. A pile of timber. Nobody. For an hour they sat, like the ark on Ararat, and wondered what they had to do to fetch people out of their houses. If they lacked the curiosity even to come and look at a three-story stern-wheeler, Everett despaired of them paying fifty cents to see a variety show. "I think perhaps I should have given the ship back to the man who thought he'd won it: let him find a way of making it pay," he muttered.

"Oh, he would've," snarled Miss Loucien. "Soon learn to stiff saps outa their life savings an' gyp babes outa their lollipops."

The children flinched. Once again Everett glanced at his wife and wondered what could have given her such a hatred of river gamblers.

"Ain't no one used this stage for a twelvemonth," said Elijah vaguely. "Tell by the nettles, look. Ain't nobody stepped through them this side of recent."

They stared at him. "So! Why we stop here?" asked Medora, and Elijah shrugged.

"Was remembering a different time, I guess." The boiler scraper was like a fortune-teller with only half a deck of cards. Little snatches of information came to him through a fog of forgetfulness. "The bigmouths are good here," he offered, holding up a fishing line with a bass still wriggling on it.

Kookie, seeing that this might be the only dramatic performance of the day, jumped impetuously off the bow and sprang through nettles as high as his chest to take a look for himself at why the people of Doldrum were ignoring them.

"How'd he do that?" asked the barber.

"Thou art rash as fire!" Curly called after Kookie.

"Power of prayer," said Elder Slater, nicely taking the credit for getting the boy through the nettles.

"He's clever like Br'er Rabbit, that's what," said Cissy proudly.

"Where there's no sense, there's no feeling," said Miss March.

After an hour, Kookie reappeared. "There's no one home!" he called. "Not a mortal anybody."

A whole town deserted? Had the river risen so high, then, that it had washed the population of Doldrum out of their windows and yards, and away down river? No, the high-tide mark was plain on the timbers and undergrowth. So had the entire settlement been evacuated against disease or rehoused by it in the neat little cemetery?

"Maybe they're all lying dead in their beds with the diphtheria!" whispered Tibbie. "How would anyone know?"

"They'll be down at Plenty," muttered Elijah, eyes jittering over the sunlit water. When they asked him how far it was to Plenty, he shrugged: "Don't recall, but it's deeper'n this puddle. New landing stage there. Made this one recumbent." Memories only came to

Elijah sporadically—like mail to an African explorer.

So they unhitched the ropes and floated off. Kookie said he preferred to walk along the bank a way and sauntered off downstream.

"Why is he walking bandy?" asked Tibbie.

And two miles farther down stood Plenty. As Elijah had said, the dock there was new and sturdy—fortunate, since otherwise the weight of people standing on it might have broken the pilings. The entire population of Plenty, hearing Miss March playing "Guide Me, O Thou Great Redeemer," had dropped what they were doing and come running. Not just them, either, but the residents of Doldrum and Blane, Hoar Hill and Sunnyoaks.

All of the Kobokins were there—that rooftop family at Patience for whom they had sung, delivered water, and invented the news. That little captive audience marooned until the water levels dropped had passed on word of the Bright Lights to every boat that sailed by. When they finally made it down off the roof, the first thing they did was to tell their neighbors about the showboat that had crashed into their jetty. The word had traveled along forty miles of riverbank.

"Tell 'em 'bout the Walleroon!" called a familiar face half hidden behind a baby. "Tell 'em 'bout them butterflies stealing the cows!" And the children on either side set off laughing again so hard they nearly tottered into the water.

Grubby and fly-blighted, desperate for some light relief after the misery of the floods, people had flocked to Plenty. Now they sat like the faithful at the feeding of the five thousand, waiting for miracles.

"Hang out our banners on the outward walls; The cry is still, 'They come!'" declared Curly delightedly, watching more arriving with every minute.

"Beginners, please!" said Everett Crew, turning to address all his cast. "Ladies! Gentlemen! Let's give these good people a show!"

Just then, Kookie boarded the boat again after his long walk downstream; his arms and hands were livid, puffy, and covered in white spots. From the way he was holding himself, it was clear that the rash covered other parts of him.

"Saints preserve us, boy, what happened to you?" asked Crew.

"Ow. Ooo," said Kookie, unusually short of words.

"You look horrid," said Tibbie, and Cissy grew a span taller with indignation.

"He might be dying!" she protested. "Never mind how he looks!"

"Oooo. Ow," said Kookie.

"Curly said you were rash," said Miss May March, and laughed with surprise; she had never made a joke before. Nor had she ever called a gentleman by his nickname.

They started at noon, thinking the crowds would want to get home by dark. But the crowd had an insatiable appetite for fun. Even when Elder Slater roared at them, crossed the gangplank waving his pistol, and stalked up and down among them, bellowing, *"Sons of Adam! Daughters of Eve! Are you ready? Are your souls prepared? If I put this gun to your head tonight and pull the trigger, are you ready? Is your conscience clear?"* they only smiled and offered him peanuts and discussed the quality of his boots and nodded appreciatively at his repertoire of big words. Apparently hellfire was small beer after the torment of the floods. If they could get through floods, Judgment Day would be a breeze. They did not understand the words of Curly's soliloquy from *The Tempest*, but they clapped hugely every time he used a word they had never heard before, as if he had invented it then and there, just for their benefit.

At eight o'clock that night the whole bank was aflicker with silver light playing on silvery faces as Medora projected her moving pictures against the side of the ship, and the light rebounded onto the audience. The offshore side of the boat seemed all the darker by contrast. That was where Loucien finally tracked down her husband, perched on the Texas.

"I cannot pass around the hat," he said as she sat down beside him. "These folk have big troubles."

Pelicans loomed white out on the river, drawn by the light, drifting like Chinese lanterns, indistinct and mysterious.

"Don't, then," she said, and refrained from mentioning that she had not eaten all day.

Five times over, Medora had to run her footage. Only then would the crowd let her pack away the Photopia. Crew need not have worried about the takings. The audience might have houses to mend, children to reclothe, gardens to excavate, animals and vehicles to replace, but they had enjoyed themselves immensely and were ready to share whatever came to hand. The Bright Lights Floating Theater Company ate and drank its fill.

As Curly put it, "Best meal I've eaten since I was in jail!"

What the *Sunshine Queen* delivered to the neighborhood was the possibility of being happy again—not just dry or back to normal, but happy, with the prospect of something coming around the river bend better than a flood. Someone in the audience even came up with calamine lotion for Kookie's nettle rash.

Only the Dog Woman was unhappy by bedtime. One of her dogs, instead of jumping into its basket at the end of the act, had run off across the gangplank and disappeared. Even when only one light was burning on the stern deck, the Dog Woman could be heard plowing up and down the towpath calling, "Binky! Binky, darling! Come here, you wretch, you!" There were plenty of answering barks from the darkened stoops of the houses, but Binky was saying nothing. Next morning there she was, curled up in her basket with a smug look on her face and grass stains on her back.

Chapter Eight

MAX THE PLANK

*E*verett left a message with the sheriff of Plenty and on a notice pinned up on the landing stage. He wrote his brother's name in big letters at the top, but he barely knew what to write underneath.

> ## CYRIL CREW
> (also Egil / Revere / Finn)
>
> NEWS OF THESE MEN WOULD GLADDEN FRIENDS AND KIN OF THE BRIGHT LIGHTS THEATER COMPANY DOWNSTREAM OF THIS POINT.

"Can we telegraph home, Mr. Crew?" asked Cissy.

"Find out how Pa is doing?"

"And if her ma's stopped religifying?" said Kookie, who was scared of Hildy Sissney at the best of times and terrified of her with the full might of Jesus behind her.

"I would if I had the funds," said Everett, and winced at the disappointment on their faces. That night they ate a stew of bluegill, bass, crappie, and drum caught by Elijah with hook and line, lying on his face on the cargo deck. It looked like the contents of a slop bucket, but it tasted pretty good if they talked hard enough about other things.

Any news of Cyril, Egil, or the others was mired somewhere upriver. News of the *Sunshine Queen* traveled, though, with the speed of a swollen river. When they docked in Branko, they did two shows a day and ran the moving pictures as a separate attraction inside the stateroom. Elder Slater toured the saloons giving out advice on how to survive Judgment Day and passing around the hat. Branko had not suffered greatly in the flood, and the people there still had coins in their pockets. Everyone got paid, and for the first time in weeks the tension slackened in Everett's jaw muscles. The first thing he did was to check for telegrams (there were none) and to send one off to Olive Town's telegraph station.

⋙⋘

Kookie's father (as town telegrapher) labored long and hard over answering the telegram. His wife asked him what was taking him so long.

"We-e-ell. You recall Mr. Crew, when he was here?" Mr. Warboys answered, scratching his head with the pencil. "How he gave us the Declaration of Independence on the Fourth of July? A man like that savors words. Eats words outa the far side of the dish with a silver soup spoon. This wire's gonna need careful crafting."

"Just pick out the meat, Pickard," said his wife briskly. "Tell him Cissy's pa is doing okay but he's still hidin' out at the barber's 'cause there's no place else for him to go. Say by all accounts Hildy is still flying around the ceiling with the angels. And tell him little Peatie . . . little Peatie . . ." Her voice slowed and filled up with tears. "Best say nothing about little Peatie."

"*Little* Peatie indeed," said her husband gruffly. He knew very well there was nothing *little* about that hulking great lummox Peat Monterey; Pickard had felt the weight of him as he helped carry the boy's coffin up to the graveyard. The telegrapher blew his nose loudly and thanked God that Kookie was safe in Missouri, even if Branko did not figure on any map in the schoolhouse. Tibbie, too.

He *could* have said in the telegram that Hulbert

Sissney was so depressed about his wrecked store, so anxious about his crazy wife, so lonely for his distant daughter, that the townsfolk were worried sick about him. But Pickard vowed to say nothing of the kind. He did not want to bring Cissy running home to be a comfort. Children were better off out of Olive Town right now. Better safe than sorry.

At the same moment Pickard Warboys was wording his telegram, the Bright Lights Theater (and Showboat) Company members were making the acquaintance of Max, a big man in lime-green dungarees and possessed of a plank. It did not seem much of an achievement in life: a plank. Max's English was limited. Very limited. Limited, in fact, to Polish. But his pride in his plank was plain to see in any language.

"It's a frabtious *long* plank," said Kookie. "Half a mile at least."

"He's a big man. I s'pose he needs a big plank," said Tibbie distastefully. Tibbie liked things delicate, including people.

"Length isn't everything," said Curly. "*Hamlet* is four hours long, but it's better done in one hour fifty."

"Does he want us to *buy* it or what?" asked Crew.

Max, who had smiled and clutched his plank while they discussed him, now took a pencil from Chad

Powers's pocket and drew on his plank. He drew two people facing each other with the plank sagging between them. A small body lay on the plank.

"Moja żona, tak?" said Max, grinning.

"Someone's dead," said Kookie, confidently guessing. The Dixie Quartet simultaneously removed their straw boaters.

"Czy ktoś może potrzymać deskę na drugim końcu?" said Max, and swung his plank into the horizontal. Everyone ducked. But Max entrusted one end to a singer and held the other himself. Then he signaled, by waving one leg in the air, for Tibbie to climb astride the plank. All eyes turned on Tibbie, who took off her spectacles, because that was what she did whenever people looked at her.

"Do it, girl!" exclaimed Kookie, admiring her daring. So Tibbie did not feel able to back down, and she laid herself gingerly on the center of the plank. It bowed almost to the ground . . . but not for long. Max, with an unforeseen flick of the wrist, flexed the thing so that Tibbie was lifted as high as the deckhouse roof. She screamed blue murder and clapped her arms and legs tight around the plank.

"Nie! Nie! Rozluźnijć sie." Max laughed and mimed "floppy" so well that he appeared to melt into his lime-green dungarees.

"He is an eccentric devotee of planks, but he is

an excellent mime, I'll give him that," said Everett, bemused.

Chad Powers was eager to volunteer, not having broken any bones for at least a month, but seemingly it had to be someone small and light.

"I'll give it a try," said Cissy casually, half hoping no one would hear but Kookie. She resolved to be as floppy as a dead rabbit if it meant impressing Kookie.

The plank flexed downward under her weight and then upward, and up rose Cissy way above their heads. At the top of its curve, the plank stopped, but Cissy's body threatened to go on rising. She was suddenly weightless, skyward bound. Her hair flew loose, her stomach lifted. Meanwhile, Max described in fluent Polish how his act had entertained and delighted circus crowds in Plock, Lublin, and Warsaw. He and his brother had worked the plank while his wife, Anka, performed leisurely acrobatics within the cradling hammock of bendy wood.

Dead-rabbit Cissy let her knuckles brush the deck, then she was rising again, knowing she had only to let go with her knees and she would fly clear into the sky. It made her dizzy, and her stomach thought it was a really bad idea. But Cissy found it thrilling.

Max's wife had run off with his brother, leaving Max nothing but the plank. Being a placid kind of fellow, he had not gone after them with wrath and vengeance; he had simply emigrated to the Mississippi basin instead.

Up and down went Cissy, feeling a little more at ease with each toss of the plank. She loosened her grip and sure enough entered free flight for a couple of seconds. None of what Max said meant a thing to those watching, but they were warming to his plank. There was something mesmerizing about watching Cissy Sissney go up and down like a kangaroo. Loucien asked if it was a fairground ride for children, and didn't they sometimes fall off, but Max understood no more English than he spoke.

"No, no. It's an act!" said Cissy, rising and falling through the haze of evening insects. "Likely, I could turn over, sort of—turn around like an acrobat."

"Akrobata! Tak jest!" cried Max, recognizing familiar ground.

Not that Cissy meant to give it a try—not on the narrow side deck of a lopsided stern-wheeler. Unfortunately, her stomach informed her she was about to be sick. Her mother had always made it clear that being sick in company was an unforgivable sin, a crime and a disgrace, and that small children had been hanged for it or chopped up for firewood.

The plank's rising curve reached its zenith, and Cissy let go. She flew like a bird. Kookie whistled with awe. Tibs Boden screamed again. Everett

Crew swore. The preacher stretched out a hand in blessing—or maybe an attempt to grab her.

"Bądź miękka! Miękka!" yelled Max. And Cissy arced high over their heads and landed in the river a stride away from the landing stage. If she had hit it, it would probably have broken her back. As it was, she stood up in waist-deep water and apologized for making extra laundry. Seventeen people ran, collided, shouted comfort, came to the rescue.

"What was it like?" called Kookie.

"Spackfacious!" said Cissy gamely as she sloshed back on board. Seeing the admiration in his eyes and how he knelt down to wring the dirty water out of her skirts, she would like to have added that it felt like being the bluebird of happiness perched on top of the rainbow.

Max joined the troupe, and Cissy apprenticed herself, unasked, to this newfound circus act. It was not flashy or glamorous, but it was novel and funny: the kind of act that sent people home thinking, *I could do that if I just had a plank.* Miss Loucien anxiously and absentmindedly covered her unborn baby with protective hands and said it was far too dangerous. But Elijah knew where straw was to be had. . . .

—"How do you know these things, Elijah?"—

. . . and a thick bed of straw was laid down for each performance, which put Loucien's mind at rest.

Cissy's heart sank the first time Max put on his makeup—white face, big red nose, a newspaper wig: this was a clown act. Cissy had been hoping for tights, leotard, sequins—but she quelled her disappointment just as she had quelled her airsickness. It was not acting, it was not Shakespeare or even *The Perils of Nancy*, but Kookie never failed to watch, and he always clapped louder than anyone else.

The plank also set Everett thinking about *The Perils of Nancy*. Touring the newly built settlements of Oklahoma the year before, his brother had given up trying to interest the locals in Shakespeare. He had turned instead to *The Perils of Nancy*. The heroine of the piece got tied to a railway track by the villain, then rescued by the hero. Everett remembered Cyril watching him glue on his villainous mustache and saying, "These people live beside the railway tracks! For mercy's sake, the trains are life or death to them in real life! They'll love it!"

And sure enough, *The Perils of Nancy* had been a great success. Kookie, Tibbie, and Cissy could still remember every twist and turn of the plot. Admittedly, someone who had never seen theater before had mistaken it for real life, and shot Everett . . . but that's drama for you: an insecure and unpredictable profession.

Everett wanted a play like *The Perils of Nancy* for the *Sunshine Queen*. Shakespeare would not cut the mustard in Ox Flats or Washford, but there had to be room for some honest-to-goodness *acting* in between the variety acts. Everett Crew was actor first and foremost. Anyway, it is what Cyril would have done: a play involving the river; a melodrama about boats.

Max's plank gave Everett the idea for *The Perils of Pirate Nancy*. He raised the subject over supper, when, by pushing together all the tables in the stateroom, they could all sit down together and eat. Seeing the glimmer of excitement in his eyes, Loucien caught light herself. "I can do that!" she declared. "I can still swing a sword and tiptoe along a plank, and get tied to a mast—long as we got enough rope to go around me!"

Everett turned pale at the very thought. "No! No, no! No! What was I thinking of? No! Absolutely not!"

Loucien Shades Crew did not take kindly to people telling her she could not do something. The very color of her hair seemed to change to a brighter red. Seeing the makings of a quarrel, Chad Powers heroically drew her fire. "It's a scientific fact, ma'am, I'm afraid. A lady in your particular condition has a higher center of gravity: that's to say, your balance goes, ma'am. It's simple physics."

Loucien pursed her lips, indignation pent up inside.

"Shouldn't oughtta mess with physics, Miss Loucien—Mrs. Crew, I mean," said Kookie. Everyone joined in the conspiracy to stop Loucien playing Pirate Nancy while expecting a baby. The question was, who would play her instead?

Cissy saw Tibbie breathe in to volunteer, then lose courage and breathe out again. Ambition crammed Cissy's heart to bursting and she leaped to her feet, spilling her water cup.

"I could do the rough bits!" she said, amid a blizzard of breadcrumbs. (She had forgotten her mouth was full.) "Let me! You can tie me to the paddle wheel 'n' hoist me up the mast 'n' shoot apples off my head—I don't mind! I can be Pirate Nancy's daughter 'n' walk the plank and get sold into slavery 'n' whatever you wanna write, Mr. Crew, an' Miss Loucien can do the cryin', 'n' actin", 'n' all the wordy bits and the songs! Then physics won't matter, will it? Can I? Oh let me! Please!"

She did not look at anyone, because people always say no if you look at them. Her cheeks burned.

"Sit down this instant, Cecelia Sissney!" said Miss March. "I told you my feelings on the subject of *theatricals.*"

Curly stirred in his seat. "Sorry to hear you still

have feelings of that kind, Miss May. I was hoping they'd tenderized since Salvation. *All the world's a stage,* you know? *And all the men and women merely players.*"

"I am *in loco parentis*, Mr. Curlitz. I owe it to her parents to try and be a mother to Cissy."

"I suppose that makes me her father," muttered Everett, appalled. Cissy was still on her feet, eyes tight shut.

Loucien, thwarted, angry, and still hankering to play Pirate Nancy herself, saw Cissy's face . . . and laid her own feelings aside in an instant. She held up a finger to silence the others. "Well, that would be real swell, honey," she said, with infinite gentleness, "but you're working the plank with Max. There's only so much one trouper can do, trust me. But we thank you for offering, we surely do."

Cissy sat back down in her chair, tears pressing against the backs of her eyes like cows in a cattle crib. Her future as an actress had just collapsed rather like a general store crushed by a grain silo. She was a clown, and she knew she ought to be grateful. But her lime-green dungarees made her behind look like a net of apples, and she never got to speak a word.

"Tibs would make a real pretty heroeen!" suggested Kookie. "Or—tell you what!—I could be Kookie the Corsair!"

"What did I just say, Habakkuk Warboys?" asked Miss March menacingly.

Kookie won the day, though. Despite Miss March trying to act like his mother, despite Tibbie changing her mind when she saw the dress Curly sewed for Nancy, despite the playwright's refusal to change the title to *The Perils of Kookie the Corsair*, Kookie Warboys did land the starring role.

When he found out he had to wear a wig, dress, and dance shoes, he almost backed out again. But he comforted himself that he was two U.S. states away from home and among strangers: if any of his classmates had turned up in the audience, he might have died of embarrassment.

The Perils of Pirate Nancy was a huge success. Somewhere between Elder Slater preaching hellfire and Max's plank act, little Nancy got sold into slavery by her own father, carried aboard ship, attacked by pirates, captured by a mustachioed pirate chief, saved from death by the beseechings of the pirate chief's beautiful (but pregnant) lover, then offered marriage by the said mustachioed pirate chief. When she refused to marry him, she was forced to walk the plank (not Max's, which was far too bendy and needed for later). At the last moment, Nancy's dashing cousin (Chad) swung to the rescue on the end of a rope, engaged in a sword fight (which he lost), but did not die, because the pirate chief's jilted jealous pregnant girlfriend shot dead the pirate chief, who fell through a hatch in the Texas roof. (There was a mattress underneath the hatch to break Everett's fall.)

After the first performance, there was another mattress, nailed to the wall of the upper deckhouse, too. Chad Powers had worked out his stunt with infinite care, using a pair of compasses and a ruler: where to tether the rope, the length of rope to use, the arc of the swing, the ideal way to spotlight this feat of derring-do. . . .

He was intended to derring-do the stunt himself, but at the first performance he forgot to put down his feet at the crucial moment, crashed into the deckhouse, and dislocated a shoulder.

So at the second performance, Nancy's cousin Chad became Cousin Benet, and one of the Dixie Quartet moved into the acting business. Nobody seemed to notice that Nancy's cousin was as black as prime molasses and wore two-tone shoes: Benet, despite his age, was as handsome and springy elegant as a mountain lion, and there was an audible sigh from the women in the audience every time he swung a sword or plunged through the light toward his rendezvous with the mattress nailed to the deckhouse wall.

At the end, Tibbie, in a red-white-and-blue, star-spangled dress, said a poem called "America the Bounteous."

The gasps, the ripples of applause, the shouts of encouragement—"*You tell him, gal!*"—the tangible hatred for the villain, the *aaah*s that greeted Tibbie in her patriotic frock, all these were more intoxicating than strong drink. Kookie quickly lost his misgivings about playing a girl and shamelessly worked up his part. He added in lines. He slipped in a joke or two. He was supposed to venture only a short way out onto the plank before Benet arrived but pushed his luck further and further until one night he actually fell in. It fetched such uproar and excitements from the audience on the bank that he made a regular thing of it. And Everett could not resist rewriting the end to include it. When Kookie fell in, pregnant lover, bold Cousin Benet, and a repentant father rushed to the offshore rails of the deckhouse roof and peered distractedly into the water. Was Nancy . . . ? Had Nancy . . . ? Were they too late to save Nancy from a watery death? They threw down a rope. They all hauled on it . . .

And up came Nancy! Back from the brink of death, and plucky to the last!

Being wardrobe master, Curly hated the change

of script. "And how am I supposed to get the costume clean and dry twixt shows? Don't blame me if it shrinks away to a dishrag!" But the audience loved it, and so did Kookie, because it meant he stole the play's climax from Benet and Miss Loucien.

"This shift is falling into holes," muttered Curly, struggling to thread a sewing needle. Cissy had never seen him tetchy before. She went and threaded the needle for him and sat with him, trying to be helpful. She missed the old Curly with his big smile and endless quotations. "What's the trouble, Mr. Curly, sir?"

The trouble was Miss May March. As for the people on the riverbank, theater was a novelty to her. She had never seen it before. So she could not quite see the join between Real and Pretend. Watching Curly (who played Nancy's father) nightly selling his own daughter into slavery, she found she could not forgive him. So she had stopped speaking to him.

Before they were even in sight of the landing at Woodpile, the Dixie Quartet was dancing up a storm on the stateroom roof.

"Save your energy, why don't yuh?" called Elijah from his own perch on the wheelhouse.

"But this is Music Land, man!" called Benet. "We's like to be reunited with the tunemakers on Hardup

Hill. Just wait till you hear us pluck them chickens!"

The three other people on the pilothouse roof—Kookie, Tibbie, and Cissy—mulled this over for a while. They never bothered to try and understand the Dog Woman's odd Boston accent, because she only ever talked to her dogs. But with the quartet it was generally worth the effort. Kookie was usually first to work it out, but Tibs was a little in love with Benet, thanks to the play, and this time she got there ahead of him. "They say they can afford to get their banjos out of hock," she said. "This is where they pawned them." She slapped a mosquito that was just then supping on her blood, but Kookie had to pull the dead body out of the crook of her arm: Tibbie did not like touching bugs.

The pawnshop in Woodpile was an Aladdin's cave of other people's belongings. Cissy did not like it. She could remember back to a time—before the *Sunshine Queen*—even before her parents had begun a new life on the Oklahoma prairie. She could remember seeing precious belongings slide across a pawnbroker's counter—her father's chess set, her mother's christening spoon, a portrait of Queen Victoria—in return for a miserable crackle of bank notes. The money had been exchanged for even smaller tags of paper: rail tickets to Oklahoma. Unlike the quartet's banjos, Poppy's chess set would never be redeemed from the pawnshop in Arkansas; Queen Victoria would never again scowl down at Cissy from the living room wall, her eyes speaking of thrones and dominions.

So Cissy waited outside the pawnshop, watching Benet, Boisenberry, Sweeting, and Oskar retune their beloved banjos.

But Curly was in clover. He scoured the pawnshop shelves for new stage props: a sword, a cloak, a baby's cot, a turban, a paste tiara. Their owners had hocked them, hoping to buy them back when happier times came along. But a year had passed, and now the pawnbroker was free to sell them—a wedding ring, a watch, a Sunday suit, a saddle—for whatever anyone would pay.

Chad Powers found himself a galvanized bucket: he was working up a sideshow trick with electricity and a silver dollar.

Elder Slater seized on some old poacher traps and a length of chain and carried them back to the ship triumphant, rattling them at passersby and shouting: *"Behold the hooks and snares of the Devil! Will you be caught in the Evil One's traps and be torn by demons for all eternity? Repent before it's too late!"* His gray hatchet face was almost cheerful.

Meanwhile, down the road, Medora bought

magnesium ribbon for her Photopia. Elijah bought a new pair of boots, Miss May March more coffee beans for her complexion. Everett found a Chinese launderer to sponge the worst of the mud and grime off his Prince Albert coat and pinstripe trousers without him having to part with them. Miss Loucien bought milk of magnesia for indigestion. "This baby must be real clever: it weighs on breakfast like the *'cyclopaedia Britannica*," she told the apothecary with a wince. "You coming to the show tonight?"

Everett sent another telegram to Olive Town, asking for news. He called in too at the offices of the *Inquirer* and placed an advertisement:

CALLING AT ALL PORTS
DOWNRIVER OF WOODPILE:
THE BRIGHT LIGHTS THEATER
AND SHOWBOAT COMPANY
CIRCUS, THEATER, AND MUSIC HALL
ALL IN ONE
A SHOW FOR ALL THE FAMILY
UNDER THE DIRECTION OF CYRIL CREW

He believed in the power of advertising, but most of all he was hoping that his brother—wherever Cyril was—might pick up a copy of the *Inquirer*, see his own name, and realize how much he was missed.

After that, Everett went to invest the bulk of the profits in emergency repairs. At present, the *Sunshine Queen* was simply drifting downstream without benefit of a paddle wheel, her feeble boiler power going only to fuel the calliope. Thanks to her rudder (and Elijah's feet), she was steerable. But without the gigantic, romantic wheel rolling at her rear, she lacked her bygone glamour. More important, she lacked the ability to speed up, slow down, turn around, or sail against the current.

George, the barber-surgeon, after buying a bottle of antiseptic, went to get himself a shave because, wherever he went, he liked to size up the competition. He dreamed of arriving one day in a place with no barbershop. There he would come to a halt, living in a two-room apartment over the shop, with real steel sinks and a hot-towel machine. Somewhere people believed in the science of phrenology and the benefit of a vigorous automated massage.

It turned out he and the Woodpile barber knew each other from school days, and they ended up drinking lemonade together and snickering at newspaper advertisements for the new safety razor. Both agreed that it would never catch on.

"Seen that paddler tied up at the dock?" inquired the Woodpile man.

"Reckon I'm ridin' it," said George, who clipped his

sentences as short as he clipped hair.

"Huh! You'll be lucky! That boat won' be goin' no place," said the local barber. He was more the chatty breed of hairdresser and could not wait to recount the story of the last time the *Sunshine Queen* had visited town. George listened, watching his own face in the mirror losing color till it matched the towel around his neck.

"It's not even the money they'll be after—more revenge for getting gypped," the other man was saying. "I pity anyone aboard. . . ."

"That right?" said George, buttoning his vest and reaching out a furtive finger toward his jacket slung over the next chair.

"We-e-ell. There's some powerful nasty men in the poker crowd around here. They don't take kindly to cardsharps from outa town. That Mr. Black was a fool to gyp a bunch of Woodpile poker players. Even bigger fool to moor up here again." As his school friend paused to wipe the razor on a towel, George leaped out of the chair, snatched up the jacket, and fled, dropping a dollar into one of the zinc washbowls near the door.

He ran around the streets, collecting members of the Bright Lights like Noah collecting animals.

Sure enough, back at the landing stage, they found that a chain had been threaded through the stern wheel of the *Sunshine Queen*, tethering her to the pier. And a notice had been tacked to the hull, labeling the ship

STOLEN

It was written in red paint—at least they hoped it was red paint and nothing more ominous, involving squealing pigs and sharp knives.

Chapter Nine

GRASSHOPPERING

"Quick! Quick! Everyone aboard!" said Everett Crew, standing at the end of the gangplank, lending a hand to the ladies. Even in a crisis he was a gentleman.

A year earlier, the Black Hand had struck again. He had sailed into Woodpile calling himself Mr. Black, with money in his pocket, a mouthful of grand plans, and a thirst to play a friendly game of poker. Here in Woodpile, a whole nest of men had been left wronged and spitting mad.

Mr. Black had played none too well that night, so eager was he to tell the men around the table his news: news of the Grand Scheme. The president of the United States had decided to move the capital of Missouri to Woodpile! Government had hushed it all up—you wouldn't see a word about it in the newspaper—but the train companies were going bust. The people of America were turning away from the iron road and looking to the waterways again. Woodpile was the up-and-coming place to be—the future state capital of Missouri.

Mr. Black said.

So Mr. Black was going to sink all his money into building a shipyard there, and he was going to get very rich indeed.

So said Mr. Black.

The local cardplayers had enjoyed their poker that night, winning money from the luckless newcomer . . . but not as much as they enjoyed the thought of Woodpile becoming the capital of Missouri. They trusted Mr. Black. He lost at cards, and what kind of cheat loses at poker? He clearly had money to spare, too, because he lost a couple hundred dollars and barely turned a hair.

By the time the poker players all stretched themselves, scratched their bellies, looked at their pocket watches, and found that it was midnight, every man had invested heavily, buying shares in Mr. Black's development: the Capital Idea Company.

"Keep this to yourselves, men. I'm letting you in early."

Mr. Black said.

They agreed to meet up again in five days' time, for the first committee meeting of the Capital Idea Company, and said good night.

Except that next morning the *Sunshine Queen* was gone. They were each hundreds of dollars down, and Mr. Black was some two thousand dollars better off . . . and nowhere to be found.

The gamblers strapped on their guns. A posse of boats scurried downriver and up. They would find him and shoot his head off for him. How can you hide a three-story stern-wheeler, after all? But on the maze of waterways and creeks, amid river mists and rain like javelins, you can do just that. The *Sunshine Queen* had simply melted away, like a sugar wedding cake left out in a downpour.

They could not believe their luck when, a year later, it tied up again at the landing stage, masquerading as a showboat.

"Step lively, now," said Everett. "Hurry up there, Mr. Powers. I strongly recommend a quick departure."

Since the *Queen*'s paddle wheel was broken and useless anyway, Chad took an axe and hacked two blades out of it so that padlock and chain slid off into the shallows. With agonizing slowness, the boat drifted out onto the river and into the grip of the currents. She was still in plain sight when the landing stage filled up with running figures pointing, shouting, cursing, shaking their fists.

"I still say we should explain the situation to them," said Miss March. "I feel sure they would understand that we have nothing to do with this Mr. Black Hand."

"On this occasion, dear lady, I think the better part of valor is discretion," suggested Curly.

"I spy strangers," said Benet, who had just done a head count of people aboard. "Who's him?" He pointed to a skinny beanpole of a boy standing behind Crew as if using him for a windbreak. The barber-surgeon, on his high-speed roundup of the company, had corralled one too many passengers.

Crew turned and gave a start. "Oh! He's the carpenter. I was in the middle of hiring him. To mend the paddle wheel."

"But he just now busted it worse 'n ever," observed the carpenter, pointing at Chad and his axe. "Ain't no wonder you need repairs if yuh's gonna chop out yer blades." And he waved a halfhearted hand toward the sorry sternwheel clattering against the stern of the ship. "You turnin' back soon? 'Cause I got no makin's." He spoke with extreme slowness, swinging his tool bag forward and back so that nails and screws tinkled pleasantly inside. He smiled, too, at the nape of Everett Crew's neck: nobody in Woodpile had trusted him with any carpentry work for months, so he looked on Crew as his friend and benefactor.

There was someone else on board whom the carpenter was happy to see. "Hey there, Mr. Bouverie, sir!" he called up to Elijah on the wheelhouse roof. "You still sailin'?"

"Looks like it, Chips," said Elijah, and kicked vigorously at the ship's wheel with his new, shiny, slimline boots.

Elijah had never laid claim to a surname before, and it came as a surprise now to find he had one; also that he was known this far downriver. They asked Elijah how he came to know Chips the carpenter but got no more than a shrug for an answer. Occasional memories nudged Elijah's brain, like flotsam banging against a boat hull, but they soon washed by. Besides, his attention was all on the riverbank.

"Are we not getting a little close to the . . . ooo!" inquired Miss March as a twig plucked undone her bun and let her hair spill down.

"Thought you'd favor that to gettin' shot, ma'am," said Elijah. "There's four comin' after us on horseback, look. Gives them 'bout three horsepower more 'n this old girl, I reckon."

Willow branches swept the *Queen*, and everybody ducked and covered their heads. Ducking was a good move, because that was the moment the riders

on the far bank opened fire with rifles and handguns. Bullets tattered the willow fronds, pitted the
pilothouse, the saloon wall. Buckshot disturbed
the river's surface like panicky schools of fish. The
posse of embittered poker players was in no mood for
parley: they were going to vent their bitterness on the
Sunshine Queen, drawing no distinction between the
boat and the crook who had owned it the year before.

So close was she to the starboard bank now that
her two tall smokestacks were smashing their way
through the boughs of trees, fetching down twigs,
sending birds squawking up into the sky.

"Chad—help me drop the chimneys!" said Crew.
"Lou, keep down! Someone get the children under
cover!"

Nobody needed much telling, except for Miss
March, who was so horrified to see the twigs and
willow fronds thrashing across her precious calliope
that she fisted up her skirts and climbed three
ladders in plain sight of the gunmen on the bank.

Curly was appalled. "They'll shoot her! They'll
shoot Miss May!"

"They wouldn't dare," said Kookie, and the two
girls nodded in agreement: anyone who had studied
at Olive Town Academy knew their schoolteacher
would never succumb to mere bullets.

Curly and the children tumbled down into the

boiler room, where the tree stump still rose crazily through the floor, while Max and Medora and the Dog Woman lay two decks above, in their cabins. The quartet helped Crew and Chad to hinge the smoke flues backward, then crouched along the starboard rail and sang hymns. Everyone knew the Dog Woman had not been hit, because they could hear her shrieking energetically, in chorus with her yipping dogs; they could also hear Elder Slater damning the gunmen to the deepest pit of hell without time off for good behavior. Medora crept under the sheet that draped her moving picture machine when it was not in use, and crouched there in the dark, her collection of movies wrapped in her skirts.

Elijah, though, was obliged to stay sitting on the roof of the pilothouse, his feet through the hatch, steering so as to stay out of range. Almost. Chips the carpenter stayed where he was, on the deck below, stolid as a bollard, gazing up at Elijah, swinging his tool bag forward and back, forward and back.

The river was wide, the riverbank treacherous, so the gunmen had to stop shooting now and then to pick their way around a mud slick, a cattle drink, a piece of flood debris, a fallen tree. But without power to drive the paddle wheel, the *Sunshine Queen* was only drifting along at the same stately speed as the current. Bullets smashed two of the windows in the stateroom before the ship drew ahead a little and their hopes lifted. Everett Crew joined his wife in the stateroom, where she sat up just high enough to slap him.

"Why did you do that? Coulda got Chad killed! Coulda got killed yourself. . . . Lower the chimneys? To blazes with the chimneys! So we lose a chimney! Who gives a . . ." The noise of her fury rang through the ship. The stateroom, with broken windows, had wonderful acoustics. Even the dogs stopped barking to listen. There was some kind of physical intervention—a hand over her mouth, perhaps. A kiss?

"Let go my hair, you damned man!"

"The chimneys might have snagged in the trees," came Everett Crew's reply, soft but insistent. "Hooked us up, you know? Like Absalom caught by his hair in that tree."

"What tree?"

"That tree in the Bible."

"Gosh sakes, Everett, I'm half Choctaw, half Minneapolis—and neither half does Bible trees! Let go my hair." But the volume waned and the voices calmed, and the shushing of water past the hull erased the sound.

"There's a good hard towpath comin' up," called Elijah to no one in particular. "No help for it: they're gonna catch up to us there, lickety-split."

Down in the boiler room, Tibbie heard this and burst into tears. Kookie put a comforting arm over her, but his eyes turned toward Cissy, and his face had not a shred of daredevilry left in it. Cissy wondered if her father would ever find out the circumstances of her death and track down her body.

"There's a side crick comin' up in 'bout a mile," Elijah called. "If I can shuffle up there, we can maybe lose ourselves. . . ."

"*Truly?*"

"Maybe."

Why should there be a creek? How could Elijah possibly know—he whose thoughts had more holes in them than a pair of worn-out socks?

But sure enough, there it was. Though it had seemed like wishful thinking, and though it was almost invisible from the open river, a side cut disgorged into the Numchuck River from behind a curtain of willows. By some deft use of the rudder, Elijah drove the *Queen* side-on into the drapery of leaves. Green leafy tongues licked the decks and windows.

For weeks they had been tripping over the two long staves of yellow wood that lay along the deck to no apparent purpose. Now they found a use for them. The entire crew both fended off and dragged their way stern-first between the narrow banks of the creek despite an ominous noise of planks grazing bottom. They worked in silence: only noise could betray their whereabouts to the vigilantes now. One of the Dog Woman's mutts began to bark—a noise a posse could have heard a mile away—and Curly shut them all in the property box, with Julius Caesar's toga on top of them, muttering, *". . . when I ope my lips, let no dog bark!"*

"Oh, you cruel—!" the Dog Woman began to shriek, but she was jolted off her feet by the boat coming to a sudden standstill.

"Yuh's aground," said Chips.

"You have a viselike grasp of the obvious," said Everett with a wan smile, and Chips beamed with pleasure. He had not been treated so decently for years.

Wedged fast in the shallows of the creek, they were at the mercy of anyone who might find them there. But they were out of sight. The river spread over them its drapery of greenery and babbling noise, like Julius Caesar's toga. A few minutes later, the posse of aggrieved gamblers pounded past on the other bank without catching a glimmer of *Sunshine*.

"They'll be back presently," said Elder Slater grimly. "Sure as the Four Horsemen of the Apollyclips. Fulla death and pestilence."

"Sure will," said Elijah, his eyes shut as if to read

off the wrinkled vellum of his eyelids. "Big chain barge at Strommaferry. They'll cross over and come up the other bank."

The others stared at him. "*This* bank, you mean. How long?" said Crew.

"How long what?"

"How long before they come back on this side?"

"Who?" said Elijah.

The *Sunshine Queen* was aground. The heavy mass of metal that made up the boiler and engine block sat on the bed of the creek with only her wooden skin parting metal from grit. In a matter of hours, the gamblers of Woodpile might ride up the towpath behind them and empty four handguns into her passengers at point-blank range. The sudden stillness made the crew unsteady on their feet. The lack of movement made them travel sick. The willows fingered their faces sympathetically.

"See them trees on a level with the bow?" said Elijah. "Rope around each of 'em. Use'm like bollards. Pull from the stern."

"That man sure has a closetful of useful tips," observed Loucien, scouring the boat for enough rope.

There were plenty of willing hands ready to haul. But when they did so, it was not the boat that moved— it was the trees. The roots came out of the soft mud banks as easily as teeth out of an old man's gums.

The upper branches splashed across the deck and put a dent in one of the chimney stacks.

Hellfire Slater exhorted the waters to rise up from under the earth, but the Numchuck River had done flooding for the season and was on the ebb. The crew contemplated lightening the boat by carrying ashore everything not battened down. But it was all too plain: the immense weight of the boiler, the engine, and the crankshafts was what was pinning the hull to the riverbed. Fish were swimming freely under the stern, but the *Queen* was fast aground where the vast engine crouched, just forward of center.

"If we all stood in the river and pushed . . . ," Kookie began, but the hopelessness silenced even him.

"Grasshoppering comes to mind," said Elijah vaguely, and Chad Powers was up there beside him in an instant, paper and pencil at the ready.

"There's yer legs," Elijah said, scowling in the direction of the yellow staves of wood. But then the concept of grasshoppering—the whole reason for talking about it—sprang out of Elijah's brain, like a grasshopper through an open window. The men yelled at Elijah to try and remember. The women took a more practical approach.

"Why's it called grasshoppering, d'you suppose?" asked Loucien. "Must be a reason."

"Maybe if we clap our hands, it'll jump clear outa

the crick!" suggested Tibbie. Miss May March gave a slightly hysterical laugh.

Chad Powers scribbled in his sketchbook, as he was inclined to do at times of stress. "Anyone remind me how a grasshopper hinges?" he asked.

Now, in the glory days before school set in, Kookie Warboys had raced grasshoppers as well as turtles and beetles. Snatching the pencil, he drew a torpedo shape with legs like a spider.

"Carrots 'n' pears, that's not it at all!" said Cissy (who had once lost all her buttons to Kookie by betting on a rheumatic grasshopper). She took the pencil and corrected the legs.

"Then I reckon . . ." Chad Powers took back his sketchbook and began to draw, tongue protruding from one side of his mouth. His diagram looked like yet another plan for a prairie sailboat, but when it was finished, they could see it was a paddleboat with spindly grasshopper legs planted on either side of its thorax. "Block and tackle at the apex, right?" he said, thrusting the drawing under Elijah's nose.

"Yep," said the old man, as if the knowledge had been there all along and he had just wanted them to work it out for themselves.

The idea was to form a hoist from the staves of yellow oak and, by rope and pulley, to lift the *Queen*'s breastbone just clear enough of the gravel and pry her a few yards forward. A few yards were all it would take to break free. Elijah watched from the roof of the pilothouse, chewing on his beard, too old to lend any muscle power and haunted by half-remembered glimpses of other groundings: ancestral grasshoppers. He looked like an oracle divining smoky visions of coming disasters. "You put them legs in the river without shoes on, and they'll let you down," he moaned to himself.

They had no idea what he meant, but they soon found out. As they hauled on the ropes—"Lou, you lay off pulling, or by God I'll divorce you!"—the A-frame of yellow wood simply sank down, down, and down into the sand and grit of the creek bed.

They scoured the boat for the "shoes" Elijah was talking about, but nothing suggested itself. Had he just known it, Curly had held them in his own two hands back at Salvation, but nothing called to mind the two "Norman helmets" he had come across, puzzled over, and stowed in the property box for some future play with knights and jousting.

The mosquitoes gathered in clouds around their heads. Frogs onshore passed rude remarks about their seamanship. Tibbie began to cry again.

"Powinniśmy śpiewać!" said Max cheerfully, and launched into a Polish folk song about a shipwreck.

"Reckon we're up Sheep Creek without a paddle,"

said Tibbie, which was something she had heard her father say.

Everett kept looking down at the watch Loucien had given him on their wedding day. Curly saw it and remarked, in an undertone, *"Our minutes hasten to their end."*

"Quite," said Everett. "Time to abandon ship. They could be here any minute. Onshore, at least we can split up and hide in the greenery."

"They'll burn the *Queen* if they find her," said Curly, casting a glance over the dilapidated wreck he had come to think of as home.

"With or without us on board, Curly, and I know which I'd prefer."

The Dog Woman waded ashore with all her mutts floating in a wooden tub. Medora wrapped up her precious equipment, and Chad Powers carried it on his head to the shore, returning to carry Medora ashore with the same infinite care. He prized her technological genius as highly as her mirrored skirt and waist-length hair. Everett had just picked up his wife in both arms, and sat down on the edge of the deck ready to slide into the water, when Elder Slater emerged from his cabin two decks up.

"Thy shoes shall be iron and brass; and as thy days, so shall thy strength be!" bellowed Slater, advancing down the passenger deck brandishing his pawnshop

poacher snares. And lowering himself into the river like John the Baptist, he drew an immense breath and disappeared below water.

Thanks to the regular shouting he did in the name of the Lord, he had a huge lung capacity and did not surface again until he had positioned the spiky metal traps, jaws open, on the riverbed. He could have stayed under for longer if he had not been reciting a psalm throughout, for fear the trap jaws might spring shut on him and rip off both his arms.

The yellow oak pilings were heaved to and fro till they could be pulled out of the soft riverbed. Now the base of each beam was lowered into the jaw of an open metal trap. The traps shut with a noise clearly audible through the water and made everybody jump. And this time, when the Bright Lights Theater Company joined forces and pulled on the ropes, the A-frame sank its iron-shod feet no more than a few inches into the riverbed before standing solid—a triumphal wooden arch capable of lifting the poor old *Queen*'s heart when nothing else could.

With a noise like an explosion, one of the yellow beams splintered and broke. The grasshopper rig collapsed. A rope was lost. Medora and the Dog Woman were left behind on the towpath, but the *Sunshine Queen* was moving—was out on the river once more! Their hair full of wet willow leaves, their clothes soaked, their hands rope burned, the salvagers clung to the rails and marveled at their own achievement.

"Who'da thought a bunch of lightweights like us could lift a ton of engine!" panted Loucien, resting on her knees, one hand supporting the great weight of the baby inside her.

"Touch the mountains, and they shall smoke!" declaimed Hellfire Slater, beaming so broadly that they caught a first glimpse of his tombstone teeth.

"Loucien Shades Crew, will you kindly lie down and rest before I rope and hogtie you?" roared her husband, scarlet with annoyance and with straining on the ropes. "And can we please get those ladies back on board before the four Horsemen of the Apocalypse come back, guns blazing?"

If they did pass the vengeful posse of gamblers farther downstream, they did not see each other. A foggy dusk draped a gray tarpaulin over the *Sunshine Queen*; her passengers lit no lights, made no sound, until they were sure they had burrowed deep into moonless night. Soon afterward, the *Queen* rammed the bank and turned clear around before nestling to a halt in an eroded hollow. Chips came and explained that Elijah had fallen asleep on his roof. "I seed him doze off," said Chips, still swinging his tool bag forward and back.

They were ashamed to have forgotten the old man perched on the Texas, steering the vessel with his brand-new boots. They felt bad about letting Elijah exhaust himself, when he had, after all, saved the day. So they all climbed to the bridge and put Elijah to bed. He barely woke as they lowered him through the roof hatch and tucked him in on the mattress taken down from the deckhouse wall. Beside his head, Cissy set down a plate of breakfast.

Or lunch if he overslept.

"I make good picture from beside river," said Medora at dinnertime, waving a glass plate in its wooden slide. They took turns peering at the blurred gray image of the *Sunshine Queen* erupting through the willows, hinged legs to the fore, very much like a three-story grasshopper. The moment had been preserved forever. Each member of the company contemplated the wonders of photography and thought of someone they would like to show this picture to—friend, father, brother, wife—in days to come.

And one by one each succumbed to tears for fear that they would never again see that person— friend, father, brother, wife. Even Max thought of his runaway wife and shed tears because now he would never get the chance to show her the photo and see her think twice about breaking up the team.

Medora looked around her at the tears running down, folded the plate away in chamois leather, and ate her dinner.

Next day, Everett persuaded Elijah to start giving him (and Chad and Curly and Benet) lessons in how to steer the boat, so that in the future they could share the work.

Chapter Ten

FEVERISH ACTIVITY

"*I*t's hot here," said Tibbie as they docked in Timberlake. Her pink cheeks and down-turned mouth made her look quarrelsome, as if Timberlake were not trying hard enough. Cissy said there was a nice smell of fresh paint. Tibs said it made her feel sick.

They stayed over in Timberlake to make much-needed repairs to the boat. Here was a town that prized the river. Every yard was home to a rowboat. There were fish traps in evidence, and eddies of stale bread in the river where local anglers were training the fish to gather. And there was a boatyard with jetties and pilings and boat cradles. In pride of place on its shoreline lay an elegant oak slipper launch. It was plain who owned it: it was called *Sheriff's Star*. There was even a ship's chandlery, selling marine paint, fenders, and the like. Not that they could afford any of these temptations. They confined themselves to patching the hole in the bottom of the hull with something better than a tree stump, getting the engine working, and giving Chips time to rebuild the paddle wheel.

It did not sound like much. Thanks to Elijah, the boiler and ducts were as clean as bagpipes. One broken piston rod, a leak in the compression chamber, some chain links that had seized as solid as an old lady's joints: how hard could it be? The local engineer they hired—a Scotsman—was so sparing with his speech that they feared he would charge by the word if they tried chatting with him, so they left him alone to bang around in the bowels of the boat with his wrench, wearing a miner's helmet with a candle in it. Elijah, who was territorial about the engine room, stood by with a bucket of water in case the candle set light to his boat.

Everett, meanwhile, went off in search of timber, taking Medora with him. In exchange for a portrait photo of him and his seven children, the boatyard owner pointed out a derelict rowboat half full of water, and said they could break it up for usable timber.

"Barter's a wonderful thing," said Everett on his

return. He told Chips the good news, and away went the carpenter, returning with useful amounts of excellent oak.

Though he generally moved with the slowness of a deep-sea diver in lead boots, give him some wood and a hammer and Chips was transformed. He climbed into the paddle wheel like a rat into a treadmill, and he fitted blades, mended struts, replaced spindles, and whopped on the paint with happy abandon. It was true that the wheel did not revolve afterward, but Chad Powers soon tracked down the problem—Chips had nailed it fast.

"Kept leaning over, kinda," said Chips discontentedly.

Chad pried out the nails, and the wheel slumped sideways.

"Piddock," said the Scots engineer, emerging from the engine room, the candle in his hat quivering with contempt.

"Only two-thirds of the blades hit the water," said Chad.

"I think it's kinda jaunty," said Loucien gamely, and linked arms with the carpenter. "At least it spins now. And two thirds of a wheel is better than no wheel at all."

The rest of the oak went to mend the hole in the hull. It did not entirely keep out the river, which wormed its way in to examine Chip's carpentry from both sides. But moving around the engine room was a lot easier now that the tree trunk was gone. Elijah splashed tar over the leaks, while everyone else hauled the *Sunshine Queen* on ropes into place alongside the Timberlake landing stage, in readiness for the evening performance.

"Where did Chips get that oak?" Elijah asked, wiping tarry hands on a rag. He and Everett were sitting on the bull rail watching Hellfire Slater harangue the gathering audience. Crew was thinking, yet again, what an odd form of entertainment it was.

"There's a hulk in the boatyard. Man said we could help ourselves."

"That oak's no junk," said Elijah. "Perfect. Varnish perfect. Nice. Take a look." So Everett and Elijah went down into the engine room. Before he got there, Everett was starting to know what he would find. Most damning of all were the words sticking out, in timber bas-relief, just below the expansion tube: SHERIFF'S STAR.

"Good. Good," Everett said, nodding and smiling and thinking back. He took a stroll along the bank, just to check that his worst fears were well founded.

The sunken derelict lay where it had, brimful of moonlight and river water, untouched. Pulled up on the slip lay the keel and ribs of a boat, like the rib cage of something vultures have stripped. Earlier in the day it had been an elegant, lovingly maintained slipper launch.

Chips had stripped the wrong boat.

Everett looked around him at the sleeping boatyard, turned up the collar of his jacket, and sauntered ever so casually back along the wharf to where Medora was showing moving pictures of timber logging in Canada.

"Early call tomorrow, folks," he said softly, each time he passed one of the Bright Lights Theater Company. "I fear we may have abused our guests' hospitality." He would have liked to make amends to the owner of the slipper launch, but the takings for the evening would not begin to cover it. With luck, the ghastly mistake would not be discovered until they were far, far away.

"Chips is a pribbling, swag-bellied skainsmate," said Curly.

"He means well," said Everett.

"He's a clay-brained scut."

"He got the paddle wheel working. We can make a quickish getaway," said Everett, but Curly only went on shaking his head in sorrow and cursing Chips in Tudor English.

Just as the fish started to rise and feast on the clouds of evening insects, the Bright Lights Showboat Company gave the good people of Timberlake *The Perils of Pirate Nancy,* and it was their best yet. Curly heartlessly sold his daughter into slavery. The dastardly pirate was all set to kill her until his pregnant lover talked him around. Then Nancy turned down his proposal flat as a skillet. Nancy walked the plank, and the audience yelped and gasped as she fell with a cry of *"I'm an American, you fiend!"*

Then somehow it all got even more exciting.

Chad lit a piece of Medora's magnesium ribbon, dropped it into a bottle—he had been aching to try it—and thrust it into Benet's grip. Benet, lit by its incandescent light, swung across the stage and made an elegant touchdown. But confronted by the villainous mustachioed pirate chief, he found he could not draw his sword, because of the flare bottle in his sword hand, so he threw it over the rail.

It narrowly missed Kookie and sank to the riverbed. But it went on burning even underwater—which is the way of magnesium. Then Loucien shot the villainous pirate chief: he should have fallen through the roof hatch, except that he remembered, in the nick of time, removing the mattress for Elijah to sleep on. So he died on the spot instead, and tried not to breathe too heavily (which is difficult after a strenuous sword fight).

"Help! Quick! Get me out!" yelled Kookie from down

below, and the fear in his voice was very convincing: he seemed to be getting the knack of acting.

"There goes Kookie, milking it as usual," said Cissy, as she hooked Tibbie into the red-white-and-blue dress in a cabin nearby.

"Mmm," said Tibbie vaguely.

Concerned parties rushed to the side of the boat and, in accordance with the script, scoured the water for signs of life, though it was all too obvious that Nancy was still alive because she was hollering:

"Alligator! Help! Get me out for the love of—"

"Aw, now he's just bein' ridiculous," said Cissy.

"That Habakkuk Warboys is *such* a fool," said Miss March.

"Mmm," said Tibbie.

From up top, Loucien, Benet, and Curly struck exaggerated poses of grief and woe, facing the bank as much as possible (because it is a rule of the theater that you don't turn your back on the audience). On the floor by their feet, the dead pirate chief growled with annoyance at Kookie messing with the script yet again.

"Pleeeease!" said Kookie, but this time very quietly. He was standing on the bottom, head and shoulders above water, arms lifted high over his head. But they could see the rest of him, thanks to the flare still burning away on the riverbed, lighting up an

underwater world. The flare had drawn fishes from far and wide into its circle of light. They were clearly visible round about him, like demons conjured by black magic. One of the shadows was torpedo shaped and so long that its tail was still in darkness while its flat snout was nudging at Nancy's white frock. Kookie was no longer calling out, but his upturned face was a round, white circle beseeching someone— anyone—to believe him.

"Frimony," said Boisenberry.

"Shotten herring," said Curly.

"Holy Simon Cameron," said Benet under his breath. "It's the genuine article. Boy's gonna get ate."

But still no one moved, because no one knew what to do. Benet feared that, if he threw the rope, the splash would startle the creature into attacking.

"Do something, Everett!" whispered Loucien, and (confusingly for the audience) the dead pirate chief got to his feet and joined the anxious knot of people at the ship's rail.

Meanwhile, in the dressing room, Cissy looked up. Without knowing it, she had developed the habit of moving her lips in time with the actors'. Now she sensed a space that should not be there, sensed a change in the schedule. "Kookie's drowned," she told Miss May, and rushed outside, lime-green dungarees or no lime-green dungarees.

In fact, the stage filled up with all manner of people who were not usually in the play. Two clowns, a Gypsy projectionist, three barbershop singers, a barber, an organist, and a woman clutching a dog to her chest.

It was Miss March who had the presence of mind to grab Moppet out of the Dog Woman's arms and throw it into the river: an alternative meal for the alligator.

"You witch!" screamed the Dog Woman, and launched a punch at Miss May. Then the commotion in the water drew them back, spellbound, to the rail.

Luckily, audiences do not give much thought to plot, and the people of Timberlake were so thrilled and bewildered that they stood up, shouting, gasping, pushing one another out of the way, holding their children up to see better or hugging them close in case the news was too upsetting for youngsters to hear.

Hand over hand, gingerly, Benet fed out the rope, which Kookie grabbed and clung to like a burr to a cat. When they pulled him up, it looked more like landing a tuna than rescuing a maiden in distress.

"Miss May, you're a wonder!" Kookie said as he came headfirst over the rail, got up, and hugged his schoolteacher. It left the audience thinking the lady with the bun must be some kind of fairy godmother, like in "Cinderella." But they really did not care. Pirate Nancy had been saved from drowning and (if they had heard right) the jaws of an alligator! Mothers assured their children that the little doggie wasn't real . . . just a puppet. The children complained they hadn't been able to see the alligator eat the dog. But they all cheered and stamped and called the actors back seven times over to applaud them. Tibbie gave a particularly wavering recital of "America the Bounteous Land" that reduced grown men to tears.

There was a pause then, because the Dog Woman had shut herself in her cabin and would not come out. So Max and Cissy and Sweeting came on with the plank and soothed the audience with the gentle comedy of their routine, and the evening ended with Loucien singing "Flow Gently, Sweet Afton" to the accompaniment of banjos, a harmonica, and a swanee whistle. No sooner had the song finished than the showboat gave a rude belch and the calliope on its roof wheezed into life. Instead of "Lead, Kindly Light," Miss March made a game attempt at "Polly Wolly Doodle." It started slow but speeded up, as she found the right key, and was positively storming along by the time the kerosene ran out in her lamp and she could no longer see the keys.

The great thing about disasters is that they feel so good afterward.

Moppet swam ashore and found her own way aboard again, showing no sign of resenting the swim. The company checked her over for missing limbs, but the alligator was either vegetarian or had been hit between the eyes with Moppet, lost its appetite, and swum off. They tossed another flare into the river, intrigued now to catch a glimpse of the monster. Fish were drawn to the light like iron filings to a magnet, but there was no sign of the alligator.

"'Gator gar," said Elijah, unimpressed by the whole spectacle.

"It was *this big*!" said Kookie for the fifteenth time.

"We saw it!" Cissy backed him up.

"Yup. They come up real big, garfish," Elijah conceded. "Take ducks. Water rats. Swans even. Seen 'em."

Kookie, who had seen the snout, seen the dark shape heading his way, felt the nudge against his hip, would have stood up in a court of law and sworn to it being an alligator. Years later, he was still describing the encounter, and by then the beast had grown to the size of Rhode Island. Everyone else was rather relieved to think the Numchuck River held nothing more deadly than giant garfish.

Curly was particularly happy. "If it means he won't fling himself in the water every opportunity

God sends, I don't care if it was a shark," he said as he wrung out the white smock and knocked the bonnet back into shape. "That fish just halved the laundry."

The great thing about disasters is that afterward it feels as if all the bad times have gone for good.

But they had not. Not if the Dog Woman had her way.

She could not forgive Moppet's plunge into the jaws of death—or even a big garfish. Packing Binky, Topper, and Moppet into their basket, she quit the *Sunshine Queen* next morning, elbows out, twitching her rear end with pent-up rage. The Boston accent made it hard to hear quite what threat she was mouthing as she left, but it seemed to involve the sheriff and hanging.

"I think avoiding action may be called for," said Everett uneasily.

"Naw! That pup's as unsad as a whistling kettle!" said Oskar.

"The dog isn't the one making the threats."

So they untied from the landing and let the *Queen* float over to the opposite bank. They could not leave Timberlake altogether, since the Scottish engineer was still aboard, banging about in the engine room like a loose tin can, tinkering with the valves, pushing exploratory puffs of steam through the system, so that the boat itself rumbled and grunted and squeaked like a bad case of indigestion.

It was not long before the Dog Woman's revenge arrived in the shape of the Sheriff of Timberlake, hailing them across half a mile of river, through a bullhorn. "You got stolen goods aboard!" he blared. It was not a question.

Throughout his acting life, Everett Crew had been coping with unforeseen, unscripted surprises: collapsing scenery, drunks climbing onstage, actors missing their cues, fans throwing flowers, hooligans throwing all kinds of things—piglets even; downpours, questions about the plot, requests for songs. . . . He reckoned he could ad-lib his way out of most crises. But he was not on dry land now. The mistake with the slipper launch had rattled him; the business of the alligator had aged him ten years. What had the Dog Woman accused them of stealing? One of her dogs? Or the ship itself? A wallet or a paddle steamer? It could be something tiny, deliberately hidden away on the *Queen* to incriminate them, something just waiting for the Sheriff to find when he searched.

Whatever it was, they could not possibly allow the Sheriff aboard without him finding large pieces of his own slipper launch patching their hull. For once in his life, Everett Crew was lost for words.

"All we got aboard is the sweating sickness!" Loucien's voice rang out from the deck above. She

produced a square of yellow silk and waved it. Half an hour before, it had been a panel of her petticoat. Now Curly had stitched a black square to it; Miss March had crocheted a loop, and it was this that Loucien looped around a wrought-iron finial. It said, in the language of the sea, FEVER ON BOARD.

"Ain't she spackfacious?" whispered Kookie in tones of awe. Sometimes he thought his one-time schoolteacher could head off a herd of charging buffalo with a single lit match.

"She surely is," said Cissy.

"It's hot," said Tibbie Boden.

"Hokum!" bellowed the Sheriff. "I'm comin' aboard to search yuh. Offer resistance and I'll shoot yuh! I'm actin' on information received. Loose women. Hooch. Hellions!"

"Loose women?!" bayed Loucien, and the Sheriff actually recoiled a step even though an entire river lay between them. *"Loose women? Wouldn't you* loosen off your corsets if you was in my condition, sir?"

The Sheriff was fazed, no doubt about it. Pregnant women are scary at any time, but a redheaded half-Choctaw, half-Minneapolis pregnant woman with a singer's lungs was truly alarming.

"She's a wonder!" said Kookie again, but when he looked around, both Tibbie and Cissy had disappeared.

Everyone was puzzled as to how the Dog Woman had informed on anyone. How, after all, had the Sheriff understood her impossible accent? Still, unusual crime was a rarity in Timberlake, and the Sheriff was not going to be cheated out of an arrest. In his own opinion, he was not some upriver hick to be taken in by a bit of yellow cloth and talk of fever. He raised one hand and led his men to the adjacent boatyard—the one where he kept his launch.

"I'm comin' over!" he warned them through the bullhorn. "I'm comin' over and I won't . . . What the—"

Finding the flayed carcass of his elegant little boat did delay the Sheriff. For twenty minutes, all thought of stolen goods, loose women, or hellions went clear out of his head. His boat, his pride and joy, had been carved up like a Thanksgiving turkey. Clear across the river they could hear him howling and cursing and kicking paint cans around the yard. But the reprieve could not last long.

Another boat was requisitioned, and the search party started out across the water, their oars leaving dimples in the gleaming surface.

"*We are contagious, as my wife told you!*" called Everett through cupped hands. The quartet tuned up for a melancholy song. Miss March tore the collar off her blouse and put it on her head like a nurse's cap.

"Please don't incriminate yourself, May," urged

Curly. "Not on our account. Remember your mother in Des Moines."

"We are in this together!" said Miss May March, and rummaged in the property box for an apron. "Besides, it was I who threw that wretched dog . . . hello, what's this?" It was the velvet choker they had all grown accustomed to seeing around the Dog Woman's throat. Its crystal buttons glittered malevolently. Could this be the "stolen property" the Sheriff had been sent to look for?

The flaw in Loucien's plan lay in the nature of sweating sickness. There was so much of it along the Numchuck River that people lived with it. They might not know where it came from or how to cure it, but it was not catching, mouth to mouth, sneeze to sneeze, hand to hand, soil pit to dining table. The sweating sickness killed children and old folk from time to time, but it was not the Black Death or cholera. So the Sheriff's search crew came on, unafraid. Now, though, thanks to the loss of his launch, the Sheriff was in the mood to shoot anyone who so much as looked at him sideways. Flicking a rope over the bull rail of the *Sunshine Queen*, he stood up, pistol drawn.

He was confronted by a ghost of a girl, about ten years old, in nothing but her short shift, arms and legs bare, hair pulled up on top of her head. Her face, her neck, her limbs, her chest were smothered in a vivid, purpling rash that made the Sheriff's men screw their faces into a communal *ouch*. She reached out to him a velvet choker decorated with crystal buttons.

"The Dog Woman from Boston gave me this," she said in a voice straight out of Edgar Allan Poe. "That's what did me in, I reckon," and real tears welled in her eyes. "Why'd she do that, mister? Why'd she want to give me the sickness?" A tear crawled awkwardly between the bumps on her cheeks.

"That ain't sweating sickness," said the Sheriff, sinking down again onto the thwart of the boat, leaving the spotted wraith holding out the choker. "How many of you is sick?"

The girl shrugged feebly. "Six? Seven? Little Johnny's been took already."

The boat pushed off—pushed off with an oar, the Sheriff's men not wanting to touch so much as the hull of the fever ship, for fear of that purpling rash. When she threw the choker down into the boat, they drew in their feet and let it lie.

The Scottish engineer chose that moment to come up from the engine room, wiping his hands on a rag. "Could they no ha' given me a ride back to the yard?" he said, peeved to see the boat speeding away, oars flailing.

The *Sunshine Queen* clicked her tongue as steam

explored her maze of pipes, metal expanded, and valves tentatively rose and fell. Her crew, by contrast, was silent and still as statues. The engineer thought he had stepped out into the middle of a stage tableau. Not until they heard the boat banging against the landing stage on the far side of the river did the Bright Lights Theater Company unfreeze and turn their faces toward Cissy.

"That's the bravest thing I ever seen," breathed Kookie.

"Moja biedna, mała akrobatka!"

"What would your poor father say if he knew? What were you thinking of, Cecelia Sissney?"

"She never slipped the lever over to 'thinking,' lady: she just gone ahead and done it."

"What she do? I never saw! Someone tell me. What?"

Cissy by this time was shivering with cold and shock and pain. The tears rolled freely down her cheeks.

"Never mind 'brave.' Where's the calamine lotion?" Loucien came swooping with a bed sheet, engulfed Cissy in linen and love, and led her away to lie down.

Loucien said it was the best piece of acting she had ever seen. She said there was not a broad on Broadway who would have been ready and willing to roll herself naked in nettles for the sake of her art.

"Mr. Everett got shot once onstage," whispered Cissy, trembling in every limb, her eyelids and lips puffy, her hands and feet swollen to twice their size.

"Not voluntary he didn't," Loucien assured her, larding on calamine like icing over a wedding cake. "No two ways, child. You're the genuine, solid-gold, thespian article!" And Cissy's heart—which was fluttering very oddly already—swelled up like the rest of her, but with pride rather than formic acid.

"How'd you do the crying bit?" asked Kookie later. In his role as Nancy, he had often wished he could do tears, but had no idea how to cry to order.

"I just thought of Sarah Waters and the Monterey boys and Ma and Poppy and all," Cissy confided. (Though she had to admit that the excruciating pain had helped quite a bit.)

Luckily there was no mirror in her cabin and no sign of Tibbie Boden to tell her how hideous she looked covered in nettle burns and dried calamine lotion, but Cissy feared the worst. Had she won Kookie's admiration only to be left looking like the Celebrated Jumping Frog of Calaveras County, lumpy with ball bearings? Now Tibbie would look all the more beautiful by comparison, and Kookie was so easily swayed by appearances. . . .

Having opened the door to jealousy, Cissy felt so

wretched that she opened the door wider and let it move in and get comfy. Would Tibbie of the golden hair and peachy skin have rolled herself in nettles for the good of the Bright Lights? Where had Tibs been with the "Thank you, Cissy!" "Well done, Cissy!" "Brave girl, Cissy!" "What an actress you are, Cissy!"? Nowhere!

Next morning, Cissy was stung by a guilt almost as fierce as nettles. For Tibbie Boden was found on her cabin bed, still fully dressed from the day before, with a fever of 104, hallucinating about alligators and sweating like a steamship's boiler. Thanks to the mosquitoes, Tibbie had contracted the genuine article: plain old sweating sickness, scourge of the Mississippi basin.

Chapter Eleven

RAISING CAIN

*G*eorge the barber-surgeon laid out his instruments on a cushion on his lap, pressing them down into deep hollows, so that they would not slide onto the floor while he wrestled with Tibbie Boden. Adults were generally pretty cooperative, but children always wrestled. Children did not grasp the science behind bleeding. Tibbie most definitely did not grasp it. Without her glasses and gripped with fever, she got the idea that George was a stage magician planning to saw her in half, a butcher intent on cutting her into joints. She screamed and sobbed and tossed her golden curls around until the ringlets snagged in the splintery bed frame.

"They are trying new remedies out East," said

Chad Powers uneasily.

Miss March was eager to believe him. She, too, was pacing up and down the cargo deck, having unsuccessfully forbidden George to lay a blade on Tibbie. She had said to his face: the idea was barbarous.

"But I *am* a barber," George pleaded unhappily. Not for the first time, he wished a barber's job consisted only of shaving beards and cutting hair, without the need for scalpels or conversation.

Chips the carpenter was particularly agitated and roamed around the boat with a mallet hammer, banging in any nail heads that were not absolutely flush, screws that had gone in crooked. Rotten wood and rusty finials fell away wherever he hammered— the *Sunshine Queen* could not stand up to rough treatment—but Chips was too distressed even to notice.

"Has the sickness himself, see," said Elijah, watching broodingly from the pilothouse. "Had it bad as a boy. Slowed him down a shade in the thinking department."

"Don't look sick none now," said Benet above the noise of Chips banging the deck with his mallet.

"Thing about the sickness," said Elijah, "it comes and goes reg'lar as Christmas."

"You've known Chips a long while then, Elijah?"

they asked, intrigued by the boiler man's past.

"Prob'ly," said Elijah, running cupped hands up and down his own forearms over and over and over.

"Those scars of yours . . . left over from being bled?" asked Everett, casual as can be.

Elijah glanced down at his arms, curious. "Prob'ly," he admitted.

"So you had it too?"

"Had what?"

The *Sunshine Queen* made steady progress now, her cockeyed paddle wheel pushing her through the water with regal dignity. The wind could still waltz her sideways over the water, but the back eddies and shoalings could no longer snatch her skirts and drag her into a dance against her will. Little tufts of smoke tore off the two tall chimneys and hung in the air like afterthoughts. Tibbie Boden, on the other hand, made less progress. After the bleeding, Miss May March wanted to get her up on deck, out of that sweaty oven of a cabin with its stucco of mildew and cornice of black mold. But the child fainted as soon as she was raised to her feet, so they laid her back down again and left her to sleep, the women taking turns to cool her forehead with damp cloths.

They sailed on for mile after mile, the wheel milling the river into silver spray, manufacturing rainbows. They passed one, two, three little settlements without mooring against their mud levees. It was as if Everett were trying to shake off a guilty conscience or a sheriff's posse. In fact he was simply eager to get to Blowville, a town large enough to have a doctor, a telegraph office, and a railway station. He had Chad Powers steer the ship during daylight hours and, instead of mooring up, allowed Elijah to continue sailing through the night. With the spokes of the wheel between his shoes, the old man sank into a frame of mind that saw nothing but the job in hand. At night he was adrift in a two-tone blackness: the darker dark the bank, the lighter the sky with its nettle rash of stars. His eyes were fixed on the "nighthawk," a metal blob impaled on the jack staff at the boat's prow. It glimmered dimly in the dark and told him, by some diviner's magic none of the others had, his distance from the riverbank. Now and then, if he detected some patch of darkness on the great shine of the river itself—something that might be a raft or a sandbar or an unlit fishing vessel, he would sound the bell by kicking at the space where it had once hung within the pilothouse. The bell itself had long since been stolen, but inside Elijah's head it still sounded out, when he kicked it, with the sweet musical clarity of polished brass.

So on the night when he saw a light on the shore,

and heard the cry of "Ahoy there!" he rang the silent ship's bell three times and made directly for the light, remembering back to his days aboard passenger steamers.

Elijah touched the bank so gently that none of the company asleep below him even stirred. The passenger who had hailed him clambered over the rail. Then the river drew the *Queen* gently back into its arms. Darkness trickled back into Elijah's old eyes and, as it did so, rubbed out all memory of what had just happened.

Chips saw, of course. Someone had to sit on the engine-room floor all the while the boat was sailing, checking the water levels in the boilers and throwing fuel into the furnace. (Chips and Sweeting took turns.) Chips could have woken someone and said that a heavily armed man had just come aboard. But why question Elijah's judgment? Elijah knew best.

So it was not until morning that the Bright Lights Theater Company made the acquaintance of Sugar Cain.

His mother had meant to call him after the sweetest thing she knew but, having lousy spelling, had managed accidentally to name him after the first murderer in the scriptures. The sprinkling of "Sugar" on top had done nothing to sweeten Cain. He was a hoodlum and a pirate, and his own preferred taste was blood.

They found him going through the various bags and crates stored in the saloon as they assembled for breakfast. Finding only an assortment of stage props, books, half-mended costumes, musical instruments, and clown noses had already worked Cain into a stew. Each person, on entering the room—yawning, dressing, humming—was greeted by the sight of a wizened crab apple of a youth sitting with his child-sized boots on the table and pointing a triple-barreled handgun at their hearts.

"Empty up," said Cain, and each person had to empty their pockets onto the table. Now and then he made a circular gesture with the awkward, lumpy weapon, to remind the early risers that he had his eye on them. Even Elijah was there, having smelled nonexistent bacon and banked the *Queen* while he ate breakfast. Only Medora had managed to hide herself under the cloth of her projection machine.

The valuables they could produce—those who ran to pockets at that time of day—only made Cain angrier. Where were the takings from their last show, he wanted to know?

"We had repairs to pay for," said Everett evenly. He described the engineer's work, the patching of the hull. He explained, too, that he had children and sickness aboard and a strong desire to reach Blowville and a doctor as soon as possible. Sugar Cain lifted the pepper-box pistol and shot out a wall lamp, which spattered the ceiling with colza oil and the people below with glass shards.

"My wife is pregnant, boy. You will desist instantly!" said Everett, and though he seemed the bigger man by it, for a moment everyone thought Cain was going to empty the gun into him, too.

Cissy's first reaction to finding a pirate aboard was to look to Loucien. Even as Olive Town's first schoolteacher, in happier times, Miss Loucien had always worn a pearl-handled pistol just below her bust, tucked into that place where hiccups come from. Cissy could remember back to when Class Two had been terrified at the sight of that pistol; now she was much more frightened by the fact that it was missing. The baby had finally grown too big to leave room for a hiccup, let alone a pistol, under Loucien Crew's bust. Worse still, at the sight of Everett placing his hunter watch on the table—the one she had given him at their wedding—Loucien burst into uncontrollable tears.

The foundations of Cissy's world rocked. It was unheard of for Miss Loucien to cry! She might shoot a hole through a pen-and-ink portrait, or take a bullwhip to a row of tin cans, or pry up a railway line with a crowbar . . . but *cry*? Cissy looked across at Benet, because he was the hero in *The Perils of Pirate Nancy*—then Chad Powers, because he was resourceful and inventive—then Elder Slater, because he owned a much bigger pistol than Sugar Cain's. But of course Elder Slater had not brought his gun down to breakfast, nor Chad Powers the blueprint for a rescue, nor Benet his heroism. Instead he and the rest of the quartet were humming maudlin spirituals about going home, stealing away, jumping aboard low-flying chariots, or otherwise pushing off to be with Jesus. Also, all the men in the room had their hands resting on top of their heads, as Cain had told them.

"Like we're all teaching ourselves phrenology," said George the barber to Cissy with an apologetic shrug, his long trembling fingers resting on his skull.

Outside the saloon, Kookie Warboys held as still as a stick insect, one foot in the air, frozen in the act of overhearing. He sucked back in through puckered lips the tune he had been whistling.

He had no idea just how many buccaneers had boarded the *Queen* or what they were doing to the people in the breakfast room, but he did not risk taking a look. Another inch, and the scuffed toecap of his boot would have appeared in the doorway. Now he backed along the deck to the nearest stairs and climbed back up to the cabin deck.

"Hey! Tibs! Wake up! You gotta wake up!"

Through a stupor of gummy sleep pitted with deep, dark nightmares, Tibbie Boden struggled to surface. She found Kookie's face close to her own. His breath smelled of river clams. Or was it Harriet Beecher Stowe? Or the Republican party?

"We got bandits downstairs tryin' to rob us. We gotta lay an ambush!"

Tibbie Boden did not want to lay an ambush. She had the sweating sickness—people had told her, as if it were a rare talent. It is hard work being ill. It leaves you worn out. She put a hand in Kookie's face and pushed it away. His face felt pleasantly cool against her sweaty palm.

Kookie made a couple more attempts to pull her out of bed, and then to stop her objecting so loudly. "Shush up, Tibs! You gotta hide, at least! We gotta lie low, so they don't know we're here! Then we can creep out and maybe cut the others loose. We gotta round up knives and tripwires and George's razors maybe. . . ." Which was all it took to set Tibbie moaning, squealing, and tossing again, fighting off Kookie with arms of rubber and as much noise as she could muster. The cabin door opened and Miss Loucien entered, big as a ship, followed by Cain, whose gun was pressed into the small of her back.

Tibbie Boden still did not stir from her bed. So she did not see Kookie join the rest of the hostages in the saloon. She did not see when he had to empty out his entire wealth of buttons and cents onto the breakfast table. She had turned over and gone back to sleep.

Elder Slater said that Sugar Cain would carry his crime on his forehead until Judgment Day, when he would be spit-roasted like a hog.

Elijah recalled a "rafter," in the old days, who had made a habit of climbing aboard the luxury paddle steamers and stealing from the passengers. One day he had been caught, and the captain of the ship had tied him to the paddle wheel and drowned him real slow, because that was what rafters deserved.

Curly shoveled on more Shakespearian insults than a Tudor stoker. Miss May March fainted, thinking Curly would be shot for sure by Sugar Cain.

Kookie was usually terrific at swearwords, because (as he had often told Cissy) he invented his, so they weren't real and he wouldn't go to hell for using them. But Kookie was wordless now.

Mixed-race Loucien knew a useful number of Choctaw curses and Minneapolis swearwords, but she could not stop crying for long enough to muster them. "I'm sorry, Everett. I'm sorry, everyone," she kept panting between sobs. "This baby's got a fist on the tap: I'm all waterworks. What good am I?"

But as far as Sugar Cain was concerned, Loucien was just perfect. He had only to jab his pepper-box pistol up against her stomach and he could stop time. Everyone in the room froze, their faces toward him, their hands reaching out unconsciously for mercy, like hoboes begging for a crust of bread. It was a heady, delectable sensation. It stirred up feelings in Cain's own belly—hot and kicking and big as any unborn demon.

"Get me stuff," he said at last, sinking into a chair.

"That's a bulliferous big gun you got there, mister," said Kookie, setting the coffeepot on the potbellied stove. "Wish I had a gun like that."

Miss May March had needed smelling salts so often that everyone in the room was twitchy with breathing in the fumes. But she raised herself now, on one elbow, and forbade Kookie to speak another word to the degenerate criminal.

Kookie curled his lip and degenerated quite a bit himself. "Huh. Who're you to tell me what I can't go doin'? Look at you. Last time I do things you say in school, *Miss* May. I'll just say 'Boo!' and you'll drop down flat like an ironing board!"

A dreadful silence piled in behind the words, but they had a galvanizing effect on Miss May, who got up, returned to her chair, and—hands sunk in her wild gray hair—looked daggers at Kookie across the table. It is impossible to look daggers at anyone while lying on the floor.

"Are you really a pirate?" said Kookie, pouring coffee into the china cup and presenting it to Sugar Cain. It was the only ship's porcelain to have survived Salvation. "I wouldn't mind bein' one of those. Bein' a pirate would suit me fine."

Cain told him his coffee tasted like dog.

"Though I 'spect you have to be real brave and courageous an' all. Saw a lantern slide of Bluebeard one time."

"Don't be dumb. They was no lantern slides in his days," said Cain.

"Sure there was! I seen one!" Kookie insisted. "Medora knows. Ain't I right, Medora?" And he deliberately pulled off the blanket covering Medora's Photopia equipment . . . and Medora herself, who had been hiding there. The very walls of the room gasped at his treachery.

Cain enjoyed it hugely. "You heard me. Get me stuff," he said, but this time he said it to Kookie in person. Having just seen the boy betray a friend, Cain trusted him better for it. "You try something dumb, I shoot your sister there. Right? And the other one upstairs."

It took Kookie a moment to work out who Cain

meant. Then his eyes focused on Cissy, and a dozen illegible emotions tugged at his face. It reminded Cissy of the look he had worn as the alligator nudged him and the company looked down from above . . . and did nothing.

Then Kookie went out and came back with Elder Slater's gun, empty of bullets; with the seven dollars and fifty cents Cissy had saved toward rebuilding the grocery store; with his own collection of cockroaches in a jam jar. On the next trip he fetched George's cutthroat razor, which he laid on the table in front of Cain.

Suddenly Cain sent Miss March to "fetch the sick kid down where I can see it." As the schoolteacher carried Tibbie, fireman style, down the steep stairs, she was whispering to herself, all the time whispering, "There must be something I can do—if I could just think!"

Tibbie, whose bones seemed to have melted during the fever, had to be laid on the table. She looked like some doomed creature out of a Dickens novel—Little Nell, maybe. She was wider awake, though, thanks to a breath of fresh air.

Kookie fetched Cain the shiniest nails from Chip's toolbox, a bottle of wine presented to them all by the Mayor of Plenty, the vanity set given to Everett by his wife on their first anniversary.

Little Nell climbed off the table and went to sit in Miss March's lap. "I think Kookie's a traitor and a Bendict Armhole," she whispered.

"Arnold, Tibbie dear," said Miss May March, cradling the child close. "Benedict Arnold. And a Judas, too."

Kookie brought Cleopatra's snaky bracelet and velvet purse from the property box; Prospero's magic staff; Hamlet's sword; Macbeth's dagger. All these he laid on the table in front of Sugar Cain, except for the tin laurel wreath worn by Julius Caesar, which he thrust at Curly. "I think *you* should give it to him, Curlitz. Like Brutus does in *Julius Caesar*. To show how great he thinks he is and how old Julius is top dog."

Curly's back straightened. He blinked at Kookie, and his eyes strained wide in their sockets. Around the clutter of assembled tables, several other spines flexed into the upright.

Miss May March breathed sharply in. "Do not do it, Mr. Curlitz! Please do not do any such thing!"

Cain was intrigued. He rested the sword point on Loucien's unborn child and demanded to have the wreath.

"It's not in me," said Curly helpless, hopeless. "I can't do it."

So Kookie took it upon himself and, holding

the tinny crown up high on fingertips, clicking his
heels and bowing, he presented it to the river pirate.
Because Cain's hands were both occupied, with the
sword and the pepper-box pistol, Kookie had, in
fact, to "crown" him. The greasy straggle of hair he
rested the wreath down on grew like seaweed on a
rock, stranded, stringy, and faintly green, inhabited
by small life forms.

"You're thinnin" on top, sir," said Kookie. "No
disrespect. You should have Mr. George do you a
head rub. Does a squissimus head rub. In the throne
there." Kookie pointed over to the barber's chair. "He
done it for me. Feels like a chantoosie licking honey
off your brains. An' look at me! My thatch was the
colora cow dung before I had that head rub!"

Cain ran an eye over the thick red hair exploding
out of Kookie's freckled head. His top lip curled back
off his child-sized teeth. "Think I'm stoopid, bean-
face? Think I'm gonna let some bum come around
behind and throttle me?" But he did get up and stalk
over to the splendid leather barber's chair, pushing
Loucien ahead of him with the sword, his wreath
catching the light, unsettling the lice. Sword in one
hand, pepper-box pistol in the other, he wriggled into
the chair's embrace. It exaggerated the smallness of
his frame, but it was clear from the look on Cain's
face that he felt the grandeur of wearing a crown and

sitting in a leather throne.

"Stoopid? No," said Kookie earnestly. "You might be a skunk, but I reckon you're a gen-yoo-ine pirate. What's a man git for bein' nice? Big turnout at his funeral. I don't plan on bein' nice, me. Sooner be no-tor-i-ous. People respect no-tor-i-ous. People lick your boots." At which he turned to Benet and asked, "You shine shoes?"

The look that came into Benet's eyes was about as dark as molten anger and overloaded as a cotton boat. Outrage. Inside-out rage. A tidal wave of anger carrying along as much ancient flotsam as the Mississippi in flood. "I only shine my *own* shoes, boy," said Benet in a voice so basso profundo that the glass rattled in the window frames.

Hamlet's sword tip tore a hole in the front of Loucien's dress. Her scarlet chemise showed through, like blood.

"Well, *I* shine 'em!" said Kookie brightly. "*I* clean boots better'n Virgil Hobbs back in Olive Town, an' he's the bootmaker! He mends 'em, but I shine 'em up for him. Don't I, sis?" he said, glaring at Cissy.

"Sure do," said Cissy and added, almost as an afterthought, "Judas."

Little Nell whispered in Miss March's ear, "No he don't," then yelped as the schoolteacher's hands tightened like steel around her arms.

"Hush now, dear," said Miss March tenderly.

"'Cause I'm a boot-shining genius, me!" Kookie was saying, warming to his theme. "It's all in the quality of the spit, see?" And in an act as fawning as that of any politician or bridegroom, he dropped down on his knees in front of Sugar Cain's throne and began to polish the pirate's cracked, flaking, mud-caked boots, using Cleopatra's velvet purse. He had to clean them in midair, because Cain's legs were too short to reach the floor.

It was probably the biggest moment in Sugar's wizened little life.

It was also the perfect opportunity for Kookie to fetch out the dime from inside Cleopatra's purse and feed it into the slot in the arm of the chair.

The chair shivered—as anyone might who wakes to find something repulsive lying on them. Startled, Cain sat up—tried to sit up, though the leather was slippery. He dropped the sword, so as to get a better grip on the chair's arm. Then the vibrating ratchets got going in earnest.

Cain's light frame was tossed around like a skeleton in a runaway hearse. The pepper-box pistol fell into his lap, whereupon he began screaming shrilly, on and on, every moment expecting it to go off and shoot him point-blank.

"Take cover!" shouted Kookie, and everyone slid

down off their chairs. But Kookie himself was ablaze with battle frenzy, lobbing more things into Cain's lap—the open cutthroat razor, the cockroaches, a handful of nails, Macbeth's dagger. . . . Benet added the pot of hot coffee off the stove. Every time Cain tried to struggle upright, the chair shook him down again onto the flat of his pelvis, where he writhed, helpless as a turtle overturned. Everyone was shouting, but no one as loudly as Kookie, who was jumping two-footed up and down on the spot, arms clamped tight against his chest, inchoate noises gargling out of his throat, nose bleeding with the strain of bawling hatred at Sugar Cain. Only when the pepper-box pistol bounced off Cain's stomach, hit the floor, and went off did the ice freeze solid around Kookie's heart and bring him to a dead halt, eyes shut. At the same instant, the dime ran out and the chair came to a standstill.

Kookie thought everyone was under the table, and that now, all alone, he would have to look and see what he had done—whether Cain was still alive and raging mad—whether the stray bullet had killed anyone he loved. But in fact, when he opened his eyes, Curly and Oskar and Crew and Benet and Miss March and Chad and Boisenberry all had hold of Cain. They had screwed him into a ball on the floor, like a boxer's handkerchief: crusty, bloodied, and damp.

Chad Powers stood up under the wrought-iron hanging flower basket and nearly knocked himself cold, but apart from that the entire company was unhurt.

Just then, Chips wandered in on the scene, having been asleep in the engine room throughout. "Something happen here?" he asked in his customary sleepy drawl.

Despite some keenness to tie Cain to the paddle wheel and drown him, they decided to shut the pirate in the property box instead, and carried him ashore in Licorice. Licorice did not really want him but promised to keep him locked up until the circuit judge next visited.

"How often does he come by?" asked Everett.

"Last time was 1891," said the Sheriff, jangling a bunch of keys in Sugar's face with sadistic relish.

Chapter Twelve

SLEIGHT OF HAND

*K*ookie was the hero of the hour. The men took turns shaking his hand, the women kissing him.

"It all goes to show the true greatness of the divine Bard!" said Curly. "Your hint was masterly!"

"I was not aware you knew the play of *Julius Caesar,* Kookie," said Everett.

"Sure! Back in Olive Town! Don't you recall? Miss Loucien hauled you in to help with the teachin', and you agreed 'cause you fancied gettin' up close to Miss Loucien, and you gave us a taste of Shakespeare. We did the 'sassination scene, and I was Brutus and stabbed old Julius in the Capitol 'fore he could dish the republicans."

Everett contemplated this. "Crudely put, but fair."

"Just as well Cain *didn't* know Shakespeare," suggested Chad.

"Ah, Mr. Powers!" said Miss May March in her most refined voice. "With a good education, Sugar Cain might not have turned out the way he did!" She did not confess her own complete ignorance of *Julius Caesar*. Kookie's toadying act had fooled her almost till the dime slipped sweetly into the slot in George's vibrating chair.

"I knew straight off, when Kookie called Cissy sis," said Tibbie, valiantly trying to keep up with all the cleverness going on.

"Terrible thought!" said Kookie. "Sister Cissy Sissney. Sounds like a steam train comin'."

Cissy retaliated. "You? Clean boots for Virgil Hobbs? Surprised anyone believed that!" Though secretly just then she thought Kookie Warboys the cleverest object on the planet.

"And a reward, too, Habakkuk!" exclaimed his schoolteacher. "Shall you open a banking account when you get home? Calculating the interest would be an excellent use for your mathematics."

Kookie could think of seventy ways of spending the fifty dollars in bounty money he had just been paid for catching Sugar Cain. None of them involved banks.

A couple of days later, as he walked down the main street in Blowville, a dozen deep-throated doorways called to him to come in and *spend*: the bakery, the tailor's, the saloon, the offices of Wells Fargo, the general store. . . . They whispered that his mother would love a new dress length, that his sisters would love . . . But once he let in the idea of buying presents for his great multitude of brothers and sisters, the sum of fifty dollars shrank quicker than boiled wool. There were so many things that would make life sweeter. With enough money, he could travel all around America! With enough money, he could buy a paddleboat like that glorious confection moored up right now on Blowville Wharf, and give it to the Bright Lights, and set them up for life! He could almost wish Sugar Cain had been a bank robber or a mass murderer with a bigger reward on his head. Almost.

The saloon won out. His older brother had once told him that bartenders don't give one cherry stone what age you are, so long as you have the money to buy. So Kookie went in and ordered himself a whiskey and orange. Sure enough, the bartender presented him with a half tumbler of whiskey with a whole orange stoppering up the top. The other men along the bar watched to see what he would do with it, grinning. Kookie considered whether to squeeze the orange into the glass in a manly sort of way, to show off his biceps. But then he might have to fish around in his drink with one finger to fetch out all the seeds. So he pocketed the orange, raised his glass to his audience, and said, "To Law and Order! I'm a bounty hunter, see. Just brought a man in." Then he drank the whiskey down in one go.

The nettles had been worse, he told himself, when the burning wore off. Well, that was the whiskey done. Now for a hat.

"Want to sit in on this game? Since your luck's in?" The young man who said it was also in need of a new hat. The one he was wearing made him look slightly simple, like a hick farm boy. His jacket was loud and tartan, too high in the waist and long in the sleeves. When he shuffled the cards, he dropped several on the floor. Kookie could have shuffled better.

"Whatcha playing?" Kookie asked, implying he had played poker and gin so often he was bored with them. (The Warboys family played only whist or pinochle.)

The tartan hick shrugged. "What's your game? Take a seat . . . unless you have enough money, what with the bounty, and don't need to win any more."

Enough? All those unbought presents for his brothers and sisters banged up against Kookie like flotsam, and suddenly fifty dollars was not nearly enough. Back in Olive Town he had been the brains behind a hundred dubious bets, wagers, dares, turtle derbies, and moneymaking schemes, and he had always come out on top. The day had convinced him he was lucky, too: the very fact that he was not full of bullets was clear proof. So he sat down at the table, split the pack, and shuffled the cards with a deft interflick of the two halves.

"This man's sharp!" said the tartan hick, and gave an admiring whistle. He was actually rather well-spoken for a farm boy, and he had good teeth.

"Tell you what," said Kookie—*très nonchalant*—"pinochle's a game you don't see much these days. You recall pinochle?" Amazingly, it so happened the tartan hick had been thinking just the same thing not five minutes before. The men around the table seemed to think it was a hilariously good idea.

And sure enough, Kookie doubled his money playing pinochle. In the course of fourteen games, he hardly missed a trick. Thanks to the whiskey, the room took on a slight tilt, but Kookie leaned into it, like a cyclist into a bend, and played even faster.

If he had just stopped then and there.

Or if he had just spotted the moment his luck changed, and called it a day.

If he had just gotten up and gone, rather than holding on and holding on, thinking that at any moment the run of play must turn around and grant him another win. But having seen his fifty dollars double, he saw it halve, and then disappear to nothing. And then the shame was so bad that he could not bear to think of heading back to the boat. "What did you buy? What did you do with all that cash?" they would ask him.

He thought his eyes must be bulging like a Pekingese's, such a weight of tears was pushing on them. Just to keep the tears from spilling out, he had to screw up his face and scowl at the cards in his hand. Diamonds slid behind one another. Spades dug themselves in. Queens and jacks eloped and left him with nothing but a handful of worthless pips.

"Don't be downcast! You're a good man—I like you," said the man in tartan, his vowels now as round as oranges. "I'll fund you."

If Curly had been there, he would have said, "'Neither a borrower nor a lender be.'" If Elder Slater had been there, he would have said that playing cards for money was a "burning sin." If Miss Loucien had been there . . . but that was too scary even to imagine. When his tartan friend—"Cole! Call me Cole; we're all friends here!"—pushed a wad of dollar bills across the table, a surge of relief went through Kookie hotter than neat whiskey. Maybe, after all, they were just playing for dollar bills the way the family played for matchsticks back home.

He lost track, after that, of how much he lost. At some stage somebody bought him another whiskey: Blowville was proving a real friendly place.

"Well! Kooks!" said Cole an hour later, pushing back his chair. "Much as I appreciate your company, you're three hundred down and we just wore the spots off the cards." He added that he had never met a bounty hunter so young and green looking before. "You write your name on there and you'll make me a happy man." And he slid a paper across the table to get Kookie's autograph.

He kept Kookie company, too, all the way back to the boat. That was where Kookie found that from being hero of the hour, he had moved on. Suddenly he was . . . invisible.

"He's underage," said Everett when Cole presented the marker for three hundred dollars and demanded payment.

"If he's old enough to sign his name to a debt, he's old enough to pay it," said Cole, sweet, cheerful, insistent.

Everett was, like all husbands in the late stage of his wife's pregnancy, overemotional. "I have a sick child aboard: I don't have time for this. Get out of here, sir, or I'll apprise your mother of the mistake she made hatching you out of that vulture's egg. Count yourself lucky I don't bring countercharges! Corrupting a minor! The theft of lollipops from babies!"

Cole smirked. "Matter of fact, you'll find I'm pretty well liked around here. . . . You bring your lawsuit. I take it you people have plenty of respectable folk upriver ready to give you character references? If so, my uncle the judge would be glad to read them over . . . though I heard you ran into a spot of trouble. That right?"

Everett looked Cole up and down with open disdain. Gone were Cole's hick hat and jacket, thrown over the boat's rail in a flamboyant gesture of swaggering, gloating vanity. From underneath them had emerged a vain, expensively dressed brat.

"The Devil marked your cards from the day you were born!" declared Elder Slater, brandishing his gun, but Everett waved him away. Like Slater, he longed to puncture the puffed-up arrogance of this low-life local dandy, but he knew there was no point. He recognized a professional when he saw one. Cole had seen Kookie coming. There was something premeditated and calculated in every move he had made. Somehow he knew of the difficulties they had encountered upstream. In short, Cole knew the strength of the hand he had to play. Here was a crooked gambler, and a gambler's only instinct in life is to win.

Everett closed his eyes, thought himself into the character of the river gambler who had come aboard back in Engedi: wily, wordly, worming . . . "Like it or not, sir, I lack the luck to have three hundred dollars. I'm short that sort of spondooly. I barely have thirty. Won't dirty your shirt pocket with thirty. Let us evolve—solve our dilemma. Say we forget all about this?" Crew reached to tug the IOU out of Cole's hand, but Cole was too quick for him. "You're a player, yes? You want to ride the river, yes? Plucking new suckers every night? A gambling booth on deck? Discreet. Be sweet. What's a paddler without sport, I say? To my way of thinking, three hundred is the purchase price of a prime pitch aboard the *Sunshine Queen*."

"And I say *double or quits*!" Loucien Crew swept into the decayed stateroom with Elder Slater at her shoulder. The preacher had been telling her the bad news. In a flame-red dress, prodigious, wild-haired and raging, she was more alarming than any hellfire preacher. "I'll bet you can't run faster than a bullet!" she threatened, pointing her pearl-handled pistol at Cole's head. "*That's* my bet. Now you prove me wrong and you get twice three hundred! Start running!"

The gambler's smile stayed wedged in his mouth, like a harmonica. He flicked his forelock of soft dark hair. "You don't want to do that, lady. My uncle's the—"

"Oh, but I do want to do it, young man! I crave shootin' all your kind. It's a crusade o' mine. Some people it's rabbits. Some folk it's roaches. Me it's gamblers." And she actually cocked the pistol.

Everett stepped between the two. Cole's cronies were even now watching from the wharf, erect as prairie dogs, spellbound. His imagination pelted ahead toward disaster. "Lou! I think this is a time for diplomacy. A little compromise!"

His wife glared at him. "Didn't I tell you? Didn't I say? *I won't have gamblers on board!*"

Cole, as smug as ever, baring his white fender of perfect teeth, raising one sardonic eyebrow, reached over Crew's shoulder, and shook Loucien's hand, pistol and all. "Double or quits, did you say, ma'am? I'll settle for double or quits. I like a game worth playing. What's yours? Cribbage? Snap?" And he allowed himself a snort of laughter that made Kookie (curled up under the tables nearby) beat his head softly on the floor.

"I know cards," said Loucien with sudden icy coolness. "I got plenty chance to learn. My first husband was a gambler." And she made it sound as bitter as any words ever spoken by a wronged wife.

Never in all their acquaintance had Loucien spoken of life before Olive Town. Not even to her husband, Everett Crew. It was a locked room, a previous address she had torn out of her address book. Now the sight of this snickering cardsharp sparked such raging recollections that the memories spilled out of her, a frozen river thawing, a flood of incoherent words.

All those years spent married to a gambling man.

His endless excuses for being short of cash; the sudden lavish gifts whenever he got lucky.

Things unaccountably missing from around the house—furniture, clocks, wedding presents that turned up in the pawnshop window.

Arguments with the landlord; moonlight flits to another town to escape the unpaid debts—debts they never shook off.

Anger—his everlasting righteous anger—because she did not understand him, because she could not make ends meet, because she whined, because a man needs a bit of excitement, a little flutter now and then. Her gloomy face had soured his luck, he said. The way she had let herself go: it was no wonder he preferred to spend time down with the backroom boys and pretty barroom girls . . . Lurline was the woman he should have married, he said: Lurline Monteverdi, queen of the gambling tables.

Loucien's past continued to pour memories down on her head, like a burst water tank. The debt collectors at the door at three in the morning. The grocer refusing any more credit. All these horrors she tried to describe, for the very first time since they had happened.

Her husband's certainty that every other cardplayer was a crimp and a cheat.

"Finally he tried it himself," said Loucien. "Bought a book mail order: *100 Ways to Cheat at Cards*. Had it in his pocket the day someone shot him for laying down five kings."

Cole's grin was still pouched in his cheeks, as big as a squirrel's store of acorns. Everett tried to put an arm around Loucien, but she shook him off. Her dead husband's crimes went on piling up around them, till it seemed the boat would founder under their weight.

Debt collectors on the day of the funeral, pushing past mourners to reach the furniture, off-loading the food onto the floor so as to carry away table and chairs. After that: nothing left in the house to eat.

"I went searching—clear through the place. Went looking for some clue, some hint. Something to remind me of the reason I married this man. Ever. Loved him. Ever. Felt something good when he came through the door. Know what I found? Gambling markers and IOUs, that's what I found. Bills shoved outa sight so I wouldn't see—huh!—so he could go on pretending the next game would make him rich.

"When the landlord came to throw me out, he

had a newspaper in his paw. Them days, I couldn't read. So I got him to read out the want ads. "Mail-Order Brides." Next day I caught the stage—for some place in Oklahoma didn't hardly exist; to marry some Swedish baker—sight unseen. That's what gambling did for me. And every day of my married life, leeches and horseflies like this . . . this . . ." Loucien took a swipe at Cole, but he ducked. "Every day these bloodsuckers sank their teeth into him, plied him with whiskey; took his money and his markers and his soul and his common sense. . . . Might as well have taken the face off his head, 'cause I didn't know him no more. When I put that man in his grave . . . felt like *burying litter.*"

Kookie, arms over his head, pulled his face so hard into the floor that the wood grain impressed itself on his forehead. A stone chisel seemed to be chipping a monumental heart into his chest: a heart, spade, diamond, and club, and underneath the words I WILL NEVER, EVER BET.

Everett was inclined to take the pistol out of Loucien's hand and shoot Cole himself. Instead, he simply withdrew his offer of a gambler's booth aboard the *Queen*. "I find I don't care to bring rats in among my family," he said, and the whole of the Bright Lights Company knew that they were included in that family.

Cole was still wearing that imbecilic grin, fanning himself with the marker for three hundred dollars. "A new wager, then! Double or quits, like the lady said! A race! A river race! You win: you get this plus three hundred more. I win, I get to keep the *Queen*."

No one in the saloon spoke. No one said yea or nay. There was a general understanding: this was where Cole had been heading right from the start.

"Just a hunch. Is that your vessel moored up on the wharf?" asked Everett.

"The *Tula-Rose*? Yah, she's mine." Cole ran a hand over his mouth, struggling to keep from laughing out loud. Taking out his wallet, he unfolded another sheet of paper and wrote out the deal, using a fancy gold fountain pen. Crossing to the potbellied stove in the corner, he wiped a hand down the soot-blackened wall above it and returned to the table to press his palm print down onto the sheet of paper.

THE SUNSHINE QUEEN
AND ALL THAT'S IN HER.
$300

"Cole Blacker," he said, beaming around him, snatching Everett's hand and shaking it. Now both their hands were dirtied by the deal. "A river race. Just like the old days, eh?"

"How would *you* know about the old days, *boy*?" asked Benet with icy composure.

But Cole "The Hand" Blacker was tucked up safe inside his good opinion of himself. He swaggered ashore over the gangplank, arms outstretched, conducting his giggling cronies, who had started up singing:

"For he's a jolly good fellow,
For he's a jolly good fellow . . ."

Chapter Thirteen

A DAY AT THE RACES

"*E*asy come, easy go," said Everett Crew. The silence snapped like old elastic. "We started off stranded, and now I surmise that the Bright Lights Steamboat and Theater Company has just run aground again. I hope that everyone . . ." Then he looked around him at the people whose lives he had disrupted—Medora, Max, Miss May, the Dixie Quartet—and his speech, too, foundered.

"But we might win!" said Kookie, crawling out from under the table. He shriveled and withdrew as a dozen pairs of eyes turned on him. The story of Loucien's past life seemed to have filled the saloon like smoke, and they were all choking on the blackness of it.

Loucien herself came to the rescue. She took a deep breath. "Kookie's right. We got two thirds of a wheel, at least. That's two thirds more than we useta! Let's ask Elijah if we stand a chance. He musta seen riverboats race when he was a boy."

But nobody did ask Elijah. Sometimes hoping for the best is better than knowing for sure. Anyway, no one had much confidence in the opinion of an antique boiler man with a defective memory and a sorrowful countenance. Instead, they did what they had come to Blowville to do: wrapped up Tibbie Boden in a blanket and carried her to the doctor, unwrapping her there like some antique heirloom they wanted valued. The doctor's office smelled of carbolic soap. The doctor did not appreciate sick people bringing their ailments into it and being sick on the floor. He gave Tibbie quinine, calomel, and a tartar emetic and advised cold baths. Three made her sick and the other made her cry, even before there was a bathtub in sight. He also advised a period of convalescence at the sanatorium in Sedalia, away from the river. Away from his office.

"And what do you get in one of those places?" demanded Miss May March. The children gave a shudder, remembering being hit with such questions in school. ("Do you think there's a right answer?" Kookie whispered to Cissy.)

"Healthsome food, good hygiene, competent nursing," said the doctor, washing his hands in a basin.

"Well, I can give her that without trekking all the way to Sedalia!" Miss May March enfolded Tibbie in her blanket again.

"Couldn't I just go home to Papa?" whimpered Tibbie, still thinking of the cold baths.

"Not till the diphtheria's past, dear." At which the doctor shot up out of his chair like a distress flare and ordered them out of his office. The sweating sickness was one thing, but diphtheria he wanted nothing to do with. There proved to be one advantage, though, to finding a doctor with a fear of illnesses: he forgot to write out a bill.

George, meanwhile, went looking for a barbershop. Even before he found one, he had gained a fair picture of the situation in Blowville. The whole town seemed to be owned by the Blacker family: he passed the Blacker Forge, Blacker's General Store, the Blacker Livery. . . . The local barber filled George in on the rest.

Cole was the youngest member of the Blacker dynasty, and the only one without a job. He would disappear for months on end, then suddenly reappear, hinting at dashing-like adventures and smelling of shady dealing. He might be the black sheep, but he was also an only child and sole heir to the Blacker fortune. Ever since babyhood he had been spoiled with extravagant presents and pats on the head. His every fad was indulged, every crime excused; every lie he told was believed, so his relations thought of him as a genius in the making.

All plans were abandoned by the Bright Lights to visit the Blackers and describe what their darling Cole had been up to higher up the Numchuck River. What was the point in telling doting parents that their son had rooked respectable citizens out of their savings—cheating, stealing, and hustling his way through the riverside communities like a fox stealing chickens? What witnesses could they produce? Nobody trusts actors: they have a reputation for exaggeration and making things up. As Loucien said, "How would you like a pack of miscellaneouses turning up on the doorstep, telling you your darlin' little boy's a shyster and a thief?"

"They may know already in their heart of hearts," suggested Curly. "Parents generally have an inkling."

"They also have a knack for denying it," said Miss May March the schoolteacher, speaking with the voice of experience.

"Just think, folks," said Loucien brightly. "There's three hundred dollars at stake here. There's Tibbie's medicine to pay for, fuel and groceries to buy, and nothing much in the kitty. Three hundred would boost funds nicely if we won."

No one else there could have dared to say it: it had to be Loucien.

"And if we lose, I say we put notices in all the newspapers upriver of here telling his victims exactly where they can find Cole 'The Hand' Blacker," said Chad Powers with a degree of venom they had never seen in him before.

"Lose?" said Cissy, pulling herself up tall. "That's not Bright Lights talk, Mr. Powers. We never lose. We just mislay our luck for a space."

So all of a sudden, the race was on. All of a sudden, everyone was finding optimistic things to say about the *Sunshine Queen*—so small and light—and what good publicity it would be for the Bright Lights— and how glad they were about that little Scottish engineer and the renovations. . . . Not a soul spoke of *why* they were having to race. No one suggested throwing Kookie to the wolves, leaving him on the quayside with his gambling debt and a whiskey headache. He was family, after all.

Elijah, asked if he had ever seen a steamer race, scoured around his coal scuttle of a brain and came up with a few dusty recollections. "They stripped down to the bones. If it weren't nailed down, it went. Course the engineer was the man. Make or break. Watching the traps; keeping the levels right in the traps." To almost everyone, Elijah's reminiscences were quaint musical nonsense. But Chad Powers squatted at the old man's feet, notebook open as if to catch and press the petals of these ramblings between the pages and preserve them forever. "Pine knots are all well and good, but if you're all steam and no water . . . well, you start in St. Joseph and end up in hell," said Elijah. "Secret is to make the river lend a hand—every mud bank, every little 'striction pushing the water on through."

It was Chad who borrowed the canoe so that Elijah could reconnoiter the course. It was not easy, though, to get Elijah into the stern of the canoe. Cissy (whose lame pa often needed a helping hand) helped him down off the wharf. Somehow she found that she was in the canoe herself, sandwiched between the two men—the inventor and the boiler man—as Chad paddled the course and wrote down what Elijah said about it. The currents and mud bars, the plants on the bank, the height of the levees— even the breeds of fish—seemed to tell the old man something. Luckily it was Friday, and Elijah tended to remember things on Fridays. Less luckily, his mind was not on the job. With one gnarled hand peaked over his eyes against the glare, he peered around him as the river slid between high escarpments of yellow sandstone. It was a stretch of rare beauty after muddy miles of sparse brush. Whenever the sun escaped the clouds, it turned the cliff to gold. High above them, overlooking the gorge, with a view down two miles of river, was a vast mansion of white clapboard and yellow brick, its windows aglitter with sunlight. Steps had been cut into the golden escarpment, which zigzagged down to the water's edge. At the bottom stood a derelict shack that the floods had reduced to a matchwood fishpen.

"Well, look at that," said Elijah. "There's my place."

Cissy's heart ached for Elijah. It had never been much of a shack: now it was uninhabitable. No wonder he had ended up living aboard the *Queen*. "My house got wrecked too," she said, and kissed the big veiny hand resting on her shoulder. She had only just remembered about the store being demolished. Up till then, Elijah's sieve of a memory had been a puzzle to her. Now she realized: it is possible to forget the most enormous things when life gets busy.

Back at the wharf, Chad and Kookie scoured the woodpile for pine knots; they burned hotter and brighter than ordinary logs because of the resin in them. It was Chad who supervised the removal of every fixture, fitting, and piece of luggage that could be carried ashore. When Medora protested that she could not possibly leave her camera equipment on the wharf unguarded, Crew told her that was fine because he would be leaving the women and children on shore, for safety.

Cole Blacker's paddle steamer, bought with the proceeds of his scams upriver, was a big vintage craft, creamy with lavish layers of new white paint, lacy with metal filigree. Golden steam whistles sprouted from the pilothouse, and two Union flags as big as tablecloths flew one on either side of the paddle wheel. The rivets in the twin chimneys were as smart as the buttons on a lady's boots. The crew (though they were simply Cole's drinking friends) had on uniform maroon overalls, and Cole Blacker, when he finally put in an appearance, was dressed somewhere between an admiral and a ringmaster.

Elijah puffed out through his soup-strainer mustache and scrubbed at his moth-eaten thatch, but said nothing. They supposed he must feel a world of disappointment at the unfairness of life. Here was this meritless, spoiled boy possessed of a beautiful vessel through cheating and lying. Elijah, who had labored his life away as roustabout, mud clerk, and boiler man, and could steer a paddler with his feet, teetered now on the brink of a penniless old age. They waited for him to say some such thing.

"She's three yards longer and two wider in the beam" was all he said. "St. Louis built. Prob'ly draws more water."

"Is that good?" asked Everett.

"Or bad?" asked his wife.

Elijah shrugged. "'Pends on the wind, I guess. Steam up, should I?"

Without knowing why, the children were given a five-dollar bill and sent to buy a side of bacon from the butcher in Blowville. It seemed a horrific extravagance.

"Gonna hold a pig roast for the crowd, you wait," Kookie stated. "Make some money that way."

"Cain't roast a flitch of bacon, silly," said Cissy. But she was unsure of her facts. Bacon was not spit-roasted in Oklahoma, but maybe in Missouri the locals were as squeamish as she was and didn't like watching a whole dead pig revolving, ears and tail hanging loose.

Five dollars would buy only one flitch. Kookie asked for two. "Send the bill on up to Mr. Cole Blacker, if you please," he told the butcher. "He sent us."

Outside the shop, Tibbie (who was still an invalid so didn't have to carry things) did her bit by getting hysterical. "That was a fearful big lie, Kooks!" she whispered, breathing too fast and biting her lip and looking back over her shoulder.

"The Hand fleeced me, so now I'm flitching him," said Kookie vengefully. "Any case, we didn't have enough money for two."

The sides of bacon were greasy and bristly and rather too much like dead bodies for Tibbie's liking, so she walked farther off, lest Cissy and Kookie bump her as they struggled along, each carrying an entire side of bacon. "What are you going to do with Mr. Crew's five dollars? You keeping it for your gambling?" asked Tibbie. The procession came to an abrupt halt, and Cissy dropped her flitch. Kookie's face was crimson with shame or anger.

"I'm never ever gamblin' ever again," he snapped. "I taken the pledge on gamblin'."

The flitches were not intended for a pig roast on the riverbank. Elijah wanted them chopped up, carried aboard the boat, and steeped in turpentine. The Bright Lights Theater Company stood around and watched, mutiny in their hungry eyes. Curly, who did a lot of the cooking, chopped up one joint and sank it in the poisonous marinade, but he kept the other intact, just in case it could be spared.

"We gonna send them around to Blacker as a gift?" Tibbie speculated. "Kill him of turpentine poisoning?" But Miss May March wrapped her in a blanket again and carried her ashore, telling her she had had enough excitement for one day and needed to give her brain a rest.

Kookie had no intention of going ashore and, instead of crossing the gangplank, peeled off sideways and hid behind a stack of life rafts. Cissy went after him to ask what he thought he was doing and if he hadn't caused enough trouble already. Then the gangplank was inboard . . . and so was Cissy . . . and there was nothing to be done about it.

When the Blacker family arrived on the wharf, the crowds parted as if for royalty. They came in a horse-drawn landau, she a big woman in purple velvet, he with a florid face and hair the color of gravy. They looked as if they ate a flitch of bacon every day for breakfast. There was an auntie or two, and a pair of hunting dogs, in the carriage as well. They all had the look of money, but not the old kind. The Blackers had spent their lives earning more than anyone in the county, and the effort was etched in their faces. Now they sat in their luxury vehicle, hands folded in their laps, and gazed with fond affection and pride at the son who had made it all worthwhile. Cole Blacker was strutting up and down the hurricane deck of the *Tula-Rose*, up and down in front of his crew, like a general inspecting troops. He climbed to the pilothouse, sounding every bell, gong, whistle, and horn, and the whole crowd cheered.

Blushing at her own daring, Miss May March called out across the water: "You can do it, boys! Pull out all the stops!"

Curly, intending to wish Miss May March a cheery farewell, climbed up to the calliope and played a couple of ten-finger chords. To his consternation, the boiler had been primed to such a pitch that the steam pressure was enormous. Instead of the usual feeble, creaky groaning, a noise like the blast of a cannon issued from the calliope pipes. People nine miles away said they heard it and thought of their Maker. Horses shied, bucked, and tried to leave. The crowds put their hands over their ears. For the first time, the grin slipped off Cole Blacker's face. The *Sunshine Queen* had shouted him down.

This was the moment when Elijah chose to forget that he was pilot aboard the *Queen*, and set to work as her engineer. Everett did not argue with him: several of the men had mastered steering since Salvation. None had mastered the intricacies of the infernal iron demon in the engine room.

The race was to be barely more than a sprint: a quick ten miles upriver—first to tie up at Boats-a-Cummin wharf. A fuel barge had been anchored in the center of the river, at the five-mile point, heaped with pitch knots and pine knots. It meant the boats ran light in the early stages, and refueling would add to the excitement. There was a gusting headwind, and a flock of fluffy white clouds was lining up to jump the sun.

At the firing of a gun, the white horses harnessed to the landau flinched and reared up in the traces. They might have bolted if Loucien had not held them by the cheek straps. The crowd got to its feet. Medora and Tibbie and Miss March called across the water that Kookie and Cissy had not come ashore—but the boats were sounding their horns, the paddle wheels were splashing, the furnaces were roaring, the tall chimneys puking out fur balls of black smoke, and the race was under way. It was a race between a swan and a one-legged duck: the *Queen* did not stand a chance. But sometimes in life you just have to eat what's put in front of you.

The *Tula-Rose* pulled steadily into the lead. Cole's friends, when they were not stoking or prodding valves, stood on the stern of the hurricane deck jeering and gesturing at the trailing boat. The *Queen*'s pilothouse was on their level, and Everett was obliged to look at their grinning, jubilant faces while beside him Chad babbled information: "Deeper channel just right of center. Reed bed on the left."

"I see it."

"Fallen tree on the next bend. You're skidding."

"I'm aware that I'm skidding, thank you, Mr. Powers."

"Ducks off the port bow."

"I don't think ducks constitute a hazard. Forgive me if I don't steer around the ducks."

Sweeting and Max were lugging pine knots. Chips and Boisenberry were feeding the port furnace, Oskar and George the starboard. Elder Slater was praying noisily, drawing the Almighty's attention to Cole Blacker's wickednesses, in case God had been busy and missed them.

"We gotta make ourselves useful!" said Cissy to Kookie.

But Elijah was checking the water levels and pressure gauges; obsessively checking, rechecking, holding the safety valve down with a huge and filthy rag, letting it go when the needles reached red, counting the chunks of wood as they went into the furnace, seeking out the perfect tempo for stoking.

"You there!" he said, seeing Cissy and Kookie loitering in the doorway. "Watch the chimneys! Tell me what comes outa the chimneys!"

"We can work! I can do proper work!" protested Kookie, not wanting to be fobbed off with a child-sized job.

But Elijah, stripped down to the waist now like

some ancient John the Baptist, only gestured them away. "Do as you're told and watch the stacks!"

Useless, helpless to help, they climbed to the roof of the Texas; Cissy collected the water that distilled on the pipes of the calliope, meaning to take it up to the pilots. Then she was fearful of how angry Everett would be when he saw she was still on board. So she and Kookie sipped the water themselves, sitting on the sand-canvas-covered roof, out of Everett's line of sight. A rain of sparks showered down on them. The air was full of soot. The thick black smoke from the *Queen*'s chimneys was tugged astern by the wind. But the smoke from the *Tula-Rose* swamped them and covered them in soot.

"Smoke's comin" out," said Cissy dubiously.

Kookie repeated the message but, finding he could not make Elijah hear a word, jumped onto the roof of the hurricane deck and relayed the news from there. "Smoke's comin' out the chimneys!"

Cole's boat pulled farther ahead. The sloping paddle wheel of the *Queen* chipped the water into a curdled foamy wake that stretched out as far behind as they could see, but the *Tula*'s wheel was churning the river into snowy drifts of spray and foam.

Back at the wharf, the landau was making hard work of turning around on the restricted space.

"Would you good people carry us up to the finish line?" asked Loucien, stepping up onto the running board of the carriage. Miss March led the horses around by their cheek straps. The Blacker family looked put out—also alarmed by Loucien's size and state. Against their will, she stowed Tibbie amid their feet. Pa Blacker began to open the carriage door to put Tibs out again, like a cat. Loucien deliberately misunderstood him. "Lor', that's kind of you to offer, sir, but you'll never fit me in there," she said, smiling him full in the face. And she closed the door again. The landau set off for Boats-a-Cummin with Miss May riding on one running board and Loucien Crew on the other.

Cissy was starting to get bored. "Smoke's comin' out the chimneys," she called yet again . . . then promptly changed her tune. Large chucks of wood began to fly out of the metal chimney stacks and shower down onto the stern decks and paddle wheel. Up in the pilothouse (which had its front shutters wide open) Crew was bombarded with hunks of charred and smoking wood, as well as a swarm of sparks.

"WOOD COMIN' OUT THE CHIMNEYS!" yelled Cissy.

Kookie parroted her in disbelief. "Wood comin' out the chimneys?"

"What are those confounded children doing here?" said Everett, who could hardly fail to see Cissy running up and down the Texas roof, kicking chunks of burning wood off it and into the river while Kookie yelled between cupped hands: "WOOD COMIN' OUT THE CHIMNEYS!"

Elijah held up a shaking hand—"Lay off!"—and the stokers stopped stoking and fell up against one another, exhausted. The steam pressure eased; the rain of cinders and timber turned back to smoke. The *Sunshine Queen* slowed to a more sedate speed.

But to their surprise, the *Tula-Rose* stayed in sight. Elijah emerged from the engine room and strolled forward to the bow, cocking his head to listen: "She's picked up a load a silt," he said matter-of-factly. "Losin' pressure."

"So we have a chance?"

Looking around him, Elijah seemed a great deal more interested in the scenery than in the race. "Familyer," he said.

"Yes, well, we're going upriver, sir," said Chad Powers. "We came through here yesterday—and the day before, going the other way."

"We did?" said Elijah. "Fancy." Curly suspected he had forgotten the race altogether—was convinced of it when Elijah said, "Tell you what: why don't we cook up some bacon?" Back in the engine room the old man clanged a bucket of bacon joints down in front of Max and Benet (who had taken over the stoking) and told them to feed the fire. Then he went back to poking the steam gauges with a broken broomstick and muttering to himself about his time as a mud clerk.

A frenzy of rising hope took over from despair. Perhaps if Cole Blacker had clogged his boilers with silt, it was still possible to catch up, still possible to overtake him. "The tortoise and the hare! The tortoise and the hare!" roared Everett from the summit of the boat, and the filthy smoke-stained Bright Lights Theater Company snuffed up the smell of bacon and felt the kick of renewed speed as the *Sunshine Queen* devoured her breakfast.

The five-mile raft came into sight. It had been moored in the center of the river, so that the racers could tie up to either side. No one but Elijah was going to be able to maneuver the *Queen* alongside a flat barge piled high with timber. But as he began to climb the four levels to the pilothouse, the man's weariness showed. There was just no telling, beneath the grizzled stubble, what age Elijah was. Sixty? Seventy? When he came to a halt on the stairs, Cissy ran and took his hand, put it on her shoulder, and felt his skeleton settle its weight on hers: a wrecked paddleboat settling on a sandbar.

"Can we manage it, Mr. Elijah, sir?" she said, meaning the race.

"Sure," said Elijah, meaning the stairs. "Only one more deck to go. Well, look at that. There's my place." They were passing through the canyon again, and there it was: that little swamped shack at the foot of a golden escarpment—one-time boathouse, maybe, of the vast mansion up top.

Elijah contemplated climbing on right up to the roof of the pilothouse, so as to steer with his feet through the hatch. But the extra climb seemed beyond him. So he simply stepped behind the wheel and steered, as if he had been doing it that way for years.

"Mud clerk, roustabout, boiler man . . . Elijah's like living with four other people, isn't he?" observed Everett, making the downward climb.

"*One man in his time plays many parts,*" observed Curly, tenderly wiping the soot off Everett's face with the tip of a damp handkerchief.

Up ahead, the paddle wheel of the *Tula-Rose* fluttered to a halt. She thudded ungently against the fueling barge, though smoke kept pouring from her stacks. Blacker's army of friends, in their natty maroon overalls, began flinging logs aboard. Their hoots of laughter and wild aim hinted at too much champagne and too little experience. They were playing at boats.

Eighty yards, sixty yards. The *Queen* approached the port side of the fuel barge. They could see Cole Blacker standing at the door of the engine room swearing down at his engineer, blaming him for the loss of power. Everett even saw the moment Cole thought of his masterstroke, turned away from the engine-room door, and ordered the *Tula-Rose* to cast off.

Heaving a tank of turpentine over the bull rails and into the river, Cole produced a handgun and emptied several bullets into it. The tank exploded under the tethering ropes, then sank amid a circle of fire. The ropes instantly severed; the raft began to move. The lads aboard it, unwarned and scared, scrambled over the log pile to try to clamber back aboard, but already the barge was drifting off its moorings, heading downriver: one boy fell between the *Tula* and the barge. One simply stood shouting: "You git back here! You git on back here, Cole!" The drifting log pile, trailing burning stumps of rope, bore down on the *Queen*. Cole had cast his friends adrift, simply to ensure that the *Queen* could not refuel. Added bonus if it smashed into the *Queen* and sank her.

Elijah steered so sharply to port that his passengers were flung to the floor, but it was not enough. Picking themselves up, they ran to the starboard rail to fend off with a broom, a shovel, and outstretched hands—faint hope!—a ton of logs accelerating toward them on the current.

"Whoso putteth his trust in the LORD!" bellowed Elder Slater. The boys aboard the wood barge squatted down among the logs, gaping faces staring at the vessel they were about to ram.

Cissy, though, was not on the river at all. She was back in Olive Town, watching a raft of logs loose a metal silo to mow down her home and everyone in its path. *"Fuller Monterey, you stink!"* she bawled at the ton of lumber bearing down on her. *"Don't care if you're live or dead. You still stink!"*

Beneath the water, a tree—uprooted in Patience and carried down a hundred miles of river before rerooting itself in Numchuck silt—snagged those trailing ropes. Ten yards short of collision, the log barge was pulled up short. It pitched wildly, dumped more timber, sent its cargo of stokers sprawling, spewed a big bow wave. The submerged tree reared up out of the water like the monster kraken . . . but sank back down, still holding fast to the raft.

Elijah had been forced so close to the bank that the port-side chimney clipped the escarpment. It tilted on its hinges and came crashing down—would certainly have killed anyone who had been standing in its path—might even now set the ship alight. But it seemed like a minor thing—almost insignificant. More important just then was the fact that they had not been engulfed by a ton of wood. Chad Powers shut down the port boiler. Smoke issued with less and less violence out of the fallen chimney. The *Queen* slowed to a stately four knots.

"Slow and steady wins the race?" said Curly, ever optimistic, but Everett Crew shook his head. Not only had Blacker almost killed them, he had deprived them of the fuel they needed to make it to the finishing line.

The lead boat, her stern wheel a thunder of foam once more, was picking up speed. But the fueling maneuver had asked a lot of the *Tula-Rose*—more than her days of genteel cruising had ever asked.

"He's cooking her," observed Elijah casually to Chips, who had trailed up to the pilothouse in Elijah's wake. "See them stacks?"

"Yep," said Chips.

The sides of Cole's chimneys looked as if mildew had broken out. Big dark patches were spreading across their pewter cladding: well, not mildew, but scorch marks, actually.

"He's strapped down his safety valves, I reckon," said Elijah.

"Yep," said Chips, always happy to agree with the old man.

"Best catch up and tell him," said Elijah, and rang the gong twice for full speed ahead.

They flung on every scrap of wood, voices crying out the water levels in the boiler, the readings on the steam gauge. Elijah rang the nonexistent ship's bell and sounded the horn, the gong, the jingles, trying to catch Blacker's attention. The rest of the crew only gradually worked out what was going on.

"*Tell* him he's burning his chimneys?" cried Kookie, sobbing with frustration and hatred. "He just half killed us!"

"Tell him? *Tell him!?*" raged Hellfire Slater, whose preaching had never dwelled long on the part about "love thine enemies." "I wouldn't tell him if the Devil was standing behind him with a club!"

"Hear that?" said Elijah, tilting his head into the cacophony of noise made by two steamer engines, a Niagara of water, piston rods thrashing, crankshafts turning, wakes hitting the shore, people shouting, joints creaking, hog chains and knuckle chains rattling. Within all that he had picked out a sound. The others were obliged to believe in it. They could hear nothing but a deafening racket.

The cockeyed paddle wheel chewed at the water like an old man with teeth in only one side of his head. The *Queen* herself refused to hurry, despite the bacon in her furnace. What would happen when they ran out of fuel altogether? Must they wash slowly down to Blowville, a powerless hulk once again? Well, let it be. With luck they would run aground and leave Cole Blacker nothing but a pile of matchwood to gloat over.

"He wanted so badly to win the *Queen*," mused Everett, "and yet he was ready to smash her to Hades. There is something grievously wrong with that young man."

And still they limped after Cole, at half power, to tell him his chimneys were scorching. Fleetingly Everett wondered what his brother Cyril would have done, but the thought only made him sadder, knowing he had just lost Cyril's showboat to a repellent little con artist.

Beside him, in the pilothouse, Elijah began to shout—an old man's creaking, croaking shout—toward the *Tula-Rose*: "Tula-Rose, *look to your chimneys! Look to your chimneys!*"

Crew left Elijah shouting and went down to the bow, where he mustered everyone possible—even calling the stokers away from their furnaces. And they too yelled forward across the foaming white wake of the boat up ahead: "Tula-Rose, *look to your chimneys! Look to your chimneys!*" Their words were swallowed up like spray.

Up on the promenade deck, deafened by the thrashing paddle wheel, Cole Blacker grinned and grimaced at them, joining his hands into a fist over his head, like a champion boxer.

That was the moment when the boiler exploded.

Chapter Fourteen

OLD MAN RIVER

*T*he noise had a shape. It was a kick that hit them in the chest and bent their rib cages. The rest was played out in pantomime, because their hearing went. For a moment, Cissy thought her eyes had shattered, too; her vision was aflicker with slits of white. Then the splintered skin of the *Tula-Rose* began to rain down: planks and slats and spars and filigree cutwork, wicker and rattan, metal chimney cladding, paddle blades and louvers reduced to matchwood. A wave spread outward from the explosion. It picked up the *Sunshine Queen* and flexed her like a rug, cracking the vertebrae of her spine—piston rod, hogging chains, rudder bars. Then something fell on Cissy. She thought it must be the *Tula-Rose* falling out of the sky, for where else could it be? In the place where it had been a moment before was nothing but a smudge, a messy rubbing out, a white patch of steamy nothing.

The weight was Everett Crew's as he threw himself on top of her to shield her from the rain of scalding water that rode on the blast, the clattering avalanche of splintered metal and wood falling out of the wind. The whole river seethed, hollowing, refilling, slapping the golden walls of the gorge with choppy little waves the shape of hands. Then a larger wave washed over the *Queen*'s cargo deck . . . and they were in the river.

Cissy barely knew it, for the water was tepid—blood temperature. Then the current brought down on her a tumbling white murrain of debris—smashed life rafts with edges jagged as knives, unbroken champagne bottles. For a few moments she was too startled to be afraid. Then the weight of her laced boots tugged her feet downward. The cloth of her skirt filled up with water and tangled around her legs. She felt for the bottom but found nothing—a shiver of shifting silt. She called out for Everett but was too deafened to hear her own voice.

Then Everett Crew surfaced beside her and told her everything was fine—a distant murmur, a movement of lips told her everything was fine.

But it wasn't.

An awning wrenched from the afterdeck of the *Tula-Rose*, shredded by the explosion, twisted by the river currents, enveloped them both—heavy wet canvas—a shroud for two dead sailors. It dragged them apart, pulled Cissy's fingers out of Everett's grip, carrying him away. And still, brittle petals of split wood were fluttering down out of the sky, chipping holes in the face of the water.

She unfastened her skirt and swam out of it, but her boots, her only good boots, her button boots that took five minute to fasten! "Ma will be livid," she heard herself say.

High above her, shapes hung snagged on thornbushes in the crevices of the escarpment— garments, sacking, the rags of chintz curtains. Bizarrely, a train passed by on the cliff top. Silent to her muffled hearing, its windows full of white faces, it looked like a ghost train. "Never even knew there was a railway," Cissy found herself saying out loud.

More strangely still, Kookie Warboys was standing on the river's surface. Water was churning around his feet, but there he stood, red hair plastered to his head, hands rubbing at deafened ears, eyes scanning the river, mouth calling her name over and over and over. . . .

There was screaming, too. She told herself there

wasn't, but as her hearing returned, it was impossible to ignore. The scalded gorge was full of screaming.

Kookie dragged Cissy out onto the mud bar, where, within moments, Benet and Curly joined them. They had no way of knowing who else had been washed off the bow of the *Queen*. The boat had nestled herself comfortably into a crook of slack water, against the foot of the cliff, and along her rail, faces began to emerge as the remains of the Bright Lights Company pulled themselves to their feet. Sweeting, Oskar, George, Max, Boisenberry, and Elder Slater:

"And Moses stretched forth his rod toward heaven, and the LORD sent thunder and hail, and fire ran along upon the ground!"

Then they turned their eyes toward the small white reef that, minutes earlier, had been the *Tula-Rose*. It was barely more than a white picket fence—as if someone had tried to tame the river with a cartload of garden gates. One of the rowboats that had moored up to watch the race was already bobbing around, looking for survivors. Another must have found one, for it came by, full of screaming. Chips had been rescued into a third and went by, dripping like a seal; but though the Bright Lights called and called, the explosion had deafened him not just to their voices, but to their very existence. He never so much as glanced toward the *Sunshine Queen*, and they never saw him again.

Of Cole Blacker, of course, there was not a sign. He would not be found. He had been standing directly above the starboard boiler when it exploded, liberating five thousand gallons of scalding water, superheated steam, and several tons of iron.

"Where's Everett?" asked Curly, missing his glasses, unable to see whether Crew's was among the faces on the *Queen*. "Is Everett there?"

"No," said Cissy. "No." And again, "No. He's in the river."

Nearby, a floating shape broke the surface of the water, rounded like shoulder blades. Kookie and Curly stumbled along the mud bar, shoes sucked off, bare feet sinking into grit and black slime. Unable to reach the shape in the water, they flopped onto their faces and swam toward it. Toward what? Some maimed corpse, clothes burned off and scalded beyond recognition? Or was it the skin pink of someone who had struggled out of his Prince Albert coat and shirt in a failed effort to swim? Kookie was a good swimmer. He was there first. His fingertips touched the bristle of hair-tufted flesh, and as he did so, the floater turned over in the water.

A bacon flitch.

"You said we should save it," said Kookie, and Curly

gave a sob of a laugh and swallowed a stomachful of dirty river. The relief gave them the strength to quit the mudbar and swim within reach of hands, ropes, and encouraging shouts aboard the *Sunshine Queen*.

Everett Crew, dragged under by the awning, a tentacle of canvas around his throat, expressed the hope that someone would look after his wife and child. The child he would never live to see. His mouth filled with water and his nose emptied of air. His vision spangled with lights as crimson as Loucien's dress. Reaching out to feel its texture, his hand touched air, and then timber.

"I am too old for this, Lou," he said as he wrapped arms and legs around the flotsam and dragged his face clear of the water for long enough to suck breath. "Should we keep to repertory work from now on?" The canvas tightened around his throat, the awning billowing beneath him dark as death. "I might even stoop to burlesque." A charred pine knot struck him in the jaw, and he tasted blood. "Or a steady nine-to-five day job?" A slew of dead fish, silver sequins for eyes, rolled over his face.

At last the awning loosed its clutch, freeing Everett to collide with the fuel barge. Its crew of stokers, still marooned in midriver, did not even notice him. They stood atop the timber pile, too horror stricken even to flinch, staring upriver toward the explosion. Up yonder, carved in steam using hammer blows of noise, was the fate that would have been theirs if they had managed to scramble back aboard the *Tula-Rose*. They were half a mile from where the boiler had blown, and yet their complexions were pecked with little burns where scalding water drops had fallen into their upturned faces.

Everett had to pull himself up out of the river. He was amused to discover that he had ridden to safety aboard Max's plank.

The owner of the rowboat that carried him back to the *Queen* was anxious to know what it signified for the betting. The *Tula-Rose* had, after all, been in front when she blew up. Then again, the *Queen* was likely to make it up to the finish even if it took a while. "I had ten dollars on the *Rose*, see."

Everett asked what line of business the man was in and, being told he was a bank teller—a regular nine-to-five man—decided to stay in acting after all. At least actors recognize a tragedy when they see one.

The Blacker family had just alighted from their fancy landau at Boats-a-Cummin wharf when the explosion happened. It was just as well, since the horses were so panicked that they turned the carriage over on its side and were left struggling in the traces. The passengers, by contrast, stood perfectly still on the jetty. Mr. and Mrs. Blacker, Loucien, Tibbie, Miss March, and an assortment of aunties. They looked up at the sky, waiting for news to settle onto their foreheads. Which of them had just lost everything?

"Yours," said Old Man Blacker. "Derelict old tub. Not seaworthy."

Loucien said nothing in reply. The baby inside her pummelled like a swimmer trapped under the hull of a sunken ship. More spectators had gathered at Boats-a-Cummin than anywhere along the course, hoping to witness the finish. They broke into a bedlam of noise now. Those in rowboats immediately cast off and started to row downriver. A train went by, and the passengers aboard had their heads out of the windows, shouting the news:

"Boat's gone up!"

"Blown to perdition!"

There were fragments of debris on the train's roof, but it did not stop to offload any better information.

"Yours!" said Mrs. Blacker, shaking Tibbie by the shoulders. "It was *your* boat!" Miss March snatched up Tibs and held her close.

"It's the *Queen*!" yelled a spectator.

"It's the *Tula-Rose*!" yelled another. Neither had any possible way of knowing.

"Look after Tibbie," said Loucien to Miss May, and began walking back alone along the bank.

As Everett stood up in the rowboat, a stampede thudded down the cargo deck of the *Queen*, and a dozen hands hauled him over the bull rail. Curly could not think of a single quotation that expressed his delight at seeing Everett still alive. Kookie told him about the bacon flitch and how they had mistaken it for him. The quartet began a soft-shoe shuffle despite having only five shoes among them. Cissy simply wrapped her arms around his damp waist and wept.

"I don't know what you children were doing aboard in the first place," said Everett, feeling the need to bring order to chaos. "I expressly said . . ."

Out on the river, a regatta had broken out, with little pleasure boats and canoes to-ing and fro-ing, taking in the sights, trawling for souvenirs, looking for survivors. Many parents in Blowville had sons who had gone out for an afternoon's sport with Cole Blacker. Some found their boys alive and safe aboard the fuel barge, and rowed them home to supper.

Some didn't.

"Where's Elijah?" asked Crew, missing a face.

They could not recall, for a moment, whether the old man had been in the engine room or steering when the explosion happened. Time had been jarred out of shape, and the details refused to fit back together.

"I shut down the port boiler," said Chad. "He wasn't in the engine room then." Their faces turned upward, necks craned. Crossing their minds were all the anecdotes Elijah had told them of pilothouses blown away in hurricanes or knocked overboard in collisions. They were relieved to see theirs still in place, perched up top like a howdah on an elephant's back.

"We forgot him," said Kookie. "Our rememb'ring's gettin' bad as his!" And he laughed, but nervously, because why after all had Elijah not put in an appearance like everyone else?

"He's not partial to stairs," said Cissy, hoping that was why.

The big ship's wheel turned a little as the wash from passing boats toyed with the rudder: clockwise to port, counterclockwise to starboard. It could not turn through more than five degrees, though, because its lower rim was wedged against Elijah.

When the *Tula-Rose* exploded, her piston rod had been fired aft through scalding air. It had hurtled, harpoonlike, out of the stern of the *Tula* and in at the open shutters of the *Queen*'s pilothouse, striking Elijah a glancing blow to the head before passing effortlessly on through the back wall. It lay now like a harmless length of bathroom piping, along the Texas, whereas Elijah . . .

Elijah was peacefully curled up like a child sound asleep, on the mattress they had laid down for him. The wheel spokes nudge-nudge-nudged at him, but he did not stir.

Hemmed in, as they were, by the walls of the gorge, the crew of the *Queen* would find it difficult to get Elijah ashore. They lowered him, on the mattress, down to the cargo deck and hailed the various rowboats plowing up and down. But the people of Blowville took no notice—blamed them for the accident, perhaps, or were just too busy picking over the floating wreckage of the *Tula-Rose*. So the company laid Elijah and the mattress on a life raft. It was not stable enough to sail all the way back to Blowville, so they headed instead for the steps by the derelict boathouse—a little flotilla of mildewed and rotten life rafts, paddled by soaked, soot stained, weary ship's rats. Their decision was helped by the figure of a red-haired woman waving to them from the bottom stair.

Until the reunion with Loucien, no one but Cissy had wept. Even now there was no flinging of arms around necks, no tender embraces, no cries of "I thought I had lost you!" There was just a general drizzling of noses, the chafing of a hand against a sleeve, an increased blood supply to the heart . . . which was just as well: it was quite a climb up those rock-hewn steps carrying between them an old man on a mattress. Loucien laid her jacket over Elijah's face, to keep the flies off the gash in his head.

"What's up there at the top, Miss Loucien? Are we trespassing?" asked Cissy.

"Like as not," said Loucien. "I came through yards of yard to get to the steps. But it was the first place I could get down to the river. It's an emergency. What kinda skunks are gonna object to us crossing their yard?"

"It's not the skunks I'm fretted about. It's guard dogs," Cissy confessed. She had a mortal fear of guard dogs.

"Yard" did not quite describe the gardens surrounding the mansion on the river bend. There were knot gardens and water fountains, an orangery and strange big trees never seeded by any Missouri bird. There was a lake and a terrace made of bricks all crisscrossing, herringbone style. The house itself looked as if it should be inhabited by Greek gods, with easy steps running up toward half a dozen stone pillars holding up a triangle full of carvings. Naked people in helmets. (They were not from Missouri either, by the looks of them.)

The house staff were all gathered in one corner of the garden, looking upriver to the scene of the explosion, pointing and fretting. Barely an hour had passed, and yet they were already wearing black armbands as etiquette demanded. Far from setting the dogs on the Bright Lights, the maids and lackeys came hopping around, smart as magpies in their uniform black and white, offering to help. A maid with a tray offered them tumblers of orange punch.

"We have laid the dead in the hall, sir," said the English butler, as if directing them to a buffet lunch.

"And the survivors?" said Everett.

"We have laid the dead in the hall, sir," repeated the butler, and his face was rigid and grim.

"Well, this one's still breathing," said Loucien decidedly. "You got somewhere a mite softer?"

The butler was transformed, energized. He summoned help to relieve them of the mattress, and a four-man team fairly ran with it up the shallow steps and into the portico. The Bright Lights caught up with them on the interior staircase. Loucien took back the scarlet jacket she had laid over Elijah's face. A couple of the maids glanced away for fear of what they might see underneath it. The stretcher bearers, though, came to a dead stop.

"Holy Mary," said the footman.

"*Oi vei! N'echtiker-tog!*" said the cook.

The butler sneezed.

"It's him. It truly is!" said the gardener.

The butler handled the situation with immaculate English efficiency, despite an allergy to excitement that always triggered a sneezing fit. He dispatched maids to turn down the bed and open the window in the master bedroom, the ostler to ride for a doctor, the cook to boil hot water, the upstairs maid to find a nightshirt.

"You know this man?" asked Everett as the sound of running feet echoed down six different corridors.

"Know him?" cried the butler, sneezing like a pepper-box pistol. "Don't you know who this is? Don't you recognize him? This is Captain Bouverie! This is the Master!"

Laid on the great expanse of his own bed, Elijah looked more frail and cadaverous than ever. Dried blood flaked the pillowcase, like iron scrapings from a boiler. His big hands lay limply open. For whole minutes together he did not appear to breathe at all; when he did, the air rasped in his throat. A bruise gradually obliterated one side of his face like a paddleboat's metal stacks scorching from within. Thanks to the disaster, the doctor was a long time coming; longer than long. The maids stood about, aprons clutched to their mouths, and when Elder Slater suggested prayers in the dressing room, they almost ran there, impatient to help in any way they could.

"Such a good man. Such a dear man," they said, as if overalls, soot, and stubble might have hidden his qualities from the Bright Lights.

Despite the clouds of glory he had trailed behind him along the Numchuck, Missouri, and Mississippi rivers, Captain Elijah Bouverie had simply slipped out of sight one day and disappeared. His impaired memory had seen him wander off before, but one year earlier he had vanished without trace from his cliff-top mansion, and no amount of searching, advertising, or heartfelt wishing had brought him home again. All that remained within the high rooms and flowery walks were his fretful staff and the proofs of his glory days as the greatest captain ever to sail the Mississippi basin.

Despite hurricanes and lightning strikes, flood, wars, and the jealousy of his rivals, he had never lost a boat or a passenger. Myths had attached themselves to his name, like barnacles on a ship's hull: Captain Bouverie had a charmed life, a pact with the Devil, a magic ship's bell. . . .

"The truth is, sir, he had genius," said Henry the butler. "Started off as a roustabout and a boiler monkey, worked his way up to river pilot and captain. He bought derelict boats and refurbished them into palaces—palaces!—not a word of a lie, sir! A fleet of forty boats. His crews were devoted to them, every man jack. It is said that he never raised an unjust hand against the meanest roustabout."

"Even the Irish," said the cook wonderingly.

"His engineering patents brought him the bulk of his fortune, of course," Henry was saying as they moved along a corridor lined with paintings and photographs of paddle steamers. "By the age of fifty he had no need to work. But the lure of the river was very strong, I fear." They paused beside a window filled with a view of the golden gorge. "I blame myself!" lamented the butler, running both hands through his dapper gray hair. "I never should have taken my eyes off him!"

The Bright Lights, meandering along behind, stopped to let him regain his composure.

"Does the Captain have folks?" asked Kookie. He was wondering—as everyone was—when Elijah's wife and children would come running.

"The master's wife and son were killed by a boiler explosion on the Platte River," said the butler, and pointed out, as they entered the sitting room, a painting of a diminutive woman dressed in silver gray, carrying a tiny boy.

"But you said—"

"Hush, Kookie."

The butler gasped. "Not aboard one of the Captain's ships! Never think it! They were traveling to meet him in Genoa."

The room contained two button-back leather sofas, also two enormous brown dogs. The members of the Bright Lights Theater & Shipwrecking Company sat and sipped sherry. "Bit like turpentine," said Kookie, trying to sound as if he liked turpentine. The dogs paced the room agitatedly, grumbling in their throats or sniffing at the base of the door.

"They sense he's home," said the butler, and his voice cracked. "Poor beasts. Poor beasts." Loucien poured him a glass of his own sherry and sat him down.

The driveway and brick terrace outside soon filled up with carriages. Saddle horses grazed the lawn. The families of missing boys moved like migrating bison through the gardens and came to a standstill in the marble hallway. Among them were Cole Blacker's parents. They stood there waiting for news and, however often they were told it, went on waiting. Their faces were blank—twin sacks emptied of coal. Emptied of Cole. They did not sob or moan or rage: they simply stood, hands hanging down. At a loss.

They had trouble understanding that there were no mortal remains to recover from the accident. "But the funeral," they said, puzzled. "How d'we bury him?"

Cissy ran and fetched Elder Slater, but his kind of comfort was of no use to the Blackers.

"We don't have God," said Pa Blacker—as someone might say "We don't take milk." A generation or two before, a Blacker patriarch had fired God from his house in a fit of temper, as he might a maid who stole the teaspoons. Since then, his children and grandchildren had been too busy making money to interview for a replacement. So Pa and Ma Blacker lacked a body to bury and a religion to bury it in. Besides, they had never planned for such a day as this. Everett thought he had never seen two lives so vaporized by disaster.

"He got his crew off the boat, you know, before it blew?" Pa Blacker said. "He saved who he could. He was a brave boy." The tone was pleading. When the old man's gaze met Everett's, the eyes were broken windows. Everett looked around him at the comrades whose lives Cole Blacker had blighted.

"Your boy was a . . . singular piece of work, sir," he said, and Pa Blacker grasped his hand in gratitude.

"Thank you. Thank you. You know anything about funerals?"

"No, sir."

Pa Blacker's thoughts kept spinning around and around this one black hole. "Don't know a thing about funerals, me. Never been to one. I mean, what do people say? What happens? Does it help? What does anyone do?"

Cissy tugged on Loucien's sleeve and whispered something to her.

Loucien leaned over and whispered in Everett's ear.

Everett, defeated by his own profession, smiled and nodded.

"Looky here, Mr. Blacker," said Loucien. "We Bright Lights—we may not look much, but we know how to put on a . . . how to polish up an hour till it shines. We'll give your boy his shining moment. You leave it with us."

Chapter Fifteen

A GOOD SEND-OFF

So they staged a funeral for Cole Blacker, even though the boy himself could not be there, the Bright Lights detested him, and the Blacker clan were strangers to God.

First, they raided the rubbish heaps for empty bottles and Golden Bend Mansion for candle stubs. They borrowed servants' uniforms, a horse from the Blacker Livery Stables, and a white duck from the town pond. Cissy and Kookie were given the job of gathering crow feathers. Tibbie was sent to pick flowers (since she was still inclined to faint if given jobs she didn't like). The men rowed over to the *Sunshine Queen* and brought back to Golden Bend anything of value—the property box, the costumes. Miss March and Loucien planned music for the funeral in Blowville.

Meanwhile, Captain Elijah Bouverie lay on his great white bed in the master bedroom of his great yellow mansion, unaware that he had made it back home. Over the bed hung a crown of gilded antlers won in a Missouri river race. In the opinion of the doctor, he was unlikely to see out the week. He simply lay, gaunt and bruised, beneath the gilded horns, as though gored by the past.

They opened the funeral in the late afternoon, with one sung note, braided and strengthened by ten more voices. It fetched people out onto Main Street. A procession appeared led by a little blond girl all in white, carrying a tin laurel wreath. Behind her came an unsaddled white horse, its withers draped with a black cloth, its mane and tail plaited with black feathers. Behind the horse, four barefoot men, their skin as black as their suits, sang in close harmony "Nobody Knows the Trouble I Seen." Behind the singers came the mourners, in a black-draped landau, their horses, too, plumed with crow feathers.

Curiosity had drawn people from their houses, some in the mood to jeer or hiss the Blackers. But sunset, music, and spectacle kept them from doing so or from turning back indoors.

As the cortege reached the wharf at the foot of Main Street, the sun was just setting. A sapling tree was planted, and the blurred shape of a pale bird flew up miraculously from its branches and took on the color of sunset. The singers started up a round that swirled and circled, capturing into its orbit the whole funeral cortege.

> *"Oh, Absalom, Oh, Absalom,*
> *my son, my son, Oh, Absalom.*
> *Would God I had died,*
> *Would God I had died for thee!"*

Then, from strategic housetops, came more lamentations—snatches of poetry, pieces of plays— nothing but turfs cut from a literary lawn . . . and yet they carried the authentic hallmark of sorrow.

Suddenly someone shouted and pointed upriver. Into sight came a host of little lights. Candle flames, flickering their way down the cold sleek slick of black water, quivered like grief itself as they came: a constellation of candles, their reflections doubling the number. There were flowers, too—weeds when they had been in the ground, but rags of luminous loveliness now aboard the darkened river. The crowd drew a single breath.

Loucien began to sing: *"I've got peace like a river— I've got peace like a river in my soul . . ."* and the crowd swayed—they could not help themselves. Children in nightclothes astride their fathers' shoulders watched the lights float by, flames reflected in their eyes. The calliope picked up the last note of Loucien's song and tumbled it into "Steal Away Home," and the crowd joined in because they had stopped being spectators and become part of the event. Max led the carriage horses back toward the Blacker mansion.

"Such a clever boy," Cole's mother said to him, her fingers fumbling the glass of the photograph in her lap. "You knew him. You know what a lovely boy he was."

"Pan Bóg jest dobry," said Max.

"Yes, yes. Absolutely!" said Pa Blacker, hearing what he wanted to hear. The mourners were invisible in their black clothing. So, too, was their draped carriage, only its wheel spokes flickering white, like coins spun to settle a bet.

The townspeople herded instinctively toward the feast laid out at the big house. The Bright Lights Theater & Funeral Company did not follow: puppeteers never show themselves after a puppet show—it breaks the spell.

"Is there anything else?" asked Everett Crew, who was a perfectionist and never entirely happy after a performance.

"There weren't no telegrams," said Kookie.

"That's weddings, silly," said Tibbie, shivering now in her thin white dress.

Kookie shook his head. "I live in a telegraph office,

me. There's always a shoal of telegrams come in after a buryin'. 'Thinking of you.' 'Carry your tears to Jesus.' 'I knowd him and he wuz spickettyboo.' That manner of thing. Ma says people don't know what to say, so they send a telegram and get it over and done in five words."

"Thank you, Kookie," said Crew. "Tomorrow I'll fix for a flurry of messages from a variety of places. It will comfort the family to think the world is full of people who liked their boy." Loucien linked her arm through her husband's. It was a whole lot easier to think gently of Cole Blacker now that he was dead.

Curly called on the Blackers next day, to ask for— if not a fee—the money they had spent staging the funeral. He and Miss May stood on the front stoop, face-to-face with the black wreath on the door knocker.

"Last night was the first time I ever heard you declaim, Mr. Curlitz. You have a fine voice."

"Why, thank you, Miss May."

A maid opened the door to them, but they were not invited in. The Blackers, she said, were not "at home" to strangers. Then she shut the door.

Everett Crew meanwhile went to the Blowville General Store so as to send a telegram to Pickard Warboys in Olive Town asking him to arrange telegrams of sympathy to the grieving family from far and wide. But he found he couldn't afford it. Still, it was not a wasted journey.

Pickard Warboys, studying an atlas night after night, had chanced sending a telegram to Cissy, care of the Blowville office. Everett had just slipped it into the breast pocket of his borrowed suit when he noticed, pinned to the adjoining post office desk, a sad mosaic of undeliverable letters. Among them was one addressed to

MR. E. CREW,
The Paddle Ship Calliope.

"Of course!" His brother Cyril had known the ship by a different name! So there it had hung, yellowing in the sunlight, unread. In his delight and gratitude, Everett gave the telegrapher the price of a beer before tearing open the envelope.

It was a long, news-filled letter. It took some time to read. Everett had to sit down on the floor to read it. He had to read it twice over and then a third time. Customers calling in to send mail or telegrams had to step over him, but he did not even notice.

Stranded and left behind in Salvation, Cyril Crew, Egil, Finn, and Revere agreed they should jump a southbound train and catch up with the *Calliope* farther downstream. Egil, Finn, and Revere had had no trouble running alongside the very next freight train, hauling themselves aboard. If they had just chosen a train going south (not east), they would have been quickly reunited with the Bright Lights.

Cyril, being an older man and a little bow-fronted under his embroidered vest, found it much harder to jump aboard a moving train. Having missed three, he finally managed to clamber onto the rear platform of a southbound passenger train, only to be arrested by an overzealous train guard and thrown in jail at the next stop. Licorice.

In prison he shared a cell with a disagreeable but optimistic young man who told Cyril they would be free in no time. And this was true, since the young man promptly broke out of jail. He did it by shooting the deputy sheriff with his own gun, and he threatened to shoot Cyril, too, if he would not tag along. As Cyril recounted, in his elegant handwriting:

I cannot imagine why he was desirous of my company, since I most assuredly did not want his. It is hard to imagine a youth less sweet than his name—"Sugar Cain"—suggested. In the light of later events, I wish I had opted for being shot where I sat. But I too fled Licorice Jail—albeit unwillingly—and the two of us achieved Roper County before we were cornered in a barn by an embarrassingly large posse and a zooful of hunting dogs. Mr. Cain was shot dead. He died in my lap, so I was found holding his gun and summarily tried for murder here at Roper Junction. Hence my present predicament. I protested that it was harsh, by any standards, to hang a man for riding a train without a ticket, but the sympathies of the audience were against me.

I have such an aversion to ropes, Everett, that I could wish a King of America could be found to grant me a Royal Pardon. That failing, I would settle for seeing my only brother again, and in this world rather than the next. Do come if you can. The party starts at sundown, Wednesday the 12th. My warmest regards to your excellent wife and miscellaneous companions. You are, be assured, constantly in my thoughts.

Your unfortunate brother,
Cyril
Roper County Jail,
Roper Junction, Missouri

When he stood up again, Everett held out, on the flat of his hand, all the coins he owned. "A telegram. How many words can I send for that?"

"Three? Four?" said the telegrapher, holding on tight to the beer money.

So Everett dictated this succinct reply:

COMING SOONEST EVERETT.

Chapter Sixteen

A QUEEN'S RANSOM

"*I*f I set off tonight, I can still maybe get there in time," said Everett. "If I can borrow a horse . . ."

"Quicker to go by train in the morning, sir," said Henry. "By my estimate, it is a five-hour journey to Roper Junction."

"We must all go. And here's us, not a cent among us!" said Loucien, brushing her hair vigorously in front of the oval mirror.

"I only need my own train fare. One way would do!" Everett did not look like a man without a cent. On returning his borrowed funeral tailcoat to the butler, his own had been given back laundered, ironed, and mended. (The servants yearned to be helpful.) He was wild-eyed but immaculate.

"We'll put on a show!" said Curly. "All proceeds to go to rescuing Mr. Cyril."

"Blowville's in mourning," said Miss March. "We won't be allowed."

"Banjos ken find they way home to the pawn shop," offered Oskar.

"I've been working up this paying trick with a bucket . . . ," said Chad Powers.

"I'll go see the Blackers tonight and pry money outa them," said Loucien.

"We could always pull a Growow. My invalid mother in Des Moines found it deeply affecting, and I have no doubt it was profitable." And Miss March went on to describe a scene from her childhood. "Two men set up a tent, claiming they have captured the most ferocious beast in the world. The public lines up to view the beast, paying a dollar a head. The Growow is said to be in the back of the tent behind a curtain, chained up (naturally) because it's so murderous. Then the gentleman behind the curtain begins rattling chains and hitting skillets together and screaming, 'The Growow has gotten loose! Argh, save yourselves, save your children!' et cetera, and the crowd understandably runs off in all haste. Not staying to ask their money back." She looked around her at a dozen shocked faces.

"Garibaldi biscuits!" exclaimed Kookie. "We gotta do that thing!"

"May!" said Curly. "We are actors, not flimflam artists!"

May March dabbed her lips with a handkerchief. "I myself was not taken in, of course, but as I say, my mother found it most stimulating. And the takings must have been good." The room surged enthusiastically into life.

Everett shook his head and groaned. "No! No, no, no! You are good, resourceful people. But there's no time! A matter of hours! And this is *my* doing. I forgot Cyril didn't know the boat's name. I should have done more to find him. It's my fault! I'll go up there and vouch for him—switch places with him, I don't know. Whatever it takes."

Over on the white bed, Elijah Bouverie was sinking. The doctor had said so; said he should be granted peace for his passing.

"Don't ever grant me peace," Loucien had said as the doctor's pony and trap bowled away down the drive. "If I'm ever lying on the brink, don't all creep off to a distance like I smell, will you, folks?"

And somehow the Bright Lights and weeping staff had believed Loucien more than the doctor and stayed put. Right now, the quartet was by the bed, crooning songs Elijah might know. Sweeting was trying to spoon water and honey into the old man's mouth without choking him. The various maids who had decided they were in love with various members of the quartet were dusting and polishing all the furniture in the bedroom so as to stay as close as possible. It was not the easiest place to plan a rescue.

Cissy, meanwhile, sat cross-legged on the foot of the bed, reading Cyril's fearful letter over and over, living through his adventures till the palms of her hands were wet with fright. Miss Loucien came and sat down beside her, tugging the letter out of her hands. Her palms, too, were wet, Cissy noticed.

"I know what Cole Blacker woulda done," said Cissy in anger. "He'da passed himself off as King of America. He'da bamboozled the whole of Roper County into giving him a golden stagecoach an' free whiskey. And he'da granted pardons, right, left, and all ways!" She only said it to Miss Loucien, but the rest of the room fell oddly silent, and then she felt just plain embarrassed.

"Heydaydie," Loucien sighed, toying with Elijah's bony old hand on the coverlet, plinking the fingers one by one. "I wonder," she added, reading over the letter, looking at the portrait of Abraham Lincoln on the wall. And then: "Hashi kuchi hunkidory," she said in half Choctaw, half Minneapolis, and kissed Cissy. She smelled of vanilla and French toast. "We can do it!" She swept over to her husband. "We can do it, sweetheart! It can be done! But we still need the danged train fare. In fact . . ." She looked around her at the strange family she had married into. "We really need the whole danged train."

Not the King of America. That would be plain unbelievable. Not Abraham Lincoln—not with him so famously dead. Not a man at all, in fact, because men are a shifty, untrustworthy bunch, most of them. (Loucien said it.) A woman, then! The Bright Lights must, within the day, produce the one woman in the world with enough influence to spring Cyril Crew from Roper County Jail! It had to be Queen Victoria herself!

"Anyone know what the lady looks like? That would be a start." Loucien Shades Crew turned sideways on to the mirror and gave a groan of regret for her lost figure. "Hope she's on the portly side."

"Oh my goodness," muttered Miss March, starting to panic. "Oh goodness me."

"Loucien Shades Crew, you are eight months pregnant!" her husband protested.

When the English butler came to round up the maids, his opinion was asked. "In England I lived in Leytonstone," said Henry. "There was little opportunity for the lady and me to become acquainted. Minnie—Leah—please go and help John fetch down the chandelier in the banquet hall. It is in need of cleaning." The maids bobbed. Everyone else was a little taken aback—it seemed an odd time to be cleaning the lamps—but perhaps Henry wanted the house restored to perfection now that the Master was home.

"I know what the Queen looks like," said Cissy deliberately. "I know exactly what she looks like. We used to have her on our wall. Looks like a dumpling, sorta, but gray all over. Cheeks like a marmot. Royal marmot, I mean, not meanin' to insult Your Majesty." To Cissy, Loucien was already a queen.

"Your hair's red as maple, Lou," Everett went on. "I am quite sure . . ."

"How tall is she, then?" Kookie demanded suspiciously of Cissy.

"Oh my goodness. Oh goodness me."

"I don' know!" Cissy retorted. "It was a head-and-shoulders picture! Her head came upta here on the wall . . . but that's only 'cause there was a nail sticking out there to hang the picture on!"

"Tell us 'bout that bucket trick, will you, Chad?" said Kookie, still thinking of the train fare they did not possess.

Then Sweeting said softly: "She's small as a dime. Wide as she long. Chil' size, that ain't no lie." It was hardly as if he had spoken; Sweeting never spoke louder than a fly buzzing at a windowpane.

The Bright Lights stared at him.

"T'ing is," said Benet, explaining on Sweeting's behalf, "back in eighty-one, we was on loan to Callander Haverley's Minstrels when the man done bless th'English with a show tour. Layin on a smack of pseudo-Nigro culture. We sung twice in fronta the Queen."

The maids gasped. Tibbie Boden gasped. To think she had sailed the Numchuck River with FOUR people who had met a real queen! The room fluttered like an aviary full of owls—*oooh! oh! oooh!*

"Oh my goodness. Oh goodness me."

"Gracious, gentlemen!" murmured Henry with unsuspected wryness. "You are very nearly royalty."

"Did she clap when you sung?" breathed Tibbie in awe.

"She didn' throw nothin', leastways," said Boisenberry.

Loucien Shades Crew was not put off by the fact that Queen Victoria was half her height, more than twice her age, and not known for her red hair. "Even *Henry* didn't know her size 'n' coloring, and he's English," she said with unruffled serenity. "Reckon Roper Junction won't know any better than Leytonstone. Henry, you got one night to teach me to talk English. After that, if you care to, you can be President of England. You ever done any playacting?"

"Prime Minister, ma'am. England does not have a president," said Henry, starting to sneeze.

"Everett, you'll be my American Ambassador . . . and Curly my money man."

"Chancellor," Henry interjected.

"And you, Elder, you can be my pastor or shaman or whatever."

"Chaplain?" suggested Henry.

Up till this point, Elder Slater had said nothing. Now he stood up, hat over his heart; his duster coat, laundered and overstarched, gleamed stiff and white as angel wings. "Mrs. Crew," he said, aiming his eyes just over her head. "Mrs. Crew, I am a lifelong Methodist. My religion allows no monarchs. God alone rules over us. This great land stepped one pace closer to godliness when it cast off king and empire." This was not Elder Slater in hellfire mode; he was visibly trembling. The room fell silent.

"I know that, honey," said Loucien, emptying her face of flippancy. "I may put on costume. Don't mean to say I ain't still a democratic American underneath."

Slater put his hat back on. 'Very good. It needed saying. Now I have a thing to do. If I am not back by dawn, leave without me." The draft, as he left, shed a strangely icy chill.

"Talking of costume," said Loucien at last, "I'll need one. Thanks to this baby, I'm down to the one dress, and that's sorta . . ."

"*Red*," said the room at large.

"Oh my goodness. Oh goodness me!"

"Hush up, May," said Curly sternly, taking the schoolmistress by both wrists. "There comes a time, in getting ready for a play, when you have to step out on the ice and walk. Or the fear'll make you heavy, and it *just won't hold*." She looked at him, breath pent up behind her lips, and a little popeyed. "Now you go see your mother in Des Moines, or you stay here and tend to Captain Bouverie, but either way, you have to start believing in us."

Miss May March looked around her at the Bright Lights Theater, Last Ditch & Final Curtain Company. She could tell from their faces that they were as one with Curly, getting ready to skate on the thin ice of an illusion, however deep the water below. "But you're family!" she exclaimed. "I can't let you all go to it without me!"

Henry the butler circulated with glasses of rich, ruby-red wine—"Don't you dare touch that glass, Habakkuk Warboys!"—then poured one for himself. "Gentlemen—ladies—may I make a toast I have not had cause to make for a great many years: *God save the Queen!*"

"And my brother," said Everett under his breath.

"And Elijah here," murmured Sweeting.

Henry wiped his eyes and raised his glass again. *"Then I say, the Queen, Mr. Cyril Crew, and Captain Elijah Bouverie—God save them all!"*

Elder Slater cycled to Boats-a-Cummin and, as night fell, leaned his borrowed bicycle against the wall of the saloon. With the Blowville saloon closed in mourning, business here was brisk. Checking his gun, settling his hat squarely, he slammed open the doors. The exciting whiteness of his duster coat caught him off guard for a moment, reflected in the long mirror behind the bar.

"Good evening, gentlemen. I mean to preach the word of the Lord here tonight, and the Lord would appreciate your attention."

A change from routine is always welcome: several drinkers turned toward him. The piano player closed his piano lid. At one gambling table, though, the players simply went on with their game, staking bets, shaking their dice. Slater drew out his gigantic pistol, cocked its hammer, and laid its barrel to the dealer's temple. "I mean to preach the word of the Lord, and the Lord *don't appreciate interruptions."*

The dealer squared up the pack and put his hands in his lap. The gaming tables froze and fell silent. The bartender turned his back and continued polishing glasses, but his eyes were on the mirror all the while, in case the sheriff needed a witness statement afterward.

Slater started loud and worked his way up to frenzied, and the empty glasses trembled on the dish rack. When he had done with the preaching, he started on the collection. "Will you help me in my mission? Will you help me ransom the life of those shipwrecked by misfortune in the valley of the shadow of death? Give generous, or ask yourself: who will ransom you in your hour of need?" He moved between the tables, hat held out in one hand, in the other his pistol held at such a level that its barrel brushed their hat brims, disturbed their cigar smoke. This was not his usual audience, come voluntarily to be shouted at. He knew that at any minute someone too drunk, too mean, too irritated to put up with him might shoot him in the back. But he raged and he whispered and he cajoled, and the bartender kept watch in the bronzed mirror.

When Slater left at last, like an avenging angel trailing dusty wings, the women clapped, the pianist played "'Tis the gift to be simple" honky-tonk style, the bartender put the safety catch back on the gun under the bar, and the dealer began dealing cards for blackjack. Only one bad-tempered ex-soldier strolled outside and fired off a couple of casual bullets at the pale figure cycling away into the distance.

The Captain's bedroom was taking on the appearance of an Arab souk, strewn with bric-a-brac, hung with clothes, and crammed with people. Even at midnight the Bright Lights were still awake and busy when Elder Slater finally made it back from his mission to Boats-a-Cummin. Medora was pinning her black photographic cloth (slightly sweat stained from its use as a funeral horse blanket) into the back of the cook's dark dress, to make it fit around Loucien. Loucien's fiery hair, meantime, had been compressed into a bun. Curly clamped it in place with the pawnshop tiara.

"Ain't she beautiful!" said Tibbie, which was not the effect Curly had been after, but which was undeniably true.

Slater swaggered in and tossed a hatful of money onto the white bedspread. "Might buy couple of rail tickets," he croaked, his voice all but gone. Blushing, he turned his back so as not to have to look at Loucien and Medora in their petticoats.

"What did you do, rob a bank?" asked Kookie. Cissy ran and hugged Slater, which was an experience new to him.

"I eased the conscience of a few sinners."

"Well! And aren't you a saint and a gentleman, Elder!" said Loucien.

Tibbie Boden picked up the money and clutched it to her chest. "Now we can all go and rescue Mr. Cyril!"

"I fear it is not enough, miss. I strove, but fell short." And Slater sat down on the dressing-table stool.

"You got red paint on your nice white coat, too," said Tibbie scoldingly. "An' you got to be the Queen's chaplain tomorrow!"

But Queen Victoria would have to manage without a chaplain on her royal visit to Roper Junction. Evangelical begging in saloons might raise cash, but they are a very dangerous game. It was not paint on Elder's coat. It was blood.

Loucien finished bandaging Slater's shoulder—the touch of her hands against his bare skin embarrassed him almost to the point of fainting—and kissed the top of his hair. She kissed Elijah, too. "Back in no time, fellas," she promised, and lowered her veil. Then the Queen's entourage descended the grand staircase of Golden Bend Mansion, Loucien leaning on the arm of her American Ambassador, a procession of tailcoats following on. A train of well-wishers chirruped down the stairs behind them.

The marble floor had been scrubbed and smelled faintly of disinfectant. Somewhere a generator was humming, fueling the pumps to the fountains. A carriage clock on a lacquered table showed its elegant spinning mechanism, intricate as a paddle steamer's engine. Just eight hours remained until Cyril Crew was due to hang.

Henry was already by the door. Despite nobody having slept all night, he had absented himself toward dawn and gone out riding: he smelled a little of horses. "You look majestic, madam," he said.

"Why thank you, Prime Minister," said Loucien in a perfectly splendid English accent. Henry sneezed with delight.

The servants had taken up a red carpet runner from an upstairs corridor and laid it down on the stone steps. The ostler had fetched up a big old eight-seater chaise. The galvanized bucket standing by the doorway, however, was not their doing. At the bottom of the bucket lay a silver dollar.

"Oh, that's mine," said Chad Powers. "I've been working up this paying trick. You see, folks can throw in money, but when they go for . . ."

As the chaise door was opened, all three children tried to get in.

"You cain't go—you got the sweating fever!"

"Well, *you* cain't 'cause you gamble!"

"Shall we toss a coin?" suggested Miss Loucien. "If it's heads, none of you get to go. If it's tails, you all stay here, and if . . ." Loucien took a backward step and reached into the bucket for the silver dollar.

"NO! DON'T!"

The back seam in her dress tore as Loucien's body gave a kind of wrenching twist and she fell sideways. There was blood and liquid and a good costume ruined. There was chaos, too. Chad explained how he had electrified the bucket, so people could throw money in but couldn't pull it out. Then Everett Crew hit him. Then Tibbie began to shriek that Chad had killed Miss Loucien and wasn't it bad enough he'd demolished the grocery store without him killing Queen Victoria as well. Kookie tried to see if the bucket really was electrified and it was, and he said so in new words more exciting than Lithuanian. Then Loucien, lying on the ground, started coming out with the kind of noise that put Tibbie in the shade, moaning and screaming in earnest, and the magpie maids all took off and ran indoors and the gardener backed off into the shrubbery, and Everett picked Loucien up and carried her indoors, and the others restrained Chad Powers from banging his head against a marble column, and Miss March corralled Kookie and Tibs in an alcove and would not let them go until order had been restored.

Cissy, meanwhile, stood stock-still by the open door of the chaise. Henry reached out and took her hand, and there they stood, still as statues, while the splintering sunshine fell around them like wreckage.

Without a word, he escorted her indoors through the French doors and to the upper floor. He led her to a china-blue bedroom, and the door of a rosewood wardrobe. The dress he took out could almost have belonged to a child—gray shantung with a white crocheted collar. Cissy had seen it before—in the portrait of Elijah's dead wife.

"Is Miss Loucien going to die?" asked Cissy.

"The electric shock has sent her into travail," said Henry, emptying mothballs out of the cuffs of the silvery gown. Somewhere in the house a clock chimed the hour. Cissy had no idea what "travail" meant except that it cropped up in the Bible a lot when people were not having a good time. "Whosoever goes in her place needs to leave right away," said Henry. "The train ride takes five hours."

"Best ask the Bright Lights, then," she answered dully.

The others, straying downstairs again, bewildered and distressed, were confronted by Henry, the gray silk dress across his two arms like the corpse of a child. "Whoever goes in the lady's place," the butler repeated, "we need to leave at once. Every minute is vital."

"It cannot be me," said Miss May March. She was not flapping, simply being realistic. "If my nerve failed, I would be a danger to Cyril and the rest of you."

"I no thing Queen Vittoria she has the Spanish accent or the dress of *Gitana*," said Medora, spreading her Gypsy skirts. "An' this little gray dress there . . . you can fit melon into skin of the grape? No."

They waited for Curly to speak, but his thoughts were trapped in a bedroom upstairs. "Don't ask me. I'm only Box Office and Costumes," he said, lifting his hands and letting them fall.

So Kookie took the thing in hand as only Kookie could. "Look now: Cissy's braver than Tibs. And she acts better. Tibs is prettier, but looks don't matter, on account of the veil. Need to stuff out the bust, 'cause Cissy's flat as a wall, but then she'll do. Won't you, Ciss? I'd do it myself, but I cain't run in a dress and I figure we may have to do some running if it all goes poodlywhop."

"Habakkuk," said Miss March, "kindly keep your uncouth opinions to yourse—"

Everett Crew appeared on the upper landing, white faced and haggard, and everyone fell silent waiting for him to say that the show was canceled, that tickets would be refunded, that no one was going to Roper Junction after all. They had never really believed in it anyway. Cyril was a dead man.

"Lou says . . . ," he began. "Mrs. Shades Crew says that we must go now if we are to be of use to my brother. Time's wasting. Kookie, take this telegram to Blowville and send it for me. It is vital to our plan." And he handed Kookie two dollars of Elder's money and a much-folded sheet of paper. "Cissy . . ."

"Yes, Mr. Crew?"

"The role of the Queen is yours, Cissy, if you'll take it. Five minutes, Henry, or we shall miss the train." And he turned away.

As the rest of the household ran to all points of the compass, the butler took hold of Cissy's chin and turned it toward him. "Though I realize, miss, that you in no way resemble a marmot, can you find it in you to put on this costume and save the day?"

No ambition surged through Cissy, except to see Miss Loucien come downstairs and play the part herself. "But I do the plank with Max. A trouper can only do so much, you know?" She could still hear the fearful yelling going on upstairs.

"Yesterday I was a butler, Miss Cecelia. Today I seem to be Prime Minister of England," said Henry. "Sometimes life has a way of asking us to take a step up."

Chapter Seventeen

THE BRIGHT LIGHTS, LAST DITCH & FINAL CURTAIN COMPANY

*F*lushed from running, Kookie slapped down Crew's note on the desk and leaned on his knees to catch his breath. The telegrapher unfolded it, turned it over, put it down again. "What's that then, some kinda joke?"

There was nothing written on the paper.

It cost Kookie five precious minutes to realize the truth. Everett had deliberately sent him off on a wild goose chase—to stop him joining the trip to Roper Junction. Why? Surely Crew did not think he was a *child* who had to be kept safe! Hadn't Kookie walked the plank and fallen into an alligator-infested river night after night? Hadn't he saved everybody from the bandit Sugar Cain and pulled Cissy out onto the mud bar after the explosion? Rage and outrage used up another five minutes, before Kookie realized: if he ran fast enough, he might still just catch the train. He told himself the Bright Lights wouldn't dare set off without him—that they would make the train wait till he got there. But no, they wouldn't! Cyril Crew's life was lost if that train ran late!

So he started to run, and as he ran, the terrible certainty grew in his breast that he would miss the train, miss going to Roper Junction, miss even saying good-bye to Cissy and the rest. And then that the Bright Lights would be found out and arrested—and then that they would be strung up in a row alongside Mr. Cyril—Cissy and Everett and Henry and Benet and George and Miss May and Curly and . . . And then that the British would hear tell some American had hanged Queen Victoria and would declare war, and then everyone in Olive Town would be massacred by invading foreigners. . . .

(Disasters grow in the thinking.)

Kookie put on an extra burst of speed.

At the last moment Tibbie had cost them yet more minutes. She had kicked up a terrific rumpus. Light-headed from her medicine, she had demanded to come: "In case Cissy gets diphtheria and dies and I have to save the day 'stead of her!" They had had to wrestle her out of the chaise three times over, before Medora volunteered to stay behind and subdue her. Another few minutes lost.

So despite the best efforts of the horses, the Bright Lights could see the morning train ahead of them, already standing in Blowville Station.

"Use the whip! Use the whip!" begged Everett.

"Should we not get out and run?" Cissy pleaded, but already it was too late. With four furlongs to go, they heard the whistle and saw the train begin to move. They had missed it. Crew gave a roar of frustration and despair.

But Henry seemed strangely unperturbed. He coaxed the chaise gently down a narrow track toward the railway sidings. "You may have wondered," he said, as they bumped over rail ties and gravel, "ours being a household of such seeming luxury, why I have not offered you financial help on behalf of Captain Bouverie. . . ."

"Oh, you have been kindness itself . . . ," Miss March started to say.

"Since the Captain went missing, there has been nobody to sign checks or withdraw cash from the bank. Oh, his money is *there* in the bank—in quantities, indeed—but we his household cannot gain the use of it. For eighteen months we have been obliged to *live off the land*, as it were."

"What, no wages? At all?" As bookkeeper for the Bright Lights, Curly had had to make do on little, but he could not imagine getting by on nothing.

"We have a roof over our heads. The kitchen-garden and the rabbit population have kept us fed. But no, no wages as such. Now and then, when absolutely necessary, we have resorted to swaps: vintage wine for a vet's visit, you know? A cut-glass vase for the doctor. The search for the Captain itself cost us ten acres of garden."

"And if Elijah dies?" asked George. But Henry was not prepared to imagine any such thing. Besides, they had arrived alongside a pair of fancy railway carriages parked up in a siding. Ahead of them, a dapper little engine was building up steam. Henry had traded the French chandelier from the banquet hall for a loan of the Blacker family's private train.

"Like Mrs. Crew, I did not think Her Majesty, Queen of the United Kingdom and Empress of India, would happily share a train with cowboys, salesmen, sticky children, three nuns, and a parcel of chickens. I believed she might travel in more *style*." When they tried to thank him, Henry simply murmured, "The Captain would expect no less of me."

Into the "royal train"—*Hurry, for God's sake! We have barely seven hours!*—climbed Cissy and Everett Crew, George, two members of the quartet, Prime

Minister Henry, Max the Plank, Curly, and Miss March. Boisenberry had to drive the chaise back to Golden Bend. Benet had to strip to the waist, mount the footplate, and fuel the boiler, since Henry's deal had not included a stoker. Chad Powers was back at the house: he had not dared to share a coach with Everett Crew.

On the carriage steps, Cissy took a last look, hoping to catch sight of Kookie running toward them. She could catch sight of hardly anything through the thick mist of her veil, and anyway Kookie would not know about these sidings or the hired train. Crew had made good and sure that neither Kookie nor Tibbie tagged along: bad enough to put *one* child in danger, without involving three.

Henry was eager to coach Cissy—as he had coached Loucien—to speak with an English accent. But behind her veil Cissy remained obstinately silent.

"You don't need to wear that all the way, Cecelia," said her schoolteacher, plucking at the netting, but Cissy tucked it firmly in at her collar like a beekeeper about to open a hive. She was Queen Victoria now, and it was her duty to think herself into the role. She knew, without a shadow of a doubt, that Miss Loucien was travailing painfully in that upstairs bedroom and would probably soon be dead. But that made it all the more important for Cissy to play her part, to behave like a queen, a frosty-faced, elderly, seen-it-all queen. Also, with her veil down, she was free to chew her lip till it bled.

Sweeting, Benet, and Oscar recounted everything useful they could remember of their trip to England: the dank weather, the ravens and peacocks, the horse guards growing horsetails out of the tops of their helmets; the castles, the sewers, the gaslit streets, the audiences who never joined in . . .

"Why in the world did you never *say* you had been there?" asked Miss March.

Benet ran the toe of a two-tone shoe over the pattern in the carriage floor. "We inclined to keep quiet 'bout England, ma'am. Patriotic sensibilities run deep in some parts. They's some daughters of the American Revolution out there still fightin' the War o' Independence. Life can be wearisome 'nough without havin' folks think we royalists too, with Union Jacks for drawers."

His words worried them. Might the people of Roper Junction be dyed-in-the-wool believers in republicanism? Exactly what reaction would they have to seeing Queen Victoria arrive in their town? Would they gawk and cheer, or would they jeer and throw eggs at the train? If Kookie had been there, the word "assassination" would certainly have gotten mentioned. Luckily Kookie was not aboard.

Kookie was, in fact, on his way to Roper Junction. In the whole of Oklahoma no one could put on a sprint like Kookie Warboys could when it was needed. Admittedly he had had to chase the morning train down the track and spend the first twelve miles clinging to an iron cleat on the back of the caboose, but having caught hold, he was far too pleased with himself to fall off and get killed. At the first signal stop, he managed to climb inside without being seen. He doubted two dollars was enough to buy a ticket.

Two, three, four times he walked through the train looking for the royal party. Nothing. No one. Five times he managed to avoid the guard checking tickets. For hours he hid out in the caboose under a pile of luggage. But every so often he convinced himself that the Bright Lights *must* be on the train, would be on the train, if he just looked hard enough, and foolishly he would creep out of hiding. Thwarted and afraid, he was cornered at last, between first class and the front of the train, the guard coming closer every second with his "Tickets, please! Tickets!" But as their eyes met, and the guard's eyes narrowed with suspicion, the train finally drew in to Roper Junction, and Kookie scrambled backward out of the carriage door.

His only luggage was a sackload of dread. Clearly

the Bright Lights had missed the train. Now the whole royal-pardon plot would have to be abandoned. Kookie was the only one to have arrived, and unless he could mount a rescue himself, Mr. Cyril was going to hang. "What time's the hanging?" he asked a boy selling newspapers.

"This side sundown" came the delighted reply. "Ma says we can stay up late to watch!" Kookie squinted up at the sun. It had to be one o'clock.

Roper County Jail was constructed to the exact same layout as the jail in Salvation: ugly government-issue architecture. (Well, no one takes civic pride in building a snazzy jail.) In the alleyway alongside, even the sewage flies were the same. If only Cyril had, like Curly, been jailed for speaking Shakespeare instead of for shooting a lawman!

"Mr. Cyril? Hey! Mr. Cyril Crew!" called Kookie. "You there?"

A pair of hands snatched hold of the bars at the farthest window.

Stuffed, quilted, stiflingly hot, damp with sweat, terrified and lonely, Queen Victoria, little by little, grew littler and littler in her seat. Was this what it felt like to wait in the wings before going onstage? If so, the Bright Lights could keep it. She would be a shopgirl in Olive Town, count herself lucky, and give thanks a million times a day.

Henry did not need to see Cissy's face to know her misery and discomfort. The way she was sitting said it all. He reached into his pocket for a treat to cheer her—sugar lumps meant for the chaise horses. His fingers touched something else that had slipped his mind, and he drew out the telegram.

"Apologies, Mr. Crew . . . er . . . Mr. Ambassador. This was in the pocket when you returned me my tailcoat after the funeral."

Bewildered at first by the yellow envelope, Everett studied it and recalled his visit to the post office. Seeing his brother's letter pinned to the wall had jolted the telegram clean out of mind. Emerging from his cocoon of worry, he saw Cissy coiled up like a hedgehog in her seat and was abashed. He was glad to have good news for her. "Look, Cissy," he said. "A telegram from home. Just for you."

The light was too poor in the carriage for Cissy to read it through her veil. Heart thumping, she sprang to the door, dropped the window, and leaned out into the sunlight, breathed deep, enjoyed the sharp breeze. Sheeny gray gloves made it hard to get the telegram out, and the wind plucked the empty envelope out of her hand—away, away. It fluttered the few stuck-down ticker-tape words as she unfolded the slip of buff paper.

COME HOME CISSY,

YOUR PAPA HAS GONE

She let go of the telegram, too. It slapped flat against the wall of the carriage, then peeled free and fluttered—away, away—like a dead bird caught in the gale.

"What's the word from back home?" asked Henry, as Cissy ducked her head back inside the carriage and sat down.

She pulled her knees up against her padded chest, hugged them to her with both skinny arms, rocked forward and back. But Miss March told her sharply to sit up straight, so she did, smoothing her silk dress, checking the fingers of her gloves for soot, sitting face front.

"Cissy?" said Crew. "Everything all right?"

Cissy nodded.

"So . . . what news?"

Her father was dead and her mother was crazy and there was nothing and no one to go home to. But Miss Loucien had once called her "the genuine, solid-gold, thespian article" and Mr. Cyril was relying on her. Cissy knew it was her duty not to be Cissy Hulbert right now, not to have a face, not to lift her veil, not to show the tears streaming down the sides of her nose and into her mouth. "Oh. Nothing. Just words," she said.

"They'll be along on the next one! They'll be along on the next train, sure as Christmas!" Kookie vowed, when he had finished explaining to Cyril the plan, the preparations. "Cissy's just lost her nerve, maybe. Or they dropped the fare money down a drain. Or old Elijah died and they stayed behind to bury him!" He did not believe one word, and he could hear it in his voice, mewling and pleading, like when he didn't have a good excuse to offer at school. Within the dark cell, on the other side of the window, he could hear Cyril Crew slapping the wall now with both hands and moaning wordlessly.

"*Is* there another train today, boy? Does another train come through before sunset?"

"Sure! I 'spect. Maybe. Don't know. I don't know! Should I go find out? Or what say I set someplace alight? Create an aversion? Make 'em put off the . . . Make them put it off till tomorrow? Should I break up the gallows?"

Having given up all hope, having passed beyond despair, having steeled himself and readied his soul for death, Cyril had managed to achieve a certain peace. Now here was the Warboys boy jumping and yapping at his window, unsettling him worse than ever. What was more, the boy himself was descending into hysterical fear and needed rescuing.

"Just tell me about the good ship *Calliope*, boy. Tell me about your adventures. Tell me about my brother. Tell me everything. Tell me anything, for God's sweet . . . It'll pass the time."

Kookie sat down in the alleyway under the window, and he tried; he did try. But the words would not come. At the mouth of the alleyway, people were passing to and fro who did not even know Queen Victoria was heading their way on a railway train. Or not. "Tell me what to do, Mr. Cyril! Should I pretend I'm King of America? I could try an' be King of America! Should I?"

Cyril Crew took a deep, shuddering breath and raked his hands through his thick white hair. Then he put a brightness into his voice as startling as a magnesium flare. "Run around, boy! Make news! Spread rumor!"

"Rumor?"

"Publicity! Terribly important before any show! Spread the word something big is about to happen—biggest day in the history of Roper Junction! People see, dear boy, what they have been primed to see. How else do you think the illusion of theater works? By the time my brother arrives, we want the whole town to be buzzing—isn't that right, my boy?"

When Kookie had gone, given his vital mission to perform, Cyril Crew sank to hands and knees on the cell floor, exhausted. He had no confidence whatsoever that a second train would be stopping in Roper Junction that day. Not in time . . . But now at least the boy had something to keep him occupied, and Cyril could be alone to gather up the grated shreds of his courage.

Kookie beamed at passers-by in the street and asked if they had heard the news. He called in at the saloon. He stopped by the school yard. Cyril had given him a job, and he hauled that job around town as doggedly as a husky pulling a sled. The more people he told, the more he believed it himself: a train would be stopping later that day at Roper Junction, and aboard it would be someone who would make everything good.

But the telegram was his masterstroke. Everett Crew had given him two dollars that morning to send a telegram. So that is precisely what he did. He had grown up in a telegraph office: he knew the places were hotbeds of gossip.

```
TELEGRAM TO CHARLIE NOBODDI,
C/O OLIVE TOWN TELEGRAPHIC OFFICE,
OKLAHOMA

WORD IS QUEEN VICTORIAS TRAIN
STOPPING HERE TODAY — STOP — BET
YOU WISH YOU WAS HERE — STOP —

YOUR PAL
KOOKIE
```

After Kookie had left the shop, the telegrapher could not help mentioning to his wife the contents of the message he had just tapped out. His wife could not resist running next door shrieking, *"The Queen's comin'! The Queen! The Queen! And look at the state of my hair!"* The people next door could not resist stepping down to the grocery store to see if the grocer had heard any such thing and to ask if it was true. The grocer said that some kid had mentioned some such nonsense—he had not thought much of it, but if the telegrapher knew better . . . After that, nobody knew where they had heard it first, but everybody in town knew that Queen Victoria was vacationing in Missouri and would be calling by in a train.

In faraway Oklahoma, Pickard Warboys tore off the ticker-tape message and read it. His heart, too, rattled like a telegraphic machine. What in the name of goodness was Kookie up to? There was no one by the name of Noboddi in Olive Town. Pickard firmly believed there was no one anywhere called Noboddi. The atlas on his desk fell open automatically now at the page showing the Numchuck River. His finger traced the river's course but could not find the town where his son must now be standing. So what was Kookie doing there? Was it true, Pickard wondered? Would the Queen of England truly be passing today through Roper Junction, Missouri? No: if Kookie and a bunch of actors were involved, it was a piece of invention, for sure. Promoting a play, maybe. Or fooling some *grandissimo* into bankrolling the company. Hence the invented Noboddi. If Kookie had needed help, he would have made himself plainer. "Don't do anything stupid, son," murmured Pickard. He dared not tell his wife: either she would get as worried as he, or she would want a new hat and a rail ticket to go and scour Missouri for a glimpse of Queen Victoria.

"Any word from the Bright Lights?" asked Mrs. Warboys from the doorway.

Pickard crumpled up the ticker tape. "Nothing today, my love, but you know what they say: no news is good news."

"Why *do* they say that?" Mrs. Warboys said. "It's never been true."

The royal train halted at signals outside Roper Junction. Henry tried not to be seen checking his pocket watch, but everyone knew there was no time left for unforeseen delays.

"Now, Cissy, remember what Mr. Crew said," Miss March fussed. "Confine yourself to those little phrases Mr. Henry has taught you. A wave of the hand. An inclining of the head. Let Mr. Crew do the rest. He is the actor."

Oskar chimed in: "You an old lady, Missy Cissy. No one don' arx nothin' of no old-lady queen."

Sweeting agreed. "Yeah. Let Everett string them greeners."

"Be great in act, as you have been in thought," Curly declaimed, taking hold of Cissy's hands.

"Wish these signals would change," muttered George, reaching for his watch and remembering, for the fiftieth time, that he had lost it in the river.

The train gave a violent lurch and rolled forward. The royal entourage squeezed through into the second coach—*"Good luck, Missy Cissy!"*—leaving the Queen and Prime Minister and American Ambassador to a lonely dignity in the lead coach.

"You give 'em what for, Missy Cissy!"

"Co robimy? Niemam mojej deski," said Max, who was under the impression that they were about to put on a show.

"At least we'll die with harness on our back!"

Everett shot to his feet with clenched fists and bawled, *"Curlitz, do me an immeasurable favor, will you, and stop quoting from danged* Macbeth!*"*

(He was, after all, an actor.)

Returning to the jailhouse to report to Cyril, Kookie was almost cheerful. But when he called out under the prison window—"Mr. Crew! Mr. Cyril Crew? Listen up!"—there was no answer.

Figures were hurrying past the end of the alleyway, all in the direction of the station—"They're here! She's coming!"—but Kookie was too busy looking for something to stand on so as to see in at the cell window. When he finally found a galvanized bucket, turned it upside down, and stood on it, tiptoe, he peered in on an empty cell. A screw of blanket, a torn jacket, a strewing of shorn hair all said that the condemned man had been fetched away by his executioners.

Everett got down first. At least he scrambled as far as the bottom of the steps. It was impossible to get any farther. The train was besieged.

Nowhere is there a truer bunch of Stars-and-Stripes, democratic Americans than in Roper Junction. Yet the rumor of visiting royalty brought them out like ants at a picnic. In ten years of selling tickets, the man in the railway-station booth had never sold so many tickets. Someone had even strung bunting across railway property. With elbows out, with umbrellas, parasols, and walking sticks to hand, the town's citizens crammed the platform as the little two-carriage train came in.

"What in blue blazes is going on?" demanded the

bank manager, passing the station gate, but the porter he asked was standing on his handcart, craning to see over the heads of the crowd.

The Mayor himself could not make his way through the crowd until the Sheriff fired his pistol to get everyone's attention. The Queen—who had just appeared in the carriage doorway—flinched visibly. The crowd roared its disapproval and the Sheriff was jostled, the pistol snatched out of his hand.

The Mayor was flustered: he had been cleaning his boots, ready for the hanging, when he heard the news, and had just realized that his hands were covered in brown polish. *"Welcome! Welcome, ma'am!"* he called, still worming his way toward the front of the crowd. "'Pologies for that. Hope my Sheriff didn't alarm you."

Crew stepped forward to deflect the question. "Not at all, sir. It is just that some anarchist took a shot at Her Majesty recently and the sound of pistols still . . . excites her. . . . How very good of you all to turn out. However did you—"

"Good day," said Queen Victoria, taking one step down.

Delighted, the Mayor reached out a hand, remembered the boot polish, and withdrew it. Their hands dodged each other. "Hoon! Mayor Hoon! Hector Hoon, Mayor of this fine town!"

The occupants of the second carriage were causing a stir. Two black men in straw boaters were an exoticism they had not been expecting. A third appeared soon after, still tying his tie.

"Her Majesty is making a *private* tour of the area," said Everett. "Permit me to introduce Her Majesty's Prime Minister . . ."

"The Right Honourable William Ewart Gladstone," said Henry, being the only one who could remember the whole mouthful.

"And this here is my American Ambassador, Sir Everett," the Queen chipped in, "and this here's the Polish one."

"Przyjemne miasto. Och, chciałbym, mieć móją deskę!"

"This is Chancellor Curlitz, and these all—well, mustn't bore you—other bits of government. Those three yonder are my good friends Mr. Sweeting, Mr. Benet, and Mr. Oskar. They come to my place in Windsor a couple of years back with Mr. Hatherley's Traveling Minstrel Show, and they told me *sooo* much about Missouri and the river 'n' all that I fair longed to see it for myself. Ask them nice and they may give you a song later. So if we could just squeeze on through . . . ?"

The Prime Minister and the American Ambassador looked at each other, rattled by the unexpected crowds, nonplussed by Cissy's sudden willingness to speak. Mayor Hoon wiped his palms vigorously on the seat of his trousers and shook the Queen warmly by the hand. "Oof, Mr. Mayor Hoon, mind the artheritees," said the Queen. Then the crowd drew in its stomachs, children, and skirts and made way for Victoria, Queen of England, and for various bits of her government and minstrelsy, all four hundred falling in behind, like a school of dolphins following a yacht.

"Ain't she tiny" someone could be heard to say.

"Heard tell she was," said another. "Child sized, I heard."

"Kinda round, too."

"Muffins," said some sage scholar of English practices. "Eat wagonloadsa muffins, them English."

The tour took in the church and the bank, the school and the civic assembly rooms (though it said DANCE HALL over the door). It stopped at the cloth and wool shop. . . .

"What did she say? What did she ask you?"

"Asked me what's the colora damson. 'What color would you call damson?' she said to me. Be able to tell my grandchildren: Queen of England once asked me what color's damson!"

And the fairground:

"Such a pity there is no fair, Mayor Hoon. We are partial to candy apples at Ballymoral."

It paused at the newspaper offices for a photograph of the entire royal party with Mayor, Sheriff, corn merchant, editor, and assorted wives. The wives spent the time urgently whispering to one another about what they ought to present to the Queen as a memento of her visit. It was exactly what the Queen wanted to overhear. Now she would be able to ask for the pardon and release of Cyril Crew.

"I see no barbershop," George observed.

"No! Sorry. Barber died of the sweating sickness back in eighty-one. Sorry. Was Her Majesty looking to . . ."

"No, I don't shave, and I don't hold with bloodletting. They got new treatments out East, you know? George is my trade person. He's runnin' a survey, is all," the Queen explained.

They moved on to the hotel:

"I fear I cannot stay over the night, can I, Chancellor Curlitz?"

"No, ma'am. The President is expecting us."

"Oh it's all right, Sheriff. Don't you go worrying on my account. There's a little bed on the train with two mattresses and a toothmug with a thing on it—lion and a unicorn."

Even the grain silo benefited from a royal visit. The Queen seemed overwhelmed with emotion for a moment by the Roper Junction grain silo, and the American Ambassador stepped closer in case she was going to faint. "You take care of that," said Queen Victoria at last. "I know some lovely people back in London got flattened by one of those." Every word she spoke was relayed backward through the crowd in a surf surge of whispers. On this occasion, the women all gasped and put hands to their mouths and looked up at the tip of the grain silo and said, "How awful." Ambassador Everett took the Queen's arm and escorted her across the dark band of shadow cast by the silo. The shadow was long. The sun was in decline.

The Sheriff and Mayor Hoon put their heads together in murmured panic. ". . . hardly a fittin' sight for . . ."

"But people come specially to see it . . ."

" . . . can postpone till tomorrow, surely . . ."

"But we already shaved and tied him!"

Cissy felt Everett Crew's arm go rigid inside hers. She squeezed it as hard as she knew how.

The Sheriff and Mayor Hoon had just agreed between them to hide the execution from the Queen's delicate gaze when a boy with startled red hair rushed the royal party and asked Victoria, "You staying on for the hangin', Majesty?" Kookie added with massive emphasis: "Because it's *happening NOW!*"

The Queen stopped dead. The crowd behind piled

into each other: a raucous starling flock of noise. Flushed with embarrassment, the Sheriff dispatched the boy with the toe of his boot. The crowd was torn by the desire to be in two places at one time.

The Sheriff selected the nicest words to phrase it—like choosing chocolates. "A felon is due to receive his just reward this evening, Your Majesty. Of the throttling variety."

"But we'll keep it discreet!" Mayor Hoon put in hastily.

"Oh, pray don't!" snapped Everett, catching everyone off guard. "Her Majesty takes a keen interest in the administration of justice." Then he forged ahead, in the direction the boy with red hair was heading. The Queen had to break into a trot.

And there it was, as if to make it all real—the stage on which the last act of the tragedy was to be played out. The scaffold. The noose.

The happy crowd was in fiesta mood by this time. They fell quiet only when Cyril Crew was brought out, but their silence was an eager, breathless excitement. His hands tied behind his back, his glory of white hair shorn down to the roots, he stumbled slightly on the sidewalk steps. A tetchy wind was catching and snatching at clothes, at bunting, at hats, at dust and street litter. The crowd looked jumpy with excitement, lids narrowed against the dust, slipping their eyes to and fro, wanting to watch both Queen and prisoner, wanting to see how queens behave at hangings. They were proud. They were proud like cats laying a chewed mouse at the feet of their visitor and looking for praise.

"Now if you were thinking in terms of a gift . . . ," Ambassador Everett observed to the Mayor's wife, "the thing that would rejoice Her Majesty more than anything . . ."

"Oh, but we have it! We have it!" she squeaked, and flapped her hands at the other ladies as if directing sheep, sending them running to fetch from the grocery store the present they had decided upon: a crate of damson jam and a gingham bag of fresh muffins.

Cyril Crew, like a ship lost in fog, fixed his eyes on the one star showing. His gaze locked with Everett's, and neither brother was capable of looking away.

"In England it is Clemency Day," said Chancellor Curlitz abruptly. "It dates back to Agincourt, when the monarch spared the life of one Sir Clement . . . doesn't it, sir?"

"Muffins. My favorite," said Queen Victoria, staring into the gingham bag, aghast.

"Ah yes, Clemency Day!" piped Lady May March, governess to the royal princesses.

"What? Yes. Quite," said Everett. "Clemency Day. If

she were in England now, Her Majesty would pardon one prisoner. . . ."

"Wouldn't pardon this skunk," said the Sheriff with the heartiest of belly laughs. "This one's scum. Food fit for the Devil to chew on. Go on, Walt!" The hangman shook out a cloth bag to put over Cyril's head.

Everett reached into his pocket for his wife's pearl-handled pistol. He wished it were a revolver; he wished it were Sugar Cain's pepper-box pistol—a weapon capable of scaring the excellent people of Roper Junction into headlong flight, rather than a one-shot lady's pistol and not even loaded. But sooner than stand and watch, stand and watch . . . Question was, if he stormed the scaffold now—if he were to grab the hangman, Walter, and hold him hostage while Cyril made his getaway—huh! faint hope!— what would the others do? Would they embroil themselves in his guilt? Would he incriminate them? Would he take them all down with him?

Cyril, despite his best resolve, snatched his head aside as Walt came at him with the bag. "I appeal to the Queen for justice!" he cried, and his once-booming voice barely had the strength to carry the distance.

The Mayor was appalled: a blot on a perfect visit! An affront to the best guest Roper Junction had ever entertained! He signaled to Walter to silence the prisoner, and Walt punched Cyril in the kidneys and felled him to his knees. Beside Cissy, Everett staggered as if the blow had struck him. He involuntarily brought his hand out of his pocket, and she clearly saw the pistol in it and shunted sideways to cover his hand with her huge dress. He put the gun away but moved toward the ladder. The Queen, though, was clinging to his arm, pulling back with all her weight.

"Let the prisoner speak!" she declared, as serenely and loudly as she could. "Does he want a pardon?"

"What he wants is horsewhipping and haltering," retorted the Mayor in a mortification of embarrassment. He actually rushed over to the ladder, climbed it, and personally grabbed the lever to open the trapdoor beneath Cyril's feet—except that Cyril was not on his feet but his knees, and half on, half off the hatch. The Mayor gestured wildly for Walter to put a swift end to this social gaffe. The prisoner made to speak, but the hood blotted out whatever he had to say.

"What was his crime?" called Curly, overly loud and sharp, grabbing for extra seconds.

"Gunned down a lawman—family man with three children. Wounded another two. Scum, like I said," gabbled the Sheriff, and the crowd mooed in agreement.

Everett made a show of leaning over to advise the Queen. "Whatever I do next, disown me," he whispered, and wrenched his arm free.

"No! Never!"

It was the Queen's tone that startled everyone: not hysterical so much as quizzical. All faces turned toward her. Even Everett stopped in his tracks. "Well?" said the Queen uppishly. "Just look at his head! That's just an scientific impossib . . . impossi . . . bleness. Sir George! Where's Sir George? There you are. Advise me, Sir George!"

George the barber fleered with alarm. No one had told him he would have to act, would have to speak! No one had given him a script! The whites of his eyes showed, and he seemed on the point of breaking into a run.

"You know more than I do, course. But I ask you, Sir George, is that . . . was that the skull of a killer? Let us take a look, what say?"

"Ah," said George to gain time. "Aha."

"Bring the prisoner here, I say!" commanded Queen Victoria.

From the top of the scaffold ladder, unable to see or hear, Cyril Crew was toppled, dragged, and manhandled over to the royal party, forced into a crouch at the Queen's feet. The American Ambassador wrenched off the hood with surprising urgency, and his fist closed on the prisoner's shirt.

To the sound of a hundred indrawn breaths, the

Queen frowned into the face of the prisoner, then pulled off her gloves, placed the fingers of two hands on his head, and actually began to . . . *feel it all over*.

"Ah! Aha!" George shouted, confidence washing over him in a flood. "Phrenology!"

Everett was quick as a wink, though his mouth was so dry that he stumbled over the words. "Yes! Her Majesty . . . expert! Judge . . . can judge a man's . . . unerringly! His character. Right down to whether he takes tea in his milk."

"Chooses all her ministers of state that way," said Chancellor Curlitz. Moving forward, taking off his hat, he dipped his own head proudly in all directions, to show off the shapeliness of his bald skull.

"*Firmness . . . benevolence . . . amativeness . . . ,*" chirped George, as the Queen ran her hands over the various territories of the skull—the phrenologist's classroom globe. "*Sublimity . . . gravity . . . memory . . . inhabitiveness . . . friendship . . . ,*" he recited, as she stroked, with sweat-sticky palms, the brow, cranium, ears, and terrible haircut of Cyril's trembling skull.

Cissy thought she had never touched anything so terrifyingly alive.

"She is magnificent," said Everett Crew, recovering that same sonorous voice that had thrown a pavilion of stars over the heads of a thousand audiences. "Her Majesty is *never* wrong!"

By comparison, the voice of the Queen herself was tiny, almost childlike. "From the shape of this skull, gentlemen, I'd swear the worst thing this man ever done was to ride a train without a ticket."

This time the gasp came from the jurors at Cyril's trial and the lawmen who had tried to beat a confession out of him beforehand. It was the exact thing—the only thing—the prisoner had confessed to.

"Point of fact, this man's as clever as that Solomon in the Bible, and I frankly wish I could have him in my government!"

The sweat on the Queen's face was such that her veil had begun to stick to her cheeks, her top lip, her forehead. Even the crabbed wind could not pick it free anymore. The Celebrated Jumping Frog of Cavaleras County seemed to have jumped into her throat and blocked it. If she opened her mouth again, she was sure she would spew up ball bearings. The quartet (three quarters of it) saved her from trying. They broke into song.

While the crowd whispered and sighed and sang along; while the hangman sneaked a cigarette; while the sweat poured down Cissy's rib cage and froze in the small of her back, the American Ambassador, the Prime Minister of England, Chancellor Curlitz, and the governess to the royal princesses closed in on Mayor and Sheriff.

"No, no. Outa the question!" insisted Hector Hoon, despite being outnumbered, despite not wanting to contradict the Queen's cockamamie beliefs. "I'd never forgive myself if I loosed this fiend on Her Majesty. Would be like setting a hound on a infant! Shoot him, Sheriff! Shoot him in the head like the dog he is!"

The Sheriff patted at his holster—then remembered his gun had been confiscated at the station, and instructed the crowd in general to give it back. The crowd was too spellbound to oblige.

"Nonsense," replied the Queen sternly. Everett felt her hand enter the pocket of his trousers . . . "No, Ciss—!" . . . and fetch out the pearl-handled pistol. This she presented, handle first, to Cyril Crew. "Given these men seem fixed on killin' you, sir, maybe you'd care to make your everlastin' mark on history 'n' shoot the Queen of England." A smoldering building takes in one gigantic breath before it explodes into flame. The town took such a breath now.

Eyes shut, swaying on his knees, Cyril cradled the pistol to his chest with hands that were shaking too much to use it, fingers too large to fit the trigger, in any case. She watched him then, with superhuman effort, pull together the scene inside his head, shut out the audience, disregard the heat of the stage lighting, and listen for his lines from the prompt corner.

"I could not . . . ," he began falteringly. "I could not shoot a fox that was stealing my chickens, ma'am. I've never fired a gun in anger in my life. I am a Quaker by upbringing and a Quaker by resolve and a craven coward by nature. But I would sooner die here like a dog in the street than take a life by violence myself." And he offered the pistol back on the flat of his two hands. His brother took it instead, and they exchanged the courteous nod of two genteel strangers. The Queen graciously invited him to rise, but Cyril found his legs would unaccountably not hold him, and he fell against the American Ambassador, who caught him and held on until Cyril was on a steady footing.

By now, if the Sheriff had moved to hang the prisoner or the Mayor to horsewhip him, the crowd would have shot or horsewhipped them both. Most were intrigued by the idea of phrenology, the rest with the charm of Cyril's voice. The romance of an innocent man saved from the gallows by a Queen's hand was already transforming itself into the happy workings of fate, into the Legend of Roper Junction.

While discussing the transfer of the prisoner into English custody, Mayor Hoon demanded assurance from Everett that he would keep the Queen safe, come what might: "'Cause she's one mighty fine lady you got there, and we've grown real fond of her."

Everett vowed on his life not to let Cyril Crew out of his sight until the felon had proved himself "as sound a man as my own brother."

Then the sun dipped below the housetops, and the royal entourage headed back to the station through the dusk. Actually it set off and had to back up again, to collect Queen Victoria. Everett bent his face so close that Cissy could feel his breath. "You did it. It's done," he whispered. "We can go now."

"Yeah, but can you steer me? Cain't see nothing no more in this danged veil."

"I'd be proud to lend you my arm, ma'am. I'd be more than proud."

Chapter Eighteen

HOMECOMING QUEEN

*T*he first thing Everett did, as they boarded the train, was to pull down the blinds and put his own hat on his brother's head.

"Is Kookie aboard?" asked Cissy.

"Sure am!" called Kookie from the carriage next door.

"So! Let's go home!"

But the train stood obstinately still, and the crowd began to regroup. A quick check by Oskar revealed that the train engineer was not in his cab. Oskar came back holding the man's denim jacket. "If he been washin' teeth in whiskey 'n' talking outa place . . . ," he said, and did not need to finish. The engineer had been told to stay at his post, expressly to keep him from careless talk in the local saloon.

"What to do, sir? Presently we will be overrun," said Henry.

"They keep trying the door!" piped Miss March in a terrified whisper, poking her head through from the second carriage. Everett Crew sat, one hand on his brother's shoulder, one hand over his face, trying to think.

"Everett and I stole a train once, didn't we, sir!"

The schoolmistress gave an involuntary gasp. "Habakkuk Warboys, you will come to nothing but a bad end!"

"What, hanged, you mean?" said Everett sharply, and stood up, taking off his Prince Albert coat and putting on the sooty denim. "We did, Kooks, we did, though you were never on the footplate, I think. Now's your chance. Come on, son."

The Queen's adoring public had begun to venture off the platform onto the rails, onto the track side of the train. Some must have seen her American Ambassador and a redheaded boy run to the engine's footplate and mount up. Everett slipped the hand brake and opened up the throttle. The jarring shock disturbed the crowd about as much as banging a table disturbs flies from a plate of meat. He slammed the engine into reverse.

"How in tarnation did you get here, Kooks?" he

said, as the boy flung coal into the furnace using his bare hands. (The shovel was too big for him to swing.) "I went to great pains to leave you behind, where you'd be safe."

"Caught the morning train like a good Christian. Miss May says punctual's next to godly."

"Then remind me to buy you a gold pocket watch when I have the wherewithal."

"Why are we going backward?"

"Because I have a yen to go home, don't you?"

"Not if we meet a train comin' up behind, I don't. This is the northbound track."

So Everett heaved the lever forward, and the train, with a massive jolt, hauled itself north, while Kookie hung off the whistle pull, and the royal train swore at a deafeningly high pitch. The errant engineer came out of the saloon at a run, felled a few passers-by like a skittle ball, and shoved his way to the front of the crowd, cursing. Seeing his train leaving without him, he found more speed than he had imagined possible in a man of fifty and managed to leap on board.

They traveled north to the points at Connor Junction, where they were able to reverse the order of the train and mount the southbound—homebound—track. Cyril Crew was left to sleep, stretched out in the "royal" carriage, using the wadding out of Queen Victoria's bosom for a pillow. Meanwhile, Kookie held court in the crowded second car, describing what a damn fine job he had made of hoodwinking Roper Junction's entire population. He had to talk with his hands on his head, because Miss March was punishing him for saying "damn fine."

"What does an ambassador do, Mr. Crew?" murmured Cissy, pinned in tight between Everett and Benet.

"Let me think. Oh yes. I believe, when the Queen's away from home, he provides a lap for her to nap in."

So Cissy laid her head on his knees. "When I wake up, I won't be Queen Victoria anymore, will I?"

"No, child," said Everett. "Someone much more wonderful."

Free at last of the veil and hat, her hair was darkly matted with sweat. "But I'll still be an actress?"

Everett was not sure what he was supposed to say. He exchanged glances with Benet, who was the only other person who could hear. "That's in the blood, child. Like the dreaded Missouri sweating sickness. There's probably a medicinal remedy for it. If it gets too much." He could feel hot tears soaking the cloth of his trousers. "What did the telegram say, Cissy?"

After a few moments she whispered: "Poppy's dead."

Kookie rattled on, bright as magnesium ribbon:

he was burning off the fear he had felt all day. Three fourths of the quartet plucked at three banjos. The train passed through two stations.

"Hush up, loud boy," Benet told Kookie. "Cecelia here is sleeping."

But she was not.

"I wish the Bright Lights could come to Olive Town," she whispered. "Give Poppy a send-off, like you done for Cole Blacker." She got no response and felt bad. She should not have spoken. Mr. Crew had worries of his own. And remembering that reminded her of what horrors might lie in store when they finally got back to the mansion at Golden Bend. Those did not bear thinking about—any more than a boiler explosion or a runaway silo or a dead father.

They rode through the night. As rail and river fell into step alongside each other, the royal train passed by the *Sunshine Queen*. Huddled against the canyon wall, pinioned on some submerged snag, one stack down, the hulk lay at such a tilt that one bull rail was underwater. The sun was just rising, kindling the windows of the mansion on the other bank, turning the canyon rose red. Everett stood at the train door, looking as if he might jump out, the sooner to reach the Captain's mansion.

As the miles piled up, separating Cyril from the

horrors of Licorice and Roper County Jail, he filled out like a sail. His voice ripened into fruity urbanity. "Now and then, the trial judge would refer to a large book on his desk, to settle a point of law. When I saw it was Volume Two of a medical encyclopedia, I knew I was in the hands of American justice at its finest."

Everett, though, drooped like an empty sail. "How shall we get from the rail yard to the house?" he asked Henry more than once.

Not knowing what time to expect the royal train, no Boisenberry was waiting at the sidings. But with ferocious determination, Henry raided the nearby livery yard and came up with a classic chaise-and-pair. With two passengers on each running board and Kookie hammocked in a fold of sunshade, the horses earned their sugar lumps toiling up to Golden Bend.

Not a soul appeared as the wrought-iron gates swung open, or at the crunch of wheels on the gravel. "What day is it? Thursday? Thursday is ferreting-for-rabbit day," said Henry, though his voice was tinged with disquiet.

Under the weight of so many passengers, the wheels sank into the deep gravel of the driveway and stopped the carriage in its tracks. All but Cyril abandoned it as they would a burning ship and set off at a run—across the lawn, over the brick forecourt and up the shallow steps, through the pillared portico and across the skiddy marble floor of the hallway. The stairs, the endless carpeted stairs, sapped the energy out of their legs, but it was the bedroom door, the door to the white bedroom and the fear of what they might find beyond it, that brought them to a halt. Henry opened it at last, the only sound the panting of thirteen people who have run up five flights of stairs.

The great white bed stood empty, its candlewick covers smooth as snow and pulled up tight over the pillows. A silence thick as milk curded around them.

Farther down the corridor, Everett pushed open the next bedroom door and gave a sharp cry, as if someone had punched him. That room too was empty: immaculate and empty. He backed to the banister and called down the stairwell, "Lou? Loucien!"

As they tumbled back down the stairs, they surprised the Thursday hunting expedition, every member of staff along with Chad, Boisenberry, and Medora, standing in the hall, a rabbit or a ferret cage dangling from each hand. Sheepish, caught in the act of breaking house rules, they hung their heads.

"I am gone for twenty-four hours and you are using the front door!" Henry reproached them.

"*Slicha,*" said the cook. "To come in the back way seems not so good, what with the *shfanim.*"

The servants struggled out of their duster coats,

torn between being improperly dressed and putting dead rabbits down on the marble floor. It was Cissy who noticed first, as their magpie-smart uniforms emerged. "Oh! Oh! Oh! *They got no black armbands!"*

Out on the sun terrace, overlooking the knot gardens and the canyon rim, Loucien, Elder Slater, and Elijah Bouverie sat, eyes shut, faces turned upward to the warmth of the sun. She was in a borrowed nightdress and wrapper, Elijah in an exotic turban of bandage. The ferreting party had used the front doors sooner than disturb them. The drone of the electric generators had covered the sound of the chaise and the shouting. The dozers did not stir until Tibbie Boden came running through the house with a cage, calling out, "I done ferreting, Miss Loucien! I done ferreting!"

"Well done, but you keep well clear of my little one, if you please. I'd like her daddy to meet her before she gets eat by some polecat." Loucien yawned, made to get up, but thought better of it. "You put that demon creature back in the shed, and then dredge up what cooking I taught you in school, and help Cook make a rabbit pie or twelve. I divine we have company for dinner. Hello, Everett. You brought Cyril home to dine, by any chance?"

Cyril Crew was still seated in the chaise, hands crossed on the top of a walking cane, as regal as the viceroy of India. His younger brother, calling from the steps of the house, looked adolescent by comparison. *"It's a girl, Cyril! I got me a daughter!"*

Cyril touched the brim of his borrowed hat. "How foresightful, dear boy. The company was in need of new blood. Do you think we may negotiate to pay her in rusks?"

Though miracles grow thick on the ground along the Numchuck River, the accident had not suddenly restored Elijah to perfect, youthful genius. Being hit in the head by a piston rod rarely has that effect. But he knew himself to be Captain Bouverie of Golden Bend, and he knew himself to be at home, among friends. At the end of a half-forgotten voyage of a life, he had sailed safely back into harbor.

He was thrilled and honored that his friends named the baby after him: Ellie. But he never fully realized how much he owed to his loyal staff, having no notion of the time he had been gone or the hardships his disappearance had caused them.

Henry made sure it stayed that way.

Mercifully, Elijah was still fit to sign checks, which made life vastly easier for the household. In commemoration, no one at Golden Bend ate rabbit for a year.

ఇం ఇ

It would be a while before Loucien was fit to travel, but with the *Sunshine Queen* a crumbling wreck, the Showboat Company also began to disintegrate and float apart. Max, lacking a plank, went back to his previous trade of gardening and got at job at the Blackers' place. Their worship of money did not trouble him, since he could not understand a word they said. Medora and her Photopia headed for St. Louis on a timber barge. But quickest to leave were the children and their schoolmistress, forlornly hoping to reach Olive Town in time for Hulbert Sissney's funeral. Chad Powers tagged along, for he could not quite get it out of his head that Oklahoma was his home. Besides, he could hardly build a prairie sailboat without returning to the prairies.

Elijah waved them all good-bye from the steps of the house, a frail, snowy-haired man in an alpaca dressing gown and lambskin slippers, leaning on the arm of a butler who was sneezing discreetly into a handkerchief. The mansion's whole magnificent facade flickered with black and white uniforms, as though magpies were perched on every windowsill.

A sign of luck.

George the barber-surgeon went with them only as far as Blowville Station. "I'm going back up to Roper Junction," he said, to their astonishment.

"But they'll recognize you!" said Miss March. "They will string you . . . I mean, they will tar and feather you for deceiving them!"

But George had been thinking things over. Not only did Roper Junction have no barber, it had just had its eyes opened to the wonders of phrenology. He wrinkled his nose. "No one looks at their barber, ma'am. If they do, they'll say I bear a passing 'semblance to someone they seen once, and I'll say, 'Oh yeah?' and they'll say 'Yeah!' and tell me about it. I'll get to hear the story of the Queen's visit twelve times a week. Sometime soon, even I won't know if I was there or not." It was the most they had ever heard George say. "Saw the perfect place. Right over the jam shop. Perfect." And he stropped his razor absentmindedly on the tail of his leather belt.

Cissy felt as small as a pea fallen out of the pod. From that packed midnight bedroom, with the maids, the music, the Bright Lights, she had shrunk back down to Cissy Sissney, one of three children in the care of their schoolmistress during an outbreak of diphtheria. Four changes of train distanced, by degrees, the heights and depths, the shoals and shimmer of the Numchuck River. With every tedious jolting mile it became less real, less part of the real Cissy Sissney. A traveler's tale.

"If Mr. and Mrs. Crew come, Cecelia, they come," said Miss May March, voice as sharp as chalk on slate. "If not, well, we have at least survived the epidemic better than some. We must give thanks."

"I got the sweating sickness!" said Tibbie, as if applying for permission not to give thanks. Miss May punished her for it with a dose of quinine. Time was winding backward. Miss May March was turning back into the snippy, unfriendly tyrant of the schoolroom.

"They'll come," said Cissy. "When they can. Mr. Crew said."

"Men," said Miss March brusquely. "As my mother says: when men promise something, even they don't know if they mean it."

The interminable prairies rolled out now on either side of the train, just as they had the day Cissy arrived in Olive Town as a settler. No house, no town, just a small patch of land (Claim Nos. 3048—9) and a big dream. Her father had been able to picture the whole thing: banks and factories and homes. And now the bank and umbrella factory and homes existed—there they were, rising out of the prairie—but not Poppy Sissney himself.

After the train pulled in, Kookie ran ahead, to the telegraph office, to the open arms of his huge family. The others trailed up Main Street, pausing only for Tibbie to be sick.

"I didn't mean to get off here," said Chad Powers vaguely. "Meant to stay on to get off at Guthrie. Force of habit, I guess."

For Cissy, the space where the grocery store had stood had become a yawning chasm waiting to swallow her up. All her instincts told her to turn and run—not go closer—not to look. But the people of Olive Town had a make-do-and-mend philosophy. Why part with a perfectly good shirt when the hole in it can be patched? The hole in Main Street had been patched. Timber framing and a roof were already in place, and clapboard walls had risen high enough to take a door, the shop door. Someone had even reattached the old shop bell to the back of the door so that it jingled when Cissy pushed on it and stepped inside.

Kookie would never have admitted it, but he felt as if he had run through a month-long clump of nettles and was just starting to smart. When he saw his mother and father and assorted brothers and sisters, it was all he could do not to embarrass himself. There was the alligator and losing his reward money to Cole Blacker and the explosion and Sugar Cain and losing his shoes on the mudbank and the flitch that might have been . . . and Cyril's hair on the prison floor that definitely was . . . and then finding out that Hulbert Sissney was dead even after everything Cissy had pulled off with the phrenology and Queen Victoria. . . . Somehow, without quite knowing why, he had told his parents about all these things within thirty seconds of bursting through the office door.

"Hulbert's not dead, honey," said his mother, trying to excavate him from under the telegraph machine, where he had curled up in a ball.

"I cabled Cissy," said Pickard, dropping to his knees to help. "Didn't she get my telegram? SAFE TO COME HOME. YOUR PA'S GONE TO FETCH YOUR MA?"

"What's wrong with Kookie?" asked the youngest Warboys.

"He's glad to see us," said Pickard, and began disconnecting the telegraph machine for fear that Kookie would electrocute himself on the cables squirled under the desk. "Hulbert's not dead, son, and Hildy has got over Judgment Day and soured down to her old miserable self."

"Where's Kookie going?" asked the youngest Warboys, as Kookie came out from under the desk as fast he had gone in there, and bolted out of the office again in the direction of the grocery store.

"To tell Cissy the good news, I guess," said Pickard, "though she's maybe found out for herself by now."

Hildy Sissney was in full cry. "What in the name of Jehosephat are you wearing, miss? I ken see they don't have hairbrushes in Missouri: if you brung nits home, you can just take 'em back where you found'm—don't hold her close like that, Hulbert; she'll have nits sure as beans are green—all right for some to go off gallivanting, leavin' others to pick up the pieces . . . Oh Lor', now we got trouble: and what do you want, Warboys-boy whichever-one-you-are? There may be too many of yuh to have names, but I know yuh by yer hair; you're the one that leads Cissy astray."

Kookie took shelter behind the shop door from the pepper-box gunfire of Hildy back in form. Living with that woman must be like Custer's Last Stand on a daily basis: how long could anyone survive it? Maybe that was how Cissy had developed such nerves of steel. "You found out about Mr. Pickard not being dead, then," he called, over the hail of abuse. "Musta lost some words off that telegram."

Cissy beamed back at Kookie from behind her pa's bath chair, arms entwined around Hulbert's neck, her chin on his shoulder. "I found out."

Kookie had to confess, as he backed out of the door: she was pretty spackfacious.

But Cissy remembered something and called him back, detaching herself from her father. With distinct overtones of Pirate Nancy and looking twice as perilous, she told him, "You're an unchivalrous dog, Kookie Warboys!" and slapped him so hard, it hurt her hand.

Hildy Sissney was instantly silent.

"What was that for, chicken?" asked her father, when Kookie was gone. "That boy get over-familyer or what?"

"Huh!" said Cissy and threw back her shoulders with the defiance of a flamenco dancer. "He said I was flat as a wall."

School reopened. The day was greeted by its pupils as a natural disaster, on a par with the Missouri floods. Like the racing lizards and turtles Kookie Warboys kept in a packing crate, children who had been freely roaming up trees and down rivers found themselves crammed back on top of one another with nothing to look at but four wood walls. Only Cissy could appreciate that there were worse kinds of imprisonment out there, and worse blights than schoolteachers.

One of her father's broken legs had been mended with steel plate, and it seemed to have strengthened his willpower as well. The deal with Hildy was off that said Cissy must leave school and start work in the store. Hulbert had put his mended foot down. "With a good education, who knows, she can maybe follow in the steps of that Loucien lady."

"What, *schoolteaching*?" Hildy had screeched incredulously.

"Mmmm," Hulbert had said, and winked at Cissy.

Now, here, sitting on a hard school bench, beside the globe of a vast and free-rolling world, even Cissy could not remember quite why she had wanted to stay on at school. Why had she felt so bereft peeping in at the window at children doing tests?

Miss May March swept in, hair oppressed into a severe little bun, mouth clamped in a determined line—"I trust, class, that you have remembered your lunches and your brains? You will be needing both."—and called their names at registration like the recording angel on doomsday. Then she passed out blank sheets of paper.

Boredom lapped around the walls of the schoolhouse as sure as the water did that rose up around Noah's ark. A week had gone by and still no word, no telegram, no letter out of Missouri.

"Today we shall be mastering the art of letter writing. The best three efforts will be sent to the State Governor, who, I am perfectly sure, abhors to see sticky finger marks or the tell-tale footprints of a dirty eraser! You will address the Governor on the following subject." And she wrote on the blackboard in squealing letters:

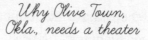

"Oh!" said Cissy and Kookie and Tibs simultaneously. Class Three buzzed like a swarm of sewage flies. Miss May swatted them.

"Assemble your arguments in your copybooks, then arrange them carefully on the page. Remember: paper costs money. This afternoon, we are going to prepare a play for the town, marking the passing of the Bad Times."

"Oh!" said Cissy and Kookie and Tibs.

"'O' is all very well, Habakkuk Warboys, but please attempt to use the other twenty-five letters of the alphabet."

Cissy was so absorbed by the task of writing to the Governor that she was last to notice when Miss May got out a hammer. (Several children flinched with fear.) Sinking a nail into the classroom wall, the schoolmistress unwrapped a framed picture and hung it from the nail. It was a sight so familiar to Cissy that all the scents of babyhood came suddenly flooding back: the very same portrait that had hung on her wall in Arkansas! Her earliest years had been overshadowed by those formidable marmot cheeks, those eyes speaking of thrones and dominions.

Queen Victoria glared across the Olive Town

schoolroom at the Stars and Stripes propped in the corner. The room was used by adults in the evenings, and several grumbled about the portrait's presence. But Miss March was adamant. "It has meaning for us" was all she was prepared to say.

Within a week, a letter arrived at the post office with an address so vague that the postmaster was unsure what to do with it and took it to Pickard at the telegraph office. Pickard Warboys was the best-informed man in Olive Town—probably because he could open an envelope and reseal it without anyone knowing. Not that he made a habit of it, but sometimes the skill came in useful. After taking a peek this time, he tossed the letter to his boy Kookie. "Take this into school and get Miss May to read it out, will you? The contents may signify something to someone."

Kookie naturally insisted on reading it out himself. He was missing his life as a performer, and letter reading to Class Three was as close as he was ever likely to get to show business, now that he was home in Boredom Country. (When he saw the handwriting inside, elaborate and curly as a wrought-iron gate, he rather regretted it.) Cissy could see at once that it was not from Miss Loucien: the ink was black, for a start, rather than green.

To Whom It May Concern:

I enclose, on behalf of Captain Elijah Bouverie, the warmest of salutations and good wishes, and trust that your homeward journey was accomplished satisfactorily.

The Captain continues to make a steady recovery, and an agreeable routine has returned to Golden Bend. We are rarely troubled by the doctor.

The sight of the Sunshine Queen so lamentably foundered on the opposite bank was causing the Captain some distress. So I have arranged for it to be towed over and moored alongside the foot of the cliff steps where, if you recall, a derelict boathouse once languished. A carpenter (who appears to know both the Captain and the ship) appeared out of the blue one day, and I put him to work converting the hulk into a large but fitting summerhouse. Here the Captain will be able to spend his days enjoying the river at close quarters. He and the carpenter—one Mr. Chips—are already catching prodigious numbers of vile-tasting fish, much to the annoyance of Cook. With the canyon steps being so taxing on the legs (even without the burden of stretcher and patient), I am intending to install a rack-and-pinion elevator of sorts. I hope you will someday have the opportunity to admire its ingenuity. The calliope was, I felt, slightly unnecessary to a summerhouse, so I have arranged for that to be conveyed to Olive Town by railroad. This upon the advice of Mr. Curlitz, who said he knew of one who could put it to good use in the church.

The house is strangely quiet since your departure, and the younger maids are quite downcast by the lack of—how shall I put it?—music. One was persuaded to repent by Elder Slater and has left with him to convert Canada: a formidable task, I feel, having consulted an atlas.

For myself, I often think warmly of my brief time as Prime Minister of England and only wish I had been free to travel to Olive Town along with the others—who will, I assume, be arriving at much the same time as this letter. (The calliope may take longer.)

> I remain your affectionate and most
> obedient servant,
> Henry (sometime Prime Minister of
> the United Kingdom)

As Kookie wrestled with the last word, a noise drifted in at the window like a whistle of admiration— the distant whistle of the morning train. There was an upheaval of papers and furniture, a bench tilted over backward, a box of chalks spilled. Everyone ran—most without knowing why, but since their teacher had headed off, as well as Cissy and Kookie and Tibs, they supposed school must be out.

Kookie went by way of the window, so he was down the street and on the station platform before the train had even stopped. But since Pickard Warboys had read the letter ahead of his son, quite a crowd of adults had already gathered there, too. Almost everyone in Olive Town, in fact.

"Now remember your ettiquette, children," said Miss March, pinkly flustered. "Barney Mackinley, don't wipe your nose on your sleeve."

Like a stern-wheeler approaching a landing stage, the train boasted four singers on its bow. Well, actually, they were balanced on the footplate playing banjos and singing "Rolling Down to Rio."

From the first-class carriage, a stranger descended first—a patrician gentleman carrying an artist's pad, who seemed startled both by the reception committee and the size of the town. "Is this it?" he said. "Is this the full extent of Olive City?"

"We plan on growing it some, with the passage of time," said Cissy's father from his wheelchair. "Give us time. Three years ago we weren't even here. Think what we can work up to in the next fifty."

The elderly man hummed, presented Hulbert with his business card, and tottered on up the street, followed by a porter with the tiniest of bags. Perhaps he mistook the cheering behind him for some quaint local custom, for he lifted his hat in thanks, without looking back.

The cheers were really for the Bright Lights, of course, who had just stepped down from third class and were cluttering up the platform with property box, costume basket, and a great number of fancy leather suitcases all stamped with Elijah Bouverie's initials. "For Bright Lights, we sure travel heavy," said Loucien, who was carrying only the smallest bundle. The baby.

"Stands Scotland where it did?" said Curly, looking around him at a town that had changed entirely since he had last been there.

Cissy rushed Loucien, without a care for etiquette, pressing her face in somewhere between baby and armpit. "I didn't lie to you, honest! You don't have to give Poppy a funeral, 'cause he isn't dead! Don't be angry! I didn't mean to waste you a journey!"

"We knew! We knew! Mr. Warboys cabled us, honey!" said Loucien, stroking Cissy's hair. "Did we need a reason to come? Beyond us promising we would? Anyways, thought you'd like to see the missing persons again. Finally found them in the small ads, you know? Like three secondhand wheelbarrows." Egil, Revere, and Finn smiled and bowed and did their best to impersonate wheelbarrows by carrying all the luggage.

"You coming to live here forever and ever and

ever?" Tibbie Boden demanded. "We're doing a play in school. You can help us with our play!"

"We'll see, Tibs. I found out a whole heapa useful stuff 'bout babies I never knew before. I could maybe teach a lesson or two, like in the old days. And while the boys are studyin' babies, we gals can maybe work up a banjo band. I missed the quartet somethin' fierce. Found them again by purest hunky-dory happenchance in a station hotel, working their ways west. They'll lend us a hand or five. I been trying to master a drum roll on a snare drum, but Ellie's a born critic—screams abuse louder'n a Chicago saloon with no whiskey. We'll stay till Thanksgiving, then we'll see."

"But I can be your noo ingenoo, cain't I, Miss Loucien, cain't I, I can, cain't I?" Tibbie's golden curls bounced around her angelic face, lustrous and sweet as buttered baby ears of corn, and Cissy felt herself shrivel into a testy little witch arriving too late with a cauldron of spells.

Loucien gasped. "Oh, but the job's taken, honey! Sorry 'bout that. Leastways, Mr. Cyril's seen the actress he wants, and he's in talks with her agent."

Tibbie shrugged and away she went, actually skipping, so as to enjoy the swish of her multiple petticoats, her ambitions altered in the blink of an eye. She would be a chanteuse instead, or a banjo player, or marry Egil, with his green eyes. Cissy paused to seal tight her cauldron of envy and nastiness, determined it would not slop over. Not ever. She could do that. Ever since Roper Junction, she had been able to do it: to pull down the veil, to seal up Cissy inside. "So . . . where did Mr. Cyril see her?" she asked, breezy as you like. "This new ingénue?"

Loucien seemed to be concentrating on her waking baby. "Saw her in a place called Roper Junction," she crooned. "Wish I'd been there. Quite a performance by all accounts. Everett said it lifted him higher'n the longest plank. I'm envious." She brushed a finger against the baby's cheek. "Her agent will stall for time, of course: he's one tough hombre. But Cyril will wear him down in a year or three. When the girl's got herself educated. The Bright Lights never give up when they've set their mind to a thing. I'm looking forward to it. Be like working with royalty." She put the same finger against Cissy's lips, which were failing to form words. "Keep it in, Cissy. Seal it up tight. You can run ten thousand mile on a furnace fulla happiness an' you won't explode. Feels like it, but take it from me: you won't."

Cyril Crew did indeed hurry over to Cissy's father, delighted to see him recovered, grasping him so eagerly by the hand that the stranger's visiting card attached itself to his palm.

"Goodness gracious," he remarked, showing it to his brother. "When the good Captain Bouverie expresses his goodwill, he does not send chocolates, does he?"

The train engineer shoved the quartet off his footplate and gave an impatient blast on his whistle. He was running late. A boy with red hair came up on him from behind, climbing onto the other footplate, tossing a piece of coal from hand to hand.

"One day I'm gonna be a train engineer," said Kookie nonchalantly. "Done it before. Piece-a pie."

"Why would you *want* to?" fumed the engineer, waving a fist at the crowd lackadaisically rambling to and fro across the tracks, making him late.

But Kookie answered him in all earnest. "Why? 'Cause trains are good. Best things happen with trains. Trains get people home."

Then, like cattle at milking time, the whole festive mob moved off up Main Street, with no particular destination in mind but a sense that things would be more agreeable thanks to the new day, more agreeable for them and for the world at large. God had given the globe a helpful spin—for luck, as it were.

A week later, the calliope steam piano arrived by train, crated and padded to a prodigious size. Kookie told everyone it was a Growow, fiercest animal in the known world, and began selling tickets. But Miss March confiscated the proceeds to buy refreshments for anyone who would help haul the contraption up the hill to the church.

No one had the first idea how to make it work. So they were glad of Chad Powers's resourceful genius. They were glad of him altogether, after weeks of berating by Hulbert Sissney for banishing an innocent young eccentric. Chad managed to hook up the calliope to the back boiler. It meant having the stove lit every Sunday, which would be a trial in high summer, but it was more than worth it to own a calliope. Now the people in towns to north, south, east, and west would be able to hear when Olive Town was at its prayers.

People stayed home the evenings Miss March gave recitals. It was not that they hated either Johann Sebastian Bach or Dixie music; it was just too deafening to stay *inside* the church when Miss March was in full flow.

"When the theater is built," said Chad dreamily, "I shall move it over there and build an organ here. I'm working up this idea for a wind-powered piano, you know? Fixing to call it the Powers Patent Aeolian Organ."

The church was full on Thanksgiving Day, of course. With certain exceptions, the people of Olive Town had a lot to be thankful for. The warmth from the boiler was welcome, and the calliope, in getting up steam, made merry little chirruping noises, like birds in the loft. Miss May March pulled out all the stops and played "The Arrival of the Queen of Sheba," and if small children howled, no one could hear them so it didn't matter. When she had finished, she rang down to Chad to tell him to ease off the steam pressure. Then she hurried down the steps, collected her bouquet from Cissy, and fairly sprinted up the length of the church. Waiting for her at the head of the aisle stood Curly, trembling with stage fright, as all bridegrooms do.

A BIOGRAPHICAL NOTE

Horace A. W. Tabor, a mining tycoon immortalized in *The Ballad of Baby Doe*, spent some of his millions building the Tabor Grand Opera House in Denver. He sent his architect, George King, to Europe for inspiration, and imported cherry wood from Japan, marble from Italy, cloth from France. The seats were cushioned, the auditorium gaslit, the curtain hand painted with a landscape of ancient Rome.

What future jobs Mr. King undertook are less well recorded, but he would surely not have let the skills and knowledge that he had gained in Denver go to waste. Who else would some rich benefactor choose, if he wanted to make the gift of theater to a town of people dear to his heart?